NOT FOR
PUBLIC CONSUMPTION

p.l. frank

Razor's Edge Publishing, Inc.
Fayetteville, New York

This is a work of fiction. Any resemblance to actual persons, living or not, is purely coincidental.

Published by Razor's Edge Publishing, Inc., 201 W. Genesee Street, #136, Fayetteville, New York 13066.

www..razorsedgepublishing.com

Printed in the United States of America

Library of Congress Cataloging-in-Publication Data
Frank, P.L.

Not for public consumption/p.l. frank—First edition.
I. Title.

2007

ISBN-978-0-9791563-0-4
ISBN-0-9791563-0-0

US $16.95   Canada $ 19.47 Fiction

ISBN-13: 978-0-9791563-0-4
ISBN-10: 0-9791563-0-0

5 1 6 9 5

9 780979 156304

2

Dedication

To all those people who prop up the illusion;
You allow the rest of us to hide in broad daylight.

And to Moshua.

Special thanks to Shadow.

NOT FOR
PUBLIC CONSUMPTION

I

"You want Indian food tonight?" The man near the aisle of the crowded subway car asks.

"Hmm...No. You know I don't like Indian food anymore...Ever since Sammy." The woman near the window replies.

"Sammy! What does *he* have to do with anything?"

"Every time I think about Indian food I think about people from India, and every time I think about people from India, I think about your boss, Sammy. He thinks he's such a shrewd businessman. In reality, he's a tyrant. A maniac. He's mentally ill, you know?"

"I know," the man says, nodding his head.

"Personality disorder. He's another Hitler. If he ever got enough power, he could *be* another Hitler. You know that?"

"Yeah. I know," he says, nodding in agreement again.

"Listen, next time that Sammy starts to give you any shit, *you* know, the next time he starts to publicly humiliate you or belittle you, or he starts yelling like a maniac like he does, you tell him like this...you tell him, '*I* saw that movie, Salaam Bombay. I know you throw your children on the streets and make them eat dogs and then turn them into prostitutes at age ten...So don't tell *me* how the world works, *okay*?' "

"You think that will do it, huh?" The man asks.

"I *know* it will. I'm telling you, I can't even *think* about eating Indian food anymore because of that guy."

"McArthur, next stop. McArthur."

The couple gets up. Murray Bardos shifts in his seat and leans back. A crowd of people huddles near the exit door. In a few moments the doors will open and another crowd will push through to take their place.

Murray fumbles around in his jacket pocket for his notepad. Two more people, a man and a woman in their early twenties, take the seat ahead of him. They are sharing a bag of Doritos, ignoring the international sign picturing a hamburger with a red line drawn through it, posted at the front of the car. Murray opens his notepad and writes, "It's because none of the signs are in English anymore. People don't get it...Doritos don't look anything like hamburgers."

The woman licks her fingers as she talks...
"If you think *that's* something, listen to *this*. Janna met this guy at Greg's party last week who told her he masturbates 15 to 16 times a *day*."
"Fifteen to sixteen times a day? How does that work?" The young man asks.
"What do you mean 'how does that work?' It works. I mean, how else do you think?"
"*No*. I mean how does he jerk off 15 to 16 times a day?"
"*I* don't know. I mean, he's probably got some pretty strong forearms, but it's not like it's a health risk or anything." The woman says, licking her fingers again.
The young man reaches into the bag of Doritos. "I don't know, dude. That depends."
"On what?"
"Well, like what does he do for a *living*?" He asks, tilting his head back and tossing the Doritos into his mouth.
"Beats me," she says, shrugging.
The young man finishes chewing and swallows hard. "I hope it doesn't have anything to do with food."

Murray begins snickering and rocking back and forth in his seat. He covers his mouth with his hand to stifle the noise, but the couple hear him and both turn around to see who is behind them. They look over at Murray and then at each other. The woman rolls her eyes and the man grins. They whisper something to one another and then get up and walk towards the opposite end of the car.

Murray shifts back in his seat again and searches in his pockets for the letter. He pulls out a thick packet wrapped in a rubber band that has been broken and knotted in two places. Murray pulls out one of the faded, tattered papers from the packet and gingerly unfolds it. He is very careful not to tear it anymore.

He reads the paper and begins to quietly weep. His hands tremble and he turns his head towards the window. Suddenly, his thoughts are broken by the realization that he can see his own reflection in the train window. He is going through the tunnel.

Murray quickly, but carefully, folds the paper, slides it underneath the rubber band, and places the packet back safely inside his pocket. He does not want to miss his favorite part.

Once he leaves the subway, Murray walks east, taking his usual route to make his weekly stop at the health food store. One hour later, he emerges with several bags. Whole wheat, oats, carob chips, brown rice and a package of incense--Patchouli. He makes use of the incense. As for the rest, no one knows. Except for the three or so bags of grain that lay in the bottom of the refrigerator covered with a layer of light green, fuzzy mold, the food from Free Earth Groceries is never anywhere to be seen, and Murray keeps to a strict diet of hotdogs and canned pork and beans.

Murray tucks all of the items into his tattered backpack and heads for his other weekly stop at the U-Save. He buys his weekly supply of toilet paper: one four-roll pack of white generic. It's just the right size to fit inside of his backpack alongside the grains.

Next, Murray heads east to Lucky's. It is 5:30 and the bar is crowded with people. Murray takes his hat off, steps up to the bar, and orders a beer. He looks around and nods at several familiar faces and makes himself comfortable. Unlike most of the other bars in the area,

Lucky's has very few college students. "Just the ones who are more serious about drinking than making a good impression," Murray once told Mollie. He does not mind them, he had said. Besides, he likes to eavesdrop on their conversations.

After twenty minutes or so, a table opens up at the back of the bar. Murray hops off the barstool, motions to the bartender for another beer, and heads over to the table. The table is sticky and holds six dirty glasses and a heaping ashtray. Murray does not even notice. He digs in his pocket for a pencil and his notepad, and in the dimly lit bar, now blaring with the sounds of laughter and Mac the Knife, he begins to take notes.

Sometime around 9:30 Murray heads home. When he opens the front door he notices the light under the door of his roommate Kirby's, bedroom. Murray's black cat Shadow runs over to greet him.

"Hi buddy," Murray says.

Shadow gives his usual greeting and holds his head up for a petting.

Before Murray can set his backpack down, the telephone rings.

"I'll get it," Murray yells through Kirby's door.

"Hello."

"Hello. I am trying to reach Murray Bardos."

"Who is calling?"

"I'm Anita Fiola. I'm calling on behalf of River's Edge Hospital."

"You have the wrong Murray Bardos."

"Are *you* Mr. Bardos?"

"Yes."

"Murray Y. Bardos?"

"Yes, but I'm not the M.Y. Bardos you are looking for. I get these calls periodically. I've never heard of your hospital. I've never been there. My number is listed in the phone book. I think someone looking for this other Mr.

Bardos looked up this number, but I am not the Murray Bardos you are looking for."

"Well, sorry to bother you, Mr. Bardos. Have a good evening."

"It's quite all right. I'm used to it. Good bye, now."

Murray carries his backpack into his bedroom. After a few minutes, he walks into the kitchen and starts a pot of water boiling for some hotdogs. As he opens a can of pork and beans he begins mumbling. Sometimes his ramblings are punctuated by loud cursing. Mostly his speech is incoherent. He does not notice Kirby walking into the kitchen.

"Hey, what's up?" Kirby asks, as he fills the coffee maker with water.

"Oh, hey there. How was your day?" Murray asks with genuine interest.

Kirby shrugs. "Okay, I guess. I spent most of the day locked up in the library searching for the back left leg of the cockroach."

"*What's* that?" Murray asks, somewhat thrown off.

"Oh, you know, I'm doing a paper on the clustering behaviors of starfish. Real minutia."

"Hmm. They do much clustering, do they?" Murray asks, stabbing his fork into one of the bloated hotdogs.

"It's amazing what these professors think is important sometimes," Kirby says shaking his head. "Especially given the fact that *I* am paying for this so-called education."

"Well, now you never know when you'll need to know about how starfish cluster in the future," Murray says, as he pours the pork and beans into a bowl.

"How was *your* day?" Kirby asks, watching the coffee finishing dripping into the carafe. "Do anything interesting?"

"Oh, well, my life isn't as interesting as yours, I'm afraid."

"Well, I've got to get back to hitting the books," Kirby says, pouring coffee into the mug with a giant chip on the rim.

"What are you studying?" Murray asks hopefully. In another couple of seconds he knows that Kirby will close himself up in his bedroom and Murray will be left alone with his own thoughts.

"Stats. I've got an exam this week. See you later...oh, help yourself to some coffee if you want."

Murray nods as he chews his hotdog. Kirby walks back into his bedroom. In a few moments, the mumbling and cursing begins again. If Kirby can hear it, he has learned to work around it. Out of all the things there were to get use to, this was probably the easiest.

Murray continues mumbling and chewing until his attention is drawn to the sounds of Shadow beckoning him back to the moment.

"Come on," Murray says, getting up from the table. "Let's go into the bedroom. How was your day, today?"

Shadow trots down the hall alongside Murray, talking the entire way.

"Oh, yeah?" Murray says, shutting the bedroom door, "and then what happened?"

Within a half an hour the sounds of Murray's manual typewriter is all that can be heard.

* * * *

The next weekend Kirby and his girlfriend Karen take off for Yosemite. Murray waits for over an hour after their car pulls away before going through Kirby's things.

"I don't know what I am looking for exactly. Mostly just being careful," he tells Shadow who is sitting atop Kirby's futon and observing Murray intently. "You never know," Murray says. "You just never know."

He is searching through a drawer stuffed with papers, magazines, and condoms, ten or so packets of rolling papers, and several loose floppy disks, when the telephone rings. Murray carefully puts everything back in place in Kirby's room before running to answer the telephone.

"Hello," Murray says, somewhat out of breath.

"Hey, Bardos, it's Sack. How's it going? What are you up to?"

"Oh, not much," Murray says peering around the corner into Kirby's room. "How are you?"

"Good, man. I was just thinking about coming over."

"Oh, yeah? Good."

"Okay, man. I'll see you in a little while, then."

Murray gives up on going through Kirby's room. After he hangs up from talking to Sack, he begins pacing the living room. He runs his hands, first the left, then the right, through his hair, and mumbles as he paces. He tries sitting down twice, finds it is too much, and quickly gives in to pacing again. He is in the middle of muttering something when the doorbell rings.

"Hey," Murray says, motioning Sack inside.

"Got to use your john, man."

"Can I get you anything to drink or eat?" Murray calls out, as Sack turns the corner and heads for the bathroom.

"One thing at a time, man, okay?" Sack yells back.

Murray begins pounding his forehead hard with his fist and muttering, "Why am I so stupid? Why am I so stupid?" He stands in the middle of the floor repeating this until the sound of the toilet flushing brings him out of it.

"I'm starving, man. You wanna' order pizza?" Sack says.

"Uh, sure. Sounds great," Murray says. He tries unsuccessfully to hide his hesitancy.

"What's the matter? You already eat?" Sack asks, putting his feet up on the stained and wobbly second-hand coffee table.

"Ah, no. I just...It's just, I was considering my finances."

"I got it covered, man. Not a problem. Where's your phone book?"

Murray hands Sack the telephone directory and walks into the kitchen to turn the fire on under his old metal coffee pot. Murray takes the opportunity to pace some more while Sack intimidates the clerk at the pizza parlor. The pizza ordered, the two of them sit down opposite each other in the living room.

"Man, this furniture is a mess," Sack says, pulling a piece of stuffing out of the sofa and throwing it on the floor. "Didn't that new roommate of yours...what's his name again?"

"Kirby."

"Didn't Kirby bring any furniture with him when he moved in?" Sack asks.

"Nah. He's a student. Travels light."

"Yeah, I remember those days. I guess he doesn't mind this dump. If the money is right, you'll take whatever you can get," Sack says.

Murray chuckles. There is silence as Sack pulls a joint out of a tin box labeled, "Altoids," and fires it up. Shadow comes into the living room and walks up close to Sack.

"Hey, Shadow. Long time no see. How you doin'?" Shadow responds by putting his tail in the air and walking over to Murray. He says something to Murray and then jumps up on the arm of Murray's chair.

"It's all right, Shadow," Murray says. "You remember Sack, don't you?" Shadow says something and Murray chuckles and gives his head a pet.

"Man, that cat still freaks me out. I swear he is actually talking to you," Sack says before inhaling. After several seconds he exhales. "I mean it's like the two of you can actually understand one another. Like you have your own secret language."

Murray chuckles. Sack hands the joint to Murray. "No, I'm telling you man, it's weird. I've never seen anything like it. Why does he talk that way?"

"He's half Siamese and half Burmese. They have a strange meow," Murray says through his exhales.

"No. I mean why does he *talk* like that? You know what I mean. He talks like a human. No. He talks like he *knows* things," Sack says shaking his head and relighting the joint.

Murray smiles and rubs Shadow's head.

"I've heard him actually call you," Sack says. "I mean, sometimes if you're out of the room for awhile, he walks around here looking for you and I *swear* he says, 'Murray. Murray'."

Murray chuckles. "Maybe we should take our act on the road," he says.

"You know," Sack says, "I read somewhere that black cats are specially chosen by seers and knowers."

"Is that so?" Murray asks with interest.

"Yeah," Sack continues. "Like wizards. They used black cats to go out and spy on whoever they wanted to get some information on."

"Whomever," Murray says. Sack gives a perturbed look.

"I'm serious, dude. Seers and Knowers always have black cats around because black cats have special powers. They can understand things and then return and communicate the knowledge to the Seer."

"Well, I really better keep him under wraps then," Murray says smiling. "No telling who might want to get their hands on something like that, right Shadow?" Murray says, petting him.

Shadow replies. Murray smiles and Sack shakes his head and leans back on the sofa.

After several minutes Sack lights up another joint. The two of them sit silently for a while. There is only the sound of their inhaling and exhaling as they take turns with the joint.

Suddenly, out of the silence, Sack asks, "So did you tell your roommate yet?"

Murray freezes up inside. He waits to exhale and then simply says, "No."

"Are you gonna'?" Sack asks, as he reaches for the joint.

"Don't see any reason why I should. It doesn't serve any purpose," Murray says.

"Any purpose for *who*?" Sack asks.

"Whom," Murray responds.

"All right, Mr. MIT, it doesn't serve any purpose for *whom*?"

"University of Chicago. And it doesn't serve any purpose for anyone. Certainly not for Kirby," Murray says.

"Oh, *no*? You don't think he would like to know? I'll tell you what, dude, if *I* signed on as a roommate, I sure as hell would like to know."

Just then the doorbell rings. "Ah, saved by the bell," Murray says and chuckles nervously. "I'll get some paper plates. Would you like a beer?"

"Yeah," Sack says. He answers the door, pays for the pizza and is already busy eating when Murray gets back with the plates and drinks.

The two of them eat and drink and belch and pause, exchange comments that they are stuffed, and then finish off the rest of the pizza.

Murray gets up, walks into his bedroom, and comes out with a small stack of audiotapes. The rest of the evening is spent reviewing Murray's interview for the underground pirate radio station. Sack is the program director...or, he would be, if anyone at the station actually got paid, or if anyone at the station, including Sack himself, bought into as he put it, "the whole bourgeois capitalist hierarchy crap." Sack is fond of reminding people that he does not.

"All right," Murray says, picking a tape out of the stack and popping it into the recorder. "Here's the interview I did last week at the City Hall meeting. This one is called, 'How the System keeps people down and tries to undermine the rights of free speech and freedom of expression'."
Murray smirks and hits the "play" button.

"We will begin this week's meeting with our usual open mike session. Those citizens who wish to speak in this forum should get your name on the list with Mr. Scalow. When the clerk announces your name, please step up to the microphone. You will each have three minutes to speak."

There is the sound of scuffling and some disagreement in the background.
"Mr. Wafier. Mr. Julius Wafier," the clerk announces.
The sounds of angry voices and more scuffling get louder. Finally, there are the sounds of Mr. Wafier approaching the microphone.
"Ah, yes," Mr. Wafier begins, his voice trembling with anger. "Mr. Chairperson and members of the City Council...I would like to address a very urgent matter. That is, the matter of the Council's overt suppression of the citizen's of this country's freedom of speech." Mutterings and rustlings can be heard in the background.
"Last week," Mr. Wafier continues, "I stood before this open mike forum to discuss the matter of police brutality and blatant discrimination on the streets of this city, and the members of this council responded by further infringement of my civil rights." The sounds of Mr. Wafier repeatedly pounding the podium with his fists as he speaks, can be heard.
"I *demand* to be heard on this urgent matter. Private citizens are being discriminated against by a plot that stems from this City Council, and is being carried out by this city's police force. Private citizens are being indiscriminately plucked off the streets, arrested, and

thrown into jail for doing nothing more than expressing themselves. And what was your response when I brought this issue to the table and attempted to open a discussion about it last week? You had *me* dragged out of here and arrested!"

Mr. Wafier's voice bellows with rage. Banging sounds can be heard throughout as he continues to strike the podium with his fists.

"I *demand* justice! I *demand* retribution! On behalf of the citizens of this community, I *demand* an apology and an immediate reversal of the current trend of discrimination, police brutality, and suppression of freedom of speech for the citizens of this community! I hereby place the *entire City Council under citizen's arrest*! You, the members of the City Council, are now officially hereby under *house arrest*! Somebody call the police. These people are under house arrest!"

There are the sounds of a great deal of commotion that move from the background to the foreground. Murray's face lights up as he listens.

"This next part is really good," Murray says, as he leans forward towards the tape recorder.

The sound of a gavel banging is heard. Once, twice, three times.

"*Sit down*, Mr. Wafier. Your three minutes are up," the Chairperson demands.

"I will *not* be silenced! I speak for every member of this community. By silencing me, you are trying to silence every innocent member of this community who has been victimized by this conspiracy."

"Mr. Wafier," the Chairperson is now shouting, "Mr. Wafier, last week we asked you to sit down at the end of your three minutes and you refused. You refused to leave the podium and let other people speak. You continued to rant and rave until we asked you to leave. When you refused to be quiet and sit down and let the meeting continue, we told you that you would be arrested for civil disobedience and for disturbing the peace in a public forum. My understanding is that your conduct with the police added a further charge of resisting arrest. These charges are a result of your own actions, Mr. Wafier, *not* a conspiracy. Now, if you do not step down from the podium and give your fellow citizens an opportunity to speak on other matters, I am afraid that you will be escorted out once again." There are the sounds of papers rustling near the podium.

"This is where Mr. Wafier looks behind him and sees that there are a line of uniformed police officers against the back wall of the council room," Murray says smiling.

"Arrest them!" Mr. Wafier shouts to the police. "Arrest the entire City Council! They have tried to silence the citizens of this community, and falsely imprison them, and they have attempted to take away our civil liberties!"

There are sounds of a loud commotion. Someone is shouting something from the back of the council room. Next, come the sounds of scuffling, and the gavel hits hard three more times. The sound of footsteps can be heard approaching the podium.

Murray says, "Some of the police officers start to move towards the podium now."

"All right," Mr. Wafier says. "All right. I'll go for now, but I am not giving up. I will be back!" This last part he says with his voice shaking.

As he addresses the Council members, he can be heard gathering up his papers from the podium and pushing past the crowd of police officers on his way to the exit.

"Okay, now here's where I get him for the interview," Murray says excitedly. Sack moves in closer towards the recorder.

"Mr. Wafier...Mr. Wafier...Liberation Radio. Can I ask you a few questions about that great speech you just made?" Murray's voice on the tape is trembling with excitement. "Could you please explain for our listeners just what this is all about? What are the incidents, in your opinion, that have infringed on the civil liberties and freedom of speech of the citizens of this city?"

"I'd be glad to tell you," Mr. Wafier says. "You just witnessed part of it in there. As you can see, anyone who confronts them on this conspiracy to silence and control the citizens of this community is threatened with arrest and imprisonment."

"But what was it that led up to your confrontation today?" Murray asks. "Can you explain to the listeners what happened?"

"Certainly," Mr. Wafier says. "Last week I came to confront the City Council on the issue of conspiracy to silence the citizens of this community and to suppress their freedom of expression. When I tried to do this, the Council members had me arrested and I had to endure police brutality and further public humiliation. I came back today as a private citizen to expose this injustice and the conspiracy and, well...you were there. You saw what happened. But I'm not giving up! I will not be silenced! I will continue to expose the conspiracy by this council and the police department to squelch the free expression and civil liberties of the citizens of this city!"

"Mr. Wafier," Murray says. "I'm sure you have the support of our listeners. Could you please explain for our audience just what happened *prior* to your first city hall meeting? What led up to your *original* confrontation with the City Council?"

"Oh, *that*," Mr. Wafier says. Well, I'll tell you. It's an outrage! A *public disgrace*, I tell you. Though, I'm not the only one this is happening to. Not by a long shot. I've started a petition on the street. I expect we'll get over a hundred signatures on this one. No one is immune. You can tell your listeners that anyone who comes into this city is at risk. All you have to do is step out onto the public street in this city and you are at risk."

"At risk for *what*, exactly, in your opinion?" Murray asks.

"To be silenced. Squelched. Controlled. To lose your freedom of speech and freedom of expression. To lose your civil liberties and your constitutional rights. *Scary*, isn't it? You're damned right, it's scary. That in a major city, right here in the United States, that you could lose your rights to peace, liberty, and the pursuit of happiness, is downright terrifying!"

Murray hits the "pause" button and says to Sack, "This guy was totally red-faced and he was shaking his fists the entire time he was talking to me."

Sack shakes his head. Murray hits the "play" button again.

"And how exactly did this happen, Mr. Wafier? How were you denied your rights to freedom of speech and freedom of expression?"

"Yes...well, it was two weeks ago. April 13th at 4:45 p.m. to be exact. I was standing at the intersection of Montgomery and Market. I was practicing my inalienable rights to the pursuit of happiness and freedom of speech, when the police come over and start screaming at me, "Move! Move!" and the next thing I know, I am a victim of police brutality. I was handcuffed, and pushed through the crowd, publicly humiliated, and then brutally shoved into the police car. They took me to the station and arrested me and threw me in jail. It was savage. It's pretty obvious to all of my friends that this is an indication of a conspiracy to silence the private citizens of this city."

"Yes," Murray says. "It seems pretty obvious. Perhaps you could just tell our listeners exactly what you were doing when the police came to arrest you. I'm sure our audience needs to hear just how egregious this arrest was."

"Pointing out the corners," Mr. Wafier says.

"Pointing out the corners?" Murray asks.

"Yes. As simple and innocent as that. I was practicing my freedom of speech and freedom of expression by pointing out the corners."

"Could you be more specific for our listeners, Mr. Wafier?"

"Yes. I was just standing at the intersection and pointing out the corners. I would turn to face each one as I went along. I would face towards a corner and point and say, 'There's a corner. There's a corner. There's a corner. There's a corner over *there*,' and so on."

"And that's *all* you were doing, Mr. Wafier? All you were doing was just standing on the sidewalk pointing out the corners, and this is the impetus for arrest and brutality?"

"Well...actually, I was in the middle of the intersection at the time...but that's all I was doing. Just pointing out the corners."

"Well, I'm sure this speaks for itself," Murray says. "This is a true testament to what our listeners have known all along. The conspiracy to silence and suppress private citizens by the capitalist bourgeois government can no longer be denied. Mr. Wafier, on behalf of our listeners, I would like to thank you for having the courage to come not once, but twice, to City Hall, and confront the bourgeoisie on their clear conspiratorial practices. You are a true freedom fighter.

"Thank you for granting us this interview, Mr. Wafier. This is Murray Y. Bardos for the Liberation Radio, signing off."

"Out of sight," Sack says, leaning back and stretching. "It's perfect. Runs a little long, but we'll adjust. I don't want to cut any of it."

Murray smiles and nods. "Here you go then," Murray says, handing Sack the tape. "I already made my copy."

"All right, man," Sack says, standing up and heading for the door. "You straight on your assignment for next week?"

"Yep. People's Park. Sunday. Rally of the activists for the homeless versus the university Regents. Should be a good one."

"All right then," Sack says. "Catch ya' later, dude."

Murray moves quickly to turn on the porch light for Sack. He nods a farewell to him, and then watches Sack leave the walkway before turning off the porch light. He checks three more times that he has turned the light off before going into his bedroom.

"It is going to be a long night, buddy," Murray says to Shadow. "There's so much to think about."

An hour later, Murray is in the middle of counting the books on his shelf, when the telephone rings. He curses when the sound breaks his concentration and walks over to pick up the receiver.

"Hello," Murray says, sounding somewhat irritated.

"Hello *yourself*. What in the world gets into you to answer the phone that way? Didn't I teach you anything? What if this had been an emergency?"

"You would have been advised where to tune for more information."

"*What*?"

"Nothing, mother. It wasn't an emergency. If it had been an emergency, you wouldn't have paid any attention to how I answered the phone."

"I just can't figure you sometimes," she says. "Anyway, the reason I called was to tell you that your cousin Dennis just received a promotion to Vice President of Marketing at that big advertising firm he works for."

"I have a cousin Dennis?"

"What? Of course you do. Well, he's your second cousin, really. George's boy. You remember. He was the one I told you drove that fancy new Lexus to the family reunion a few years ago. Good looking. Very smart. He has that wife who is always leaving the children with a nanny to run off and go to conferences or some such thing," she says.

"Hmm. I don't remember him. But good thing he got that promotion. I heard the price of a new Lexus is really going up," Murray says.

"Why do you always have to be so sarcastic all of the time? Can't you be happy for other people?"

"Only if it directly effects my life. Otherwise, I don't bother to feign happiness," Murray responds.

"You know," she begins, "There's really no reason for you to be so bitter. If there is anyone who should be bitter, it's me. I'm the one who can't hold my head up at family get-togethers. Every time someone asks me, 'So how is your boy doing? Where does he work now? Is he ever going to get married?' how do you think it makes me feel? I can't even give them an answer. What am I to do? Should I keep saying, 'Oh, time will tell' forever? Time did tell. I can't even say my own son has a *job*, for God's sake. You're hardly a child anymore. And you think *you* have a right to be bitter?" She pauses for just a moment.

"All that schooling," she continues. "That expensive education. I don't even know what it is you *do* all day. I can't believe I call you to share a little good news about the family and this is what I get. What is it, Murray? If your father was here, God rest his soul, *he* would know what to do. I don't know. I can't believe at my age and in my condition that I should have to worry about you. Oh...that reminds me. Did you get my message about your Aunt Mira? She's visiting the Bay Area next month and I offered her to stay over at your place while she is in the area."

"She can't stay here," Murray says. "I have to go now."

"What do you mean she can't stay with you? I already *told* her she could!"

"Well, she can't," Murray says.

"Why not, Murray? She's *family.* "

"I haven't seen her since I was *five*. Besides, there's no room here and she can't sleep on the sofa. We need it quiet here because my roommate is always studying. I've really got to go. I'll talk to you later."

"I can't believe you are at this point in your life and have a roommate. You should be married by now. With *children*, for God's sake. I never thought I would live this long with no grandchildren. What am I going to tell your Aunt Mira? Do I tell her that her own family, her own flesh and blood, do not want her? She cannot stay in the home of *family* because she is not welcome? Perhaps if you had done as well as your cousin Dennis, you would be able to have a home with a guest room and you wouldn't have to turn your own flesh and blood out into the *streets*."

"There are plenty of good hotels in San Francisco. I've really got to go now," Murray says.

"Why? What would you have to do at this hour?"

Shadow meows and Murray rubs him with his foot. "I've *got* to *go*, mother. Talk to you later. Good bye."

Murray returns to his bedroom and searches for the remote. He turns the television to San Francisco Cable Access and is relieved to see he has only missed the first few minutes of The Bee Babe Show.

As usual, she is dressed in her bee costume. Murray's eyes dart back and forth. He knows the routine but he never tires of the details. Wings on a black and yellow striped, tight-fitting tunic. Breasts fully exposed save the nipples, black fish-net stockings. Tattoo of a giant heart and a row of Weebles wobbling, but apparently not falling down, on her upper left arm. Bleached white-blond hair, fried at the ends. Thick, heavy makeup.

"A beauty to behold," Murray mutters. "A beauty to behold."

As usual, she sits in the living room of an apartment filled with dolls and stuffed animals, and rambles on in front of a stationary video-cam.

"Cable Public Access. What did people do before its invention?" Murray says to Shadow.

Tonight Murray is in for a treat. The Bee Babe is lamenting about how her parents were part of the Yuppie Generation who pushed educational and enlightenment-inducing playthings on her during her childhood. From the Bee Babe's perspective, it was their complete and utter lack of sensitivity for her childlike tendencies and the ever-present flow of gifts that were never "age appropriate" that makes her yearn for stuffed animals to this day.

Tonight the Bee Babe complains about one book in particular that she received for her seventh birthday. It was by Kaftka, and, as she puts it, "Didn't even have any pictures in it." The Bee Babe tells her audience that her parents' child-rearing practices were designed to give her a "thousand and two IQ" and, as she puts it, is exactly what created her current penchant for pink plastic.

"Relative deprivation," Murray says, snickering.

In childlike fashion, the Bee Babe then chooses several of her talking dolls. To demonstrate how cute they are, she walks them over, one by one, to just inches from the camera. Murray finds it difficult to focus on the filthy, tattered Big Bird doll. Every time Bee Babe pulls the string to make Big Bird talk, she leans forward and shakes, her breasts spilling out of her bee costume. Murray reaches forward as if to catch them.

"So there's something else I wanted to show you," Bee Babe says, shaking her way back to the sofa. "That is, my favorite kitty purse."

Bee Babe proudly displays a large, gray purse with two cats painted in acrylic and covered with glitter. "Now, I get a lot of compliments on this purse," Bee Babe says. "Especially when I wear this purse with my leopard-print outfits. Now, I also have a leopard-print purse, but I don't like to use the leopard-print purse with my leopard-print outfits. The reason is because it's too easy. It's just too easy. What's *really* challenging in life is to put together a *theme*. Now, if you take the leopard-print theme, and then figure out to use the purse with the kitty-cats on it, *that's* hard. *That's* something to be proud of..."

As usual, Murray is mesmerized straight through until the credits roll.

"That Bee Babe is a goddess," he says to Shadow. "Real women like her just aren't around anymore."

Murray shuts the television off and starts typing. After just a short while though, he stops, gets up, and begins pacing around the cluttered bedroom. Within minutes, the tension has begun to build.

"O*hhh*. Oh, no," Murray mutters as he runs his hands through his hair, his pacing becoming more frenzied.

Finally, Murray gives in to the mounting pressure. Everything had been too much tonight...between his mother and the Bee Babe, the pressure had become almost unbearable. Murray walks into the bathroom and locks the door. He lifts the toilet lid, grabs the plunger, and gets to work.

"It's going to be a long night," Murray mutters. There was so much to get rid of.

II

Murray is dead. He hovers above everyone at the memorial service, getting just close enough from time to time, to make each person shudder. His mother is sobbing. This makes Murray grin. For the first time ever, he relates a pleasurable feeling in connection with her.

The people from the hospital are there, and the university, and the underground radio station, too. So are the people from all of the activists groups he belongs to..."belonged to," Murray reminds himself. The people from the free clinic and Lucky's are there, too.

Mollie and Sack are there, of course, and all the ex-psychiatric patients. Murray chuckles as he watches them...all the ex-mental patients who volunteer to give therapy to other mentally ill people. He listens as one of them tries to explain to his mother why they are so opposed to, as they put it, "psychiatric assault by the traditional medical community." The 51-50'd group they call themselves...all those people who had been forcibly restrained inside psychiatric wards and given mandatory treatment for "their own good." Psychiatric Rape, they called it. Murray watches as his mother asks, "But how did you know Murray?" and then shakes her head.

The people from his writing group are there, too. They are all there. Murray is delighted at the shock his friends bring to his old colleagues, mother, and other relatives. He had been waiting for this moment for so long.

Per his instructions, all of the visitors at the memorial service take a small portion of his ashes and ride the subway together, San Francisco to Berkeley, round-trip, while scattering his ashes in and around the BART. Murray is ecstatic as he watches pieces of himself scatter onto the floors and seats of the Bay Area Rapid Transit system.

"Embarcadero, next exit. Embarcadero."

Murray is jolted out of his trance. And not a moment too soon. His daydream had been so pleasurable that he now must shift uncomfortably in his seat to conceal his excitement.

The doors open at the next stop and two young women take the seat in front of Murray. They are both carrying briefcases. Murray notices they are both wearing upscale, designer clothes. Their shoes, earrings, and bags match their outfits. "It's too easy," Murray writes in his notepad.

The women's hair bounces back and forth as they lean in close to one another to speak.

"Today I went to Debbie to get my nails done," the one near the window says, holding her hands out and wiggling her fingers.

"That's nice," the one near the aisle says. "What color is it?"

"Cafe Ole`. Anyway, you won't believe what Debbie told me."

"Isn't she the one whose husband makes her do all that funky sexual stuff?" asks the one near the aisle.

Murray shifts in his seat and coughs quietly.

"Yeah. Remember last time she did my manicure, she told me her husband makes her wear *surgical gloves* and then forces her to do all that stuff to him?" asks the one by the window.

"*Ewwwh*, yeah. Disgusting!"

The two women make motions with their hands and faces that look to Murray as though they have both discovered worms in their spaghetti.

"So what did she tell you *this* time?" asks the one near the aisle.

"Oh, God, you won't believe it. She said she's 'kind of upset' because she came home from work early a week ago and walked in on her husband sitting naked on the edge of the bed with their 18 month old daughter, who was also naked, on his lap. He was just sitting there with no clothes on, reading from a children's book! Is that sick, or what?"

"*Gross.* What did Debbie do?"

"She said she asked him what he was doing and he said he was telling the baby about the Three Bears. When Debbie said, 'You don't have to be naked to read the Three Bears', he started yelling at her to get out and to shut the fuck up, so she just let it go. But she says she is upset and doesn't know what she should do."

"What did you say to her?"

"I told her she should make sure she's at home when her husband is telling bedtime stories."

"Oh, do you want to see what I bought at Macy's today during lunch?" asks the girl nearest the window as she rummages through her briefcase.

"Yeah, what?" asks the one near the aisle.

"Oh, shit. I left it in my office. It's this really great Betsy Smith sweater."

"What color?"

"Kiwi. Did you hear the consultant that Bill brought in rambling on about 'Enlightened Management' today in that meeting? Does he really expect us to 'relate' to our employees and be *empathic*? If he wants the numbers, he can't expect us to play therapists. I mean, does he really expect us to *care* about these people? If I start acting like I care about their failing marriages, wayward teenagers, and daycare traumas, I'm not exactly going to be able to keep them in line and get the most out of them. You want profit, you've got to manage by fear, not soft, warm fuzzies."

"Here's our stop," the one by the aisle says. "Do you want to get a cappuccino?"

"I can't. I'm going to my chi-kung class. You should really think about joining. It gives you a totally balanced view of reality."

"Next stop, Civic Center. Watch your step please. Have a good evening."

After the women leave, Murray pulls out his notepad and begins to write furiously. When he finishes making notes, he begins printing the words, "Polymorphism. Polymorphic Perversion" over and over again on his notepad. Sometimes he writes it out, sometimes he prints it in block letters, and sometimes he draws pictures around what he has written. He is so absorbed in writing the words that he nearly misses his stop. He grabs his backpack and races out just before the automatic doors slam shut.

Murray adjusts the pack on his back and heads towards the escalator. When he is about six feet from the escalator he hears some commotion behind him as some man in a suit and tie tries to hurriedly push his way through the rest of the commuters heading in the same direction. "Excuse me!" Murray hears over the sounds of the sighs of the commuters being gently pushed aside as the man tries to get past them.

"*Excuse* me," Murray hears just behind him. He turns to look at which direction he should move to step out of the way of the hurried man. Just as Murray turns around, the man thrusts his hand towards Murray to introduce himself.

"I thought I wasn't going to catch up to you," the man says, out of breath. Murray freezes in place as the rest of the commuters sigh and shift their path around the two men.

"I thought it was you when we were on the platform earlier, but you got on a different car, and I was afraid I was going to miss you." Murray gets a confused expression on his face.

"Oh, I'm sorry," the man says, once again thrusting his hand forward to shake Murray's hand. Murray remains motionless, unsure of what to expect.

"Dr. Yardley, right?" The man asks. "Kenneth Caldwell," the man says, smiling. "Pritzker Medical School...University of Chicago? You were my advisor and professor. Psychiatry."

Murray takes two steps backwards. "I'm sorry," Murray says. "You are mistaken. A case of mistaken identity, I'm afraid."

The man looks stunned. "I'm...I'm sorry," he stutters. "You are a dead ringer for someone I knew. Sorry," the man says staring at Murray from head to toe and shaking his head slowly.

"It's quite all right," Murray says. "Happens to me all the time."

Murray tips the brim of his hat and turns toward the escalator. At the last minute, he changes his mind and heads towards the stairs.

"Have a good evening," he says to the man who has now begun to ascend the escalator.

"Yes," the man mutters, still staring at Murray and looking genuinely confused. "You too," he says. But Murray cannot hear him. He is bolting up the steps two at a time and racing for the street level. He usually enjoys being below ground in the subway. Tonight, however, he cannot wait to be among the crowds of people on the street.

When he reaches the top of the stairs there is a homeless man standing near the exit. "When a thought gets in the air, it's out there!" he screams at Murray. "You'll start hearing people all over the place, people who don't even know each other, talking about it...They'll all be saying the same thing without anyone having made the thought public...It's because it's airborne!" The man shouts, shaking his fists at Murray.

* * * *

"Ah-ha", Murray says closing the front door of his apartment and taking his hat off. "Engaging in some intellectual stimulation, I see." He bends down to acknowledge Shadow's greeting.

"Yep," Kirby says through an exhale. "Just finished midterms. Thought a tape of some old Stern reruns and a couple of doobies would help me to regain perspective."

"Achieving an altered state of consciousness is good for expanding one's thinking," Murray says with a chuckle.

"Why don't you join me when you get settled in?" Kirby asks.

"Thanks. I will. Did I get any messages?"

"Yeah. I wrote them down by the phone. I don't know if you can read my handwriting. One was from Joe, no, *John*, from Meals-Not-Militia. And you also got a message from some woman who said it was urgent that she speaks with you. She said she was calling from some law office from somewhere back East. Chicago, maybe?"

"What did you say to her?" Murray asks.

"I told her she should call back tomorrow."

"Thanks," Murray says. "Anything else?"

"No. That's it. We got the electric bill today. I put it on the kitchen counter." Kirby hits 'play' and the tape resumes just as Howard Stern begins verbally molesting two fans who have come down to the studio to show him their breast implants.

Murray goes into his bedroom and closes the door. After about fifteen minutes, Murray goes out the back door carrying a paper-bag. He returns a few minutes later, empty-handed, and heads for the living room.

"So," Murray says sitting down in the beat-up recliner, "Do you have any more of that joy weed?"

"Yeah. Here. Fire one up." Kirby hands Murray a small suede drawstring pouch filled with joints. He does not take his eyes off the screen. One of the Stern fans is taking off her clothes and giggling.

"What do you suppose these women see in him?" Murray asks, as he lights up the joint.

"You got me," Kirby says. "Power, maybe? I don't know. These chicks are a bunch of half-wits. Maybe it doesn't take much to turn them on."

Murray chuckles. "They don't need to be intelligent," Murray says. "*Look* at them. It's not like they have to depend on their brains to get what they want out of life. Anyway...I wouldn't kick this one out of bed," Murray says, motioning towards the screen.

The two men laugh. "Tell me," Murray continues, "Why don't any of these types of women exist in *real* life?"

"Oh, they do. You just haven't been trolling in the right places," Kirby says opening a beer.

"I guess I wouldn't know what to say to 'em even if one of them were right here in this apartment," Murray says.

"I don't think you would have to worry about *saying* anything."

The two laugh. Kirby switches the video recorder off and turns the television channel to local Cable Public Access. He turns off the volume on the television and puts the radio on. Images of penises, homosexuals embracing, and transvestites in wild makeup and costumes flicker across the screen in time to the music of Sublime. "Imagine," Murray says pointing toward the television screen, "a bill had to be passed in Congress to make sure *this* got on the air."

Kirby smirks. "It does make for interesting background," he says.

Murray watches the screen for several minutes. "Do you ever get the feeling there's an entire world going on out there all around you, that you know nothing about?" He asks motioning towards the television.

"It's all an illusion anyway," Kirby says, adjusting the pillows and stretching out on the lumpy sofa.

"How's that?" Murray asks.

"Life. Reality. It's all constructed on illusion," Kirby says. "People create the reality they *want*. We construct reality according to how we need it to be."

"In that case," Murray says, "maybe we ought to reconstruct the reality of this furniture. If it's all an illusion anyway, I'm for turning all this junk into a few Ethan Allen pieces."

"Seriously, dude," Kirby responds, "*You* created this reality. This furniture is part of it. It's just backdrop, of course, but it's all a part of the illusion you created because you needed and wanted your reality to be just the way it is."

"And what would that be?" Murray asks. "What exactly is this reality I supposedly created for myself? I mean, if I constructed this reality, then why didn't I do a better job?" Murray asks, chuckling.

"I don't know, dude. Only *you* can answer that. Maybe it's because you couldn't do any better than this. More likely, you didn't *want* to do it any differently. I mean, you're always exactly where you want to be," Kirby says.

"I don't know if I agree with your analysis," Murray says, shifting in his chair. "What purpose would it serve to create *this*?" He says, gesturing around the living room.

"Like I said, only you can determine that. Maybe you like the bohemian lifestyle. Maybe you prefer freedom above comfort. This lifestyle gives you freedom, right? I mean you are not committed to some job you hate, working seventy hours a week to pay for a lot of expensive furniture, right?"

Murray nods.

"Maybe," Kirby continues, "you crave a life free of commitments. I don't know what it is. You would be the best judge."

Murray rubs his chin for several seconds.

"You said earlier that there is an entire world out there you feel you know nothing about, right?" Kirby asks.

Murray nods.

"If that's true," Kirby continues, "it's only because it's not part of your schema. It's because you have created a reality that neither wants nor needs things like perversion..."

"Well," Murray interrupts, "I wouldn't go *that* far."

The two men laugh.

"My point is," Kirby continues, "that whatever you think reality is, it's just an illusion. It's all a matter of your perception...and I guarantee you, your perception of this place, this city, this lifestyle, and so on, is probably nothing at all like mine." Kirby takes another drink of his beer and sits thoughtfully for several minutes. "It's like you and your cat," he says, finally.

"How's that?" Murray asks with interest.

"You know. You have some special kind of relationship with him."

"You noticed, huh?" Murray asks, smiling.

"Kind of hard not to. Let's face it, it's not your typical relationship between pet owner and pet. Am I right?" Kirby asks.

Murray lights a cigarette and leans back in his chair. "Agreed," he says.

"Well, how did that happen?" Kirby asks. "I mean, the two of you are strangely..." Kirby pauses to search for the right word. "To use Karen's terminology, the two of you are strangely *connected*."

Murray shifts in his chair. Just then Shadow enters the living room, looks up at Murray and speaks. "Come here, buddy," Murray says. Shadow remains standing in the middle of the floor and speaks again, this time with more emphasis.

"What is it?" Murray asks him. "Is someone trapped on the ice, Lassie?"

Kirby laughs. Shadow repeats the same emphatic cries.

"Okay," Murray says, groaning as he hoists himself out of the easy chair. "Let's see what you're talking about."

Murray follows Shadow. Shadow trots along, talking all the way, and stops abruptly at his food bowl. "Hmm," Murray says, bending down.

"Is he telling you he's out of food?" Kirby yells from the living room.

"Nah," Murray replies. "This is an old trick of his. He's just inviting me to come over and be with him while he eats." Murray mixes up the dry food with his fingers. "There you go, buddy. You're not getting any more for the day. You're too fat as it is."

Murray waits a couple of minutes while Shadow eats and then he walks back into the living room.

"How long have you had him?" Kirby asks.

"Eight years. He's eight years old. He adopted me. We've been through a lot together. We've traveled all over the country together," Murray says, stretching the chair out into the reclining position.

"Well, there you go," Kirby says. "As I was saying, the two of you have a special connection. A bond that is highly...well, let's say...unusual. Some animal behavior experts might even argue that such a relationship is not even possible."

"Yeah, well, let them come in and see for themselves, and then see how they explain it," Murray says.

"That's just my point," Kirby says reaching for his beer. "*Their* perception of reality is that animals are incapable of anything beyond what is instinctual. They would say that Shadow cannot possibly communicate with you in any way that requires emotion or reason."

Murray grunts.

"But *your* perception of reality is something quite different, right?" Kirby asks. "I mean you *know* that you and Shadow communicate. You know that you and he are bonded. And how did that happen? Because it was a reality you wanted and needed." Kirby sets his beer bottle down and leans back on the sofa.

Just then, Shadow enters the living room and jumps on the arm of Murray's recliner. "Did you have a good dinner?" Murray asks. "*Rroow*," Shadow replies.

Kirby laughs and shakes his head. "Unbelievable," he says.

Several moments of silence pass as Murray rubs Shadow's face and head. Finally, Murray says, "Just what is *your* perception of this place?"

"Well, temporary," Kirby says. "Ephemeral. It's backdrop. It's not what is central to who I am, or what I am about, or my life in general. I could be anywhere, really. So nothing in my surroundings have that much meaning to me, personally. I guess you could say that for me, the setting is not what is salient."

"And what about the poor?" Murray asks. "Do they create their reality too? And, if they do create their own reality, then why don't they create one in which they are better off?" Murray leans back, pleased with himself. He has a knack for keeping people talking. And, right now, more than anything, he wants Kirby to talk.

"No, man," Kirby says, leaning forward. "You're not getting it. First of all, I think the Bleeding Hearts of the world are too often guilty of not giving other people the respect they deserve."

Murray shifts in the recliner until he is sitting bolt upright. Shadow jumps down and sits on the floor.

"You see," Kirby continues, "you demean people by not giving them ownership of their own choices. First off, why is *your* way the *best* way, or the only way? Why do you think that money is what *everyone* strives for? Believe it or not, there are people who do not have money who are actually happy...besides, for some people, living without money is simply a compromise...a trade-off for something they want or need even more."

Murray shifts in his chair. "Like what?" he asks.

Kirby thinks for several seconds. "Well, like freedom, for one thing," he says. "You can have freedom without money, you know. Maybe not comfort, but freedom. For some people, freedom may mean not needing to go to work each day and do something they hate. Anyway...I digress. My point is that everyone, other than children, that is, we're talking about adults here. Anyway, everyone is responsible for their own choices...and the consequences."

Kirby sits up, takes another joint out of the pouch, and lights it. When he has inhaled and exhaled a couple of times, he passes it to Murray and resumes his thoughts.

"Anyway, as I see it, if poor people choose to act in ways that to middle-class people, seem not to be in their own best interest, it's only because the middle-class have their own perception of reality. A perception of how things 'should be.' That perception of reality is no more real or valid than the poor person's reality. Either way, it's just an illusion that people create for themselves."

Kirby gets up from the sofa and stretches his arms. "I've got to take a leak," he says.

Murray is left feeling exhilarated. He hopes he will be able to remember most of Kirby's words. He considers going into his bedroom to write down some notes, but changes his mind when he hears the sound of the toilet flush.

Kirby heads for the kitchen. "I hope we have something to eat in this place. I've got the munchies." Kirby begins opening one cabinet door after another and then slamming each one in disappointment.

"Oh. I just remembered," Murray says. "I bought some Trail-mix the last time I went to Free Earth. It's in a bag in the cabinet next to the 'fridge."

"Found it. Thanks. Excellent...I'm starving," Kirby says pouring the Trail-mix into a bowl.

"So, Kirby," Murray calls into the kitchen. "This theory of yours, that we all construct our own reality...We do this based on the perceptions and illusions we create to fit our own needs...right?"

"Yeah?" Kirby calls back, moving bottles and cans around inside the refrigerator.

"Did you ever use this theory to, uh, to create a reality for yourself where you pretended to be something you weren't?" Murray asks.

Kirby walks to the edge of the living room with a confused look on his face. "You mean like fantasizing that I am already successful and not living in this dump?" he asks. "Yeah, I guess I've done that."

"No," Murray says, looking down towards his shoes. "That's not what I had in mind."

Murray pauses for a couple of moments and then sits back in his chair. "Does this theory of yours work for the homeless, too?" Murray asks. "I mean, do they create their own reality, too? Are they exactly where they want and need to be?" Murray is careful to keep his tone one of genuine curiosity. He does not want to sound antagonistic.

"Oh, don't even get me started on that one," Kirby says, taking a handful of Trail-mix and shaking his head.

"No, seriously," Murray says. "I'm genuinely interested in hearing your take on the topic."

Just then the telephone rings. Kirby looks at the clock and mutters, "Who could be calling so late?"

Murray shrugs and heads toward the bathroom.

"Remind me to tell you my homelessness take later," Kirby says, as he gets up to answer the phone.

"Hello," Kirby says, with concern in his voice.

The caller is a woman who sounds distressed. She asks to speak with Murray. Kirby lays the phone down and heads toward the bathroom to get him.

"Murray. Phone call...it's a woman. It sounds real important."

"Thanks," Murray yells from behind the bathroom door. "I'll be right there."

Kirby returns to the sofa and continues to surf the channels with the mute still on. When Murray picks up the phone, Kirby can hear some of what the woman on the other end is saying.

"It's Mollie...she's sick. She's..." The rest is unclear.

"What is her temperature?" Murray asks authoritatively. Kirby gives a start at how dramatically different Murray's voice sounds.

"Did you take her blood pressure? Are her pupils dilated? Hmm...uh-huh...Any other symptoms? Have you called anyone else? 911?"

"No" Kirby can hear from the other end of the phone. And then, "She's afraid of going to the hospital." And then something that sounds to Kirby like, "She's scared she'll be locked up again if she goes to the hospital."

"I'll leave right now," Murray says. "I'll be there as soon as I can," he adds firmly. "Try and get her to drink some fluids."

Murray hangs up the phone, runs his hands through his hair a few times, mutters under his breath, and heads for his bedroom. After a few minutes, Murray comes out with his pack on his back.

"I've got to shove off," he says to Kirby.
"Do you need a lift?" Kirby asks.
"No thanks. I'm going to take the BART."
"At this hour? Isn't that dangerous?"
"No one would dare mess with me," Murray says nervously. "Oh, and uh, don't worry if you don't see me until tomorrow. The train stops running in a couple of hours. I might have to wait until the morning to get back."
"Take care," Kirby says. "Call if you want a ride or anything."
"Thanks. See you later." Murray bends down and gently wakes Shadow. "I've got to go out, buddy. I'll be back tomorrow morning, okay? See you later."

Murray walks much brisker than he normally does. He arrives at the BART station a full ten minutes quicker than usual. Murray fumbles for his pass as he heads through the entranceway. He walks down the stairs to the subway, completely unaware of the five young men in over-sized clothing and red bandannas that step out from behind the concrete barrier, flick their cigarettes across the pavement, and fall in line behind him.

When Murray approaches the final stairs down into the subway, two of the young men pass him and block his way on the bottom step. One of the men moves to the left of Murray, and the other two stay close behind him.

"What's in the backpack, little man?" asks one of the young men blocking Murray's path.

"Yeah, little man. What you got in there?" asks the one on his left.

One of the men directly in front of Murray takes his fingers and jabs them into Murray's chest, pushing him just enough to cause him to lose his balance. Murray tips backwards, into the young men standing at his back.

"Give us your money, old man," says one of the men behind him, as he grabs hold of one of the straps of Murray's backpack. "Or we'll make it so your own mama won't recognize you."

Murray straightens his back, tips his head backwards and then forward. He looks straight ahead, beyond the two men standing in front of him.

"All right," Murray says. "You want to know where the drugs are?" he shouts. "You want to know where the drugs are? *I'll* tell you where the drugs are, all right."

Murray's voice is strange, his face distorted. The five young men start to shift and fidget.

"Bosnia!" Murray shouts. "*That's* where! Bosnia! That is, if you can get that son-of-a-bitch, Kadaffi out of the way…Baby-killers, the whole lot of them!" Murray's voice moves to a shrill pitch.

"What the fuck is he talking about?" asks one of the men in front. The others shrug.

"Give us your money, man!" Shouts the one on the left, shoving Murray's body into the railing on his right.

"You know they killed my father!" Murray shouts. "They kidnapped my daughter to increase their profits. No one should buy their ketchup *or* their soup! They're all murderers! Capitalists murderers!" Murray's body is shaking as he screams. His face and neck are bright red. He clinches his fists and pounds his head repeatedly. His body rocks rapidly back and forth, back and forth.

"No!" Murray screams. "They killed him. Everyone knows they did! They use the body parts in the Cream of Mushroom soup…The government knows it, but they don't do anything about it because the FDA is in bed with the food companies!"

With this, Murray lets out a blood-curdling scream. "The country is eating dead bodies in their fucking soup and the government just lets it go on!"

"Man, let's get out of here. This guy is fucking crazy!" says one of the men in front, pushing his friend on

Murray's left up the stairs. The two men standing behind Murray turn to follow.

"Yeah," one of the men says as Murray begins another round of rocking, shaking his fist, and screaming. "This motherfucker's insane. He's gonna' attract attention."

The five young men bolt up the stairs. Their footsteps can be heard for several seconds as they run across the concrete on their way out of the station.

Murray continues to rock and mumble and shout obscenities for several minutes more. When he is sure the five have gone and he is safe, he walks to the automatic gate, slides his pass through, and heads down the final flight of stairs to the subway.

Once he is on the platform, Murray looks at his watch and shakes his head. When the train pulls in several minutes later, Murray steps aboard and collapses into the closest seat. There is no one else on the car. He closes his eyes and tilts his head back. This time he doesn't even bother to look out the window.

At the next stop, two men in their late-twenties get on. They sit several seats away, facing in Murray's direction. Murray notices the two look so much alike, that they could be identical twins.

"Did you see that chick Jeff was hitting on tonight?" The one closest to the window asks.

"Oh, man. Great body, but what planet did she come in from?" The one near the aisle says. They both laugh.

"She made me think of old times," the one by the window says. "Remember that place we had in Newport Beach while we were in college," he continues, "and we had those wacky neighbors who lived on the corner?"

"Oh, yeah," the one by the aisle says. "I remember. What was that guy's name? Donald. That's it. Yeah, he was one of those aging hippie-types. Mid-forties, bald on top, with long hair in the back. That guy was *always* on acid. It used to completely freak me out to talk to him."

They both laugh.

"He was out of work every other week, remember?" The man by the aisle asks. "He was always complaining about what idiots all of his bosses were, and he'd quit every job after about ten days."

"Actually, I was thinking about his *wife*," the one by the window says with a smile on his face.

"Oh, yes. Sweet Cassy. She had an incredible sense of timing. As I remember it, she would go outside to water her flowers in her string bikini every morning just at the time you would be getting back from surfing," says the one near the aisle.

"Yeah," the one near the window says, smiling. "She'd be bent way over with her little watering can every morning at 6:30. I'd be walking back from the beach with my surfboard and I'd see the traffic on Balboa Boulevard slowing down almost to a stop, and I'd know Cassy was out watering her flowers again." He shakes his head and laughs.

"Remember when mom and dad came down to visit that time, and Cassy was out cleaning her windows in her bikini?" The one near the aisle asks, laughing as he speaks. "And she asked dad to give her a hand putting the screen back in her window..."

"Yeah," the one near the window says, laughing. "And mom came out and Cassy was hanging half way out the window. Cassy was falling out of her bathing suit, and there was dad standing in the middle of her garden, looking up at her and trying to attach the screen.

"Mom came back in the house and said, 'Are you boys sure this is the sort of place you should be staying? There seems to be so many...well, *distractions* to your studying'." The two men laugh.

"She worked in a law office in Irvine, didn't she?" The one by the window asks.

"Yeah, but remember? She used to make extra money on the weekends by putting on her tiny, red string bikini and selling those stupid stickers on the beach for a *dollar* a piece.

"Every time she went out there she had every kid with a skateboard lined up for blocks to buy a sticker. They would usually drop their money as they were handing it to her just to get her to bend over. I watched it happen like ten times one day," he says, laughing. "She never caught on."

"Yeah. She was also great for the tourists," the one by the window says. All of those people vacationing from Wisconsin snapping pictures of her bending over...that's probably what they remember most about their trip to California." They both laugh.

The brothers sit thinking in silence for several minutes. "Oh," the one by the aisle says, finally. "Remember Rick, the macho *fireman*? He used to order all of that stuff from Frederick's of Hollywood and we'd usually be the only ones around during the day to sign for the UPS deliveries. Remember? And for the longest time we couldn't figure out who he was ordering all that stuff for."

"Yeah!" The one by the window says. "I remember him. He'd get drunk on all of his days off, and blast his stereo so high our windows would shake. And then one night you got so upset you went over at two in the morning to ask him to turn down the music. It was so loud he couldn't hear you, so you looked through his window to try and get his attention, and there he was..."

"Yeah," the one near the aisle says, "There he was...Fire Fighter Rick, dancing and prancing around to the music in the middle of his living room, wearing fuck-me pumps and a black lace tank top and panties from Fredericks!"

The two men both laugh so hard that tears come to their eyes. When their stop finally comes, they exit the train doing impressions of the firefighter and laughing.

Murray searches in his pockets for his notepad. He writes straight through for the next three stops. When he finishes, he turns to a clean page, and writes the words, "Title: PARADOX." A few moments later, he crosses out the word, "paradox" and replaces it with the word, "ILLUSIONS." After a couple of minutes, he crosses the last entry out and writes, "THE PARADOX OF ILLUSIONS."

Murray carefully replaces his notepad in his pocket, puts his knapsack on his back, and stands up near the automatic doors. As he waits for his stop to approach, he notices that someone has written graffiti on the aluminum partition separating the entrance area from the seats. "NO ONE CAN SAVE YOU BUT YOURSELF . . . URINATE !!! "

As he reads it, a smile comes across Murray's face. Almost as an afterthought, he reaches into his shirt pocket for his felt-tip marker, bends down and writes, "ENURESIS RULES !!!" just before the doors open.

III

Murray starts his morning coffee and turns on the oven. He walks to the corner of the kitchen for his recipe books. Shadow comes into the kitchen and speaks in his usual, "It's time for breakfast" meow.

"Ah, so it is, little buddy," Murray says. "Let's see how much food you have left in your bowl."

Murray grunts as he bends down to get Shadow's bowls. "Ah-ha. You're eating like a little piggy still, I see. You could stand to lose a couple of pounds, you know?"

Shadow responds by lifting his tail in the air.

"All right, maybe we'll work on the diet some time later then," Murray says, filling Shadow's bowl with food. "Interesting. You polished off most of your water, too. Were you running around here yesterday?" Murray places Shadow's food and water bowls on the floor and returns to the recipe book.

"Well, Shadow," Murray says, "it's a good thing we are postponing that diet of yours, because I'm going to make your favorite today." Shadow looks up from his bowl.

"That's right," Murray continues, as he flips through the recipe book. "Mollie is finally starting to recover so I'm going to bake up a batch of homemade oat bran muffins. If you're real good today, you can have some." Shadow walks away from his food bowl, meows and circles around Murray.

Murray moves through the kitchen digging out the ingredients, muffin tins, paper fillers, bowls, spoons, and a sifter. Shadow jumps up onto one of the kitchen chairs and watches Murray prepare the muffins.

When the muffins have finished baking and finally cooled, Murray places a small portion of a muffin on a plate and gives it to Shadow, who quickly gobbles it up. Murray then places a couple of muffins in the refrigerator for later, wraps the rest, and heads off to take the subway to Mollie's.

* * * *

"Some guy was here looking for a Dr. something-or-other, yesterday. Here, I wrote it down someplace," Kirby says as he balances his jellied toast and reaches for a paper on the kitchen counter. "Oh, yeah. Dr. Barry Yardley. Do you know anybody by that name?"

"No. Can't say as I do," Murray says, filling up his metal coffeepot under the faucet.

"It was weird, actually," Kirby says. "I mean, he didn't act like he was asking *whether* this Dr. Yardley lived here or not. It was more like he was certain that he *did* live here and was asking if he was in, and when he would be back."

"Did this guy give you any indication of what he wanted with this doctor?" Murray asks.

"No. He did say to tell this Dr. Yardley he would be in town for the next three days and that he could be reached during the day at the university hospital. He left an extension to reach him on the back of his business card, but I don't see it here...I thought I laid it on the counter. Anyway, I guess the guy is some doctor, too. His business card was from some hospital back east. Actually, I'm pretty sure it was Chicago. Do you think this Dr. Yardley could have lived here before you moved in?"

Murray chuckles. "I don't know why a doctor would ever live in this dump."

"You've got a point there," Kirby says, finishing the end of his toast. "Maybe he lived here to study the effects of all the mold spores growing on the walls."

Murray smirks. "Yeah," he says. "I suppose we should do something to clean this place up one of these days."

"Well, not today, unfortunately. I've got a lab this morning, and a full schedule today," Kirby says putting his dish in the sink. "As a matter of fact, I've got to jet. If that Berkeley Curve is backed up anything like it was yesterday, I'm in trouble."

"Oh, hey," Kirby adds, looking for his backpack, "I keep forgetting, if you ever want to use my computer for whatever it is you're working on, feel free."

"Oh, thanks, but I'm sort of attached to doing things the old-fashioned way," Murray chuckles. "Thanks, though. Have a good day," Murray says, pouring himself a cup of coffee. "Maybe you can solve the mysteries of the universe today."

"Are you kidding?" Kirby asks, grabbing his keys off the counter. "I'll have a hard enough time just figuring out how to keep my car from getting towed away...See you later."

"Bye, now," Murray says, giving a wave.

Murray takes his coffee mug and heads towards his bedroom. "Come on, Shadow," he says, as he leaves the kitchen. Shadow gives a meow response and gets up and prances behind Murray.

Once inside, Murray closes the door. "Listen," he says to Shadow, "We've got to talk about something important."

Murray grunts as he sits down in the battered and torn leather high-back chair opposite the television set. Shadow jumps up on the Ottoman across from Murray.

"All right, old buddy," Murray says. He takes a sip of his coffee, sits the mug down on an inverted Berkeley Farms crate, and lights a cigarette.

Murray inhales, exhales, shifts in his chair and then begins, "It looks as if it's getting to be time to shove off in a bit, little buddy. Things are heating up around here." Shadow pricks up his ears and looks at Murray.

"It's time to blow this Popsicle stand anyhow. Too much mold. Too much doom-and-gloom. Too much fog." Murray takes a gulp of coffee and sits the mug back down.

"Too many gangs. Too many vampire-wanna'-be's. Way too much whining...Too many people letting their freak-flags fly." Murray laughs. "Anyway, Shadow, we may have to take off soon. If anything were to happen to me, who would take care of you, buddy?" Shadow closes and reopens his eyes slowly. "Who could ever appreciate you, my little kitty-Einstein?"

Murray reaches over and rubs Shadow's head. "It's for your own good, Shadow. You don't like it here, anyway. All the fleas. Besides, you have to stay trapped up here in this apartment all the time hiding out from that old witch Gail, the landlady." Shadow replies with. "Rrah, Rraah" and swings his tail from side to side.

"I'm planning on in a bit we could get our own little place with a yard and sunshine. You could play out in the yard all day with me. Would you like that?" Shadow replies and jumps off the Ottoman and onto the arm of Murray's chair.

"If anything happened to me and we were separated, I couldn't bear to think about what might happen to you." Murray's jaw tightens and tears flow down his face. He puts his face against Shadow's. "I love you, buddy," he says through sobs.

Murray sits up and wipes his face and blows his nose with his handkerchief. "Anyway, Shadow, it will be a lot better for both of us..."

Just then the doorbell rings. Murray freezes. Shadow pricks up his ears. "*Shhh,*" Murray whispers to him. The doorbell rings two more times. Murray and Shadow remain still. There is the sound of footsteps nearing the sidewalk just outside the bedroom, and then the outline of someone trying to see in the windows.

Murray holds on to Shadow. Both remain still. After a few seconds, the footsteps move towards the back of the two-flat, and then around the side, to the front of the building. Murray gets up from the chair and quietly tiptoes to the living room. He peeks through the blinds just as a man in a dark suit gets into a black car. He writes something down and then Murray sees him talking on the phone. After several minutes, the car pulls away.

Murray returns to the bedroom and gathers up some clothes. "Like I said, Shadow, we may have to get out of here. I'm going to shower now. I've got an important appointment today."

* * * *

"Murray, Murray," George Pelton says, chuckling and patting Murray on the back as he enters the room. "Well, I've finished it, old boy," George says, patting a stack of papers lying on the desk. "Looks like you've got a real winner here."

Murray's facial expression changes from anticipated rejection to the look of sheer child-like joy. "You liked it?"

"*Liked* it? I *loved* it." George says patting Murray on the back again.

"In fact," he continues, "the reason I asked you to come by a little early is to tell you I'm going to make an announcement to your creative writing group today. I'd like to give it a dry run. If the group doesn't have any major changes to suggest, I say we get ready to send it out. We could have this thing on stage with Dolan's group possibly within half a year or so."

Murray's eyes open wide as if he is trying to physically absorb all he is hearing.

"Listen," George says, "as I told you before, one of my students from the play-group I ran back in the eighties now owns his own playhouse. It's in the Tenderloin. Very cutting-edge. He usually writes or co-writes his own stuff, but he's on the lookout now for something fresh and interesting from other writers. I know he's especially interested in anything that could be classified, 'Theatre of the Absurd'."

Murray chuckles. "Well," he says, "it's certainly *that*."

"Murray, this work is really special. What you want is *exposure*. Start off in small theatre companies and get it seen. That's the most critical step. It's not as good as having your own agent, mind you, but these days, unless you are either supremely connected or supremely lucky, that's next to impossible."

Murray nods. "I'm appreciative of any break I can get," he says. "I've been working on it for so long now...I can't believe it may actually be going somewhere," Murray says as he smiles and looks at the floor.

"Let's have your group do the first reading," George says. "I'm sure they'll agree with me. If, after hearing it played out, you feel it's ready, we'll send it over to Dolan and see what he thinks."

"Sounds great," Murray says, barely able to conceal his excitement. He takes his seat and pulls out his notepad and begins writing. Within a few minutes, the other members of the creative writing group enter, chattering with one another. Murray stops writing and makes small talk with them about how their week has been and how their writing is coming along. For some, the writing group is merely a social event. For most, however, the writing and the group are the only things that hold their lives together.

Murray looks at the clock on the wall. He checks his shirt pocket for his cigarettes and matches and heads for the door. He walks down the long corridor underneath the sign marked, "Psychiatric Ward: Outpatient," and turns left towards the outside exit.

Once outside, Murray lights a cigarette and begins pacing nervously. He paces and smokes, and then paces some more. Finally, he puts his cigarette out in the sand of the outdoor ashtray, tugs at the waistband of his tattered, tan-colored cotton pants, clears his throat, and heads back through the entrance marked, "Outpatient: Activity Area."

Murray enters the room just as George is finishing up his instructions. All heads turn towards Murray. His classmates smile, offer kudos, and start a round of applause. Red faced, Murray stumbles to his chair and picks up the packet of his play from his seat. As he settles in, he notices that all of his classmates already have their own copies.

"Well now, we all have our parts assigned," George says, taking his seat in the circle, "Shall we begin?"

~ ~ ~ ~

ACT I

The scene opens up on a subway car. Two men are seated on opposite ends of the car. One of them is dressed in drab, worn-out clothing. He is wearing a wool plaid cap. There is a backpack on the seat next to him. The man is intently writing something on a small notepad. The other man is dirty and homeless. He is talking loudly, perhaps to the man at the opposite end of the car, perhaps, to no one at all.

Homeless Man: You know what all of them do, don't you? *All* of them. They start picking away just as soon as they get the chance. What's your name there, young man?

(The other man looks up, a little startled.)

Barry: Uh, Barry.

Homeless Man: Barry, eh? Is that an interring name? Well, as I was saying Barry, they *all* do it.
Barry: What's that?
Homeless Man: Picking away. Within just a few minutes they start in. They'll say, "Is this the *original* door on here?" or "This isn't the *original* hood on here, is it?" or "Did you have the trunk replaced? This isn't the original." They *all* do it. Mechanics. Car salesmen. People who come out to help you when you break down. People who work in auto part stores. Even this guy who fixed my lock once after my car had been broken into. I think its part of their training. They all do it. No matter what car you have. And they don't even know one another! One of these times I'm gonna' say, "Yeah, it's not the original. Nothing on here is original. *The whole fucking car's been replaced.*" You know what *I* think?
Barry: Sorry?
Homeless Man: What *I* think? I think they're up to something. Sending you a message. Trying to belittle you by putting down your property. What other motive would they have?
Barry: What reason do you suppose they would have for putting people down?
Homeless Man: Basic instincts. You've said it yourself a thousand times.
Barry: How's *that?* (expressing surprise)
Homeless Man: *You* know. Aggressive Display. We're no different than other animals. Than all of nature, for that matter. You've said it a thousand times.
Barry: How do you know *that?*
Homeless Man: The mechanics try to show you who's boss. Who's in control. That way, their word, or their final bill, is not questioned. It's no different than

the rest of the Animal Kingdom to hear *you* tell it. Only instead of puffing their chest out, or aggressive gesturing, they point out the flaws in your property.

Barry: Interesting theory.

Homeless Man: Oh, not nearly as interesting as some of your *other* theories.

Barry: And what might *those* be?

Homeless Man: Speaking of mechanics, wasn't it you who said medical doctors are no more than auto mechanics? I believe you once said that doctors lack the ability to do creative, expansive, and critical thinking. Rote memory, is what you said their training was. They memorize the parts of the human body in much the same way as auto mechanics memorize the parts of a car. When something goes wrong, the doctor, like the mechanic, looks for the most likely thing first. If that doesn't work, they pull out their manual and look for the thing that has the next highest statistical likelihood, and so on.

Barry: (snickering) Yeah, and if they still can't figure out the problem, they refer you to a specialist. Audi or neurologist--not much difference. I told that theory once at a lecture on the bio-psycho-social approach to the patient...(voice trails off)

Conductor: (From somewhere off-stage an unintelligible announcement of stop)...Watch your step please.

(Barry returns to writing. The Homeless Man leans back in his seat. A woman enters the subway car and sits several seats away, facing Barry. She is silent for several minutes and then addresses Barry.)

Diane:	You know, Barry. You had better climb out of your hole.
Barry:	What hole is that?
Diane:	You know. That hole you got yourself dug into. You're going to lose everything if you don't. What's the matter with you, anyway? Couldn't you see it coming?
Barry:	See what coming?
Diane:	The hole! Couldn't you even see what you were doing? Digging your self into a hole?
Homeless Man:	(chuckling) That's some hole you got yourself in, Barry.
Barry:	I don't know what you are talking about, Diane.
Diane:	You don't? What about your career? What about your life? What about *me?*
Barry:	*You're* a hole? (Homeless Man chuckles)
Diane:	See. This is exactly what I mean. Everything is a joke to you. What are you doing about your career? Nothing. I don't even know what it is you do all day, but it's not what you are suppose to be doing, that much I do know.
Barry:	And just what is it, according to you, that I am *supposed* to be doing?
Diane:	Be like everyone else, *that's* what. Why can't you be like everyone else? Instead, you are holed-up in your own little world. It's like you burrowed yourself into your own little hole and you are refusing to come out.
Homeless Man:	Is that "hole" as in "Hell-Hole," or "hole" as in the domain of an "Ass-Hole"?
Barry:	What do you want from me?
Diane:	A commitment, for starters. I am not even sure I can depend on you.
Barry:	I'm there when you need something.

Diane:	That's not what I am talking about. I want a *commitment*, Barry. Here I am raising my teenage son alone, who, as you know, is driving me crazy.
Homeless Man:	Driving Miss Daisy?
Diane:	(giving Homeless Man a look of annoyance) I need to know if you are going to be there for me. I need to know I can depend on you. Why can't you just be like everyone else? What about our future?
Barry:	I'm not going anywhere.
Diane:	I can't rely on if you will be able to support me or if you'll keep on insisting on being this "*free spirit*" you're always yammering on about. I don't get it Barry. Why can't you just be like everyone else? The rest of us aren't *free*, for God's sake. You think the rest of us wouldn't like to be free and happy? We would. But it's not realistic. Real life is about taking responsibility and doing what we have to do; not just what we *want* to do.
Barry:	And here, all along, I thought we had free choice to decide how to live our lives.
Diane:	What would the world be like if everyone decided to be *free* and *happy*?
Barry:	A better place to live?
Diane:	Oh, grow up, Barry. No one has that. Sure, it would be nice if we all just did what made us feel good. What's that you call it? *Self-actualize*. But the reality is that the rest of us have a lot of crap in our lives we have to deal with.
Barry:	But isn't that of one's choosing? Don't people *choose* to have children, make commitments, accumulate a lot of stuff, and then choose to work at jobs they hate, to pay for all of their other choices?

Diane:	You just don't get it, do you? Why do you think you're so special? Why do you think you're *entitled* to be happy?
Barry:	Isn't *everyone?*
Diane:	That isn't what life is about!
Barry:	Life is not supposed to be an endurance test, at least from my perspective...(trails off)
Diane:	I need to be with someone who will make a commitment to me. I have to look out for my future. I just don't know where you are going. You seem intent on this idea to "drop out" as you are so fond of saying. *Normal* men *want* to be successful. *Normal* men *want* to build careers. They *want* to compete.
Barry:	Do they also want to go to work each day to a job they hate? Do they want to have heart attacks? To feel unfulfilled? To die unhappy?
Diane:	There you go again, talking as if people should just give up their normal lives.
Barry:	No, I don't want people to give up anything. I just don't want any part of that rat race. It's my choice. Not for me, thanks.
Diane:	That is exactly the attitude I am talking about. I just don't think I can stay together with you anymore. I need someone who I can depend on. Not someone who may disappear at any moment and run off into the Redwoods. I can't be with someone who is chasing some elusive dream of being *happy.*
Barry:	(chuckling) I guess I am just a square peg in a round hole.
Homeless Man:	Hole: (1) an opening through something, (2) something missing: a gap, (3) serious discrepancy: a FLAW, weakness, (4) a defect in a crystal, (5) cavity, depression, cave, pit,

hollowed-out place, (6) burrow, (7) wretched or dreary place, (8) awkward position or circumstance: a fix, (9) a score below zero, (10) being at a disadvantage. She's right, Barry, anyway you look at it, you've got to get out of that hole.

Barry: (holding his hand up as if it is a gun and pointing it towards Diane)
Bang! You're gone.

(Diane slumps forward. The lights flicker in the subway car. The conductor speaks, an unintelligible stop is announced. The doors open and a man enters and sits directly across from Barry.)

Mosh Pitt: Hey, Barry, how's it going?

Barry: (looking over at man) Mosh! Hey, man, it's great to see you. How long has it been?

Mosh Pitt: What's wrong with *her*? (pointing his thumb towards Diane)

Barry: Dead. (chuckling)

Mosh Pitt: Oh, man, it's so easy, isn't it? If only people knew. They hang around forever in these pathetic, miserable relationships with everyone, like girlfriends, spouses, family, bosses, neighbors. And there's no need for it. No need at all. It's so easy, but no one sees it. (both men chuckle)

Barry: It's really great to see you. What are you doing now?

Mosh: Hangin'. I'll probably jump in sometime soon, but for now, I'm just hangin'.

Barry: Man, I've really missed you. I've had no one to talk to in so long.

Mosh:	Yeah, (chuckling) I've noticed. What about your roommate?
Barry:	Ahh. He's getting ready to move out. Business school major waiting to happen.

(Mosh snorts)

Barry:	Hey, that reminds me...I was walking past the old coffee shop last week. It's now this nouveau-chic import shop for yuppies. Filled with three-hundred dollar gourds that are hand-painted by some farmer's wife in Peru while he's out herding llamas.
Mosh:	That's beautiful. (snickers)
Barry:	Anyway, so I'm standing outside this place and I start looking at all these notices posted on the door. There's all these people scrambling around looking for rooms to rent, but only one of the signs posted has any numbers torn off. This one has like all of the tabs with the phone numbers gone except two. So I start reading it, and at the top it says in big letters, "WANTED: Room to Rent. DYKE and DOG." (Mosh laughs) It has these two pictures and above one picture it says, "The DOG" with an arrow pointing towards one of the pictures, and above another picture it says, "The DYKE" with another arrow. So I start reading it because, of course, now it has my attention. So under the picture that says, "The DOG" it reads, "FUN-LOVING. ENERGETIC. WELL-TRAINED. HATES JAZZ MUSIC." (Mosh laughs)

	And under the picture that says, "The DYKE" it reads, "AGGRESSIVE. BUTCHY JEW. LOVES TO COOK!"
Mosh:	Well-trained?
Barry:	Apparently not. So anyway, I took one of the tabs with the phone number.
Mosh:	You *called* her?
Barry:	Yeah. I called and said I was inquiring about the notice posted for a room to rent.
Mosh:	Dude, you're kidding. You told her you were considering her to be your roommate?
Barry:	Listen...So I say I'm calling about the rental notice and that I want to talk to the person who placed the notice. She says real butch-like, "speaking," and I say, "I'll take the dog."
Mosh:	(laughing) You *said* that? What did she do?
Barry:	She hung up. (both men laugh)
Mosh:	(still laughing) Man, that was good. So how are things going in general?
Barry:	(clears throat) I don't know. Things were a lot easier to swallow when you were around. Now...I don't know, I feel like I'm spinning around out there all by myself. Remember when we used to say it was a curse?
Mosh:	Yeah. I remember.
Barry:	Is it any easier for you now?
Mosh:	Nah, man. You don't lose it. Not ever. Once you have it, you can never go back. Not ever.
Barry:	There are so many times I wish I could just be like the rest of them. It would be so much easier.
Mosh:	My grandmother used to say, "It's a curse, but it's also a gift." I know it might not always seem like it, but it really *is* a lot better to be able to know and see what you do than to be like the rest of

	them. Do you think you would really rather go through life not being able to know what you do or see what you see?
Barry:	Sometimes. I'm telling you, sometimes it's so damned ugly, I think I'd just as soon live in ignorance. Then I could be like everyone else. Clueless. Just get your job, your house, your car payment, your cemetery plot. Cut and dried. Besides, I feel so damned alienated.
Mosh:	Well, no one is making that happen except you. There's no rule that says you can't be with other people.
Barry:	Yeah, but you remember how it is, don't you? All the relationships I *do* have, the ones I can tolerate, that is, are all so superficial. What can I talk to them about? There's nothing about their lives I really want to hear, and even less I want to say. (Mosh nods) There's no one that understands. No one that sees what I see, even when I point it out, most people just don't get it.
Conductor:	(From somewhere off-stage an unintelligible stop announced) Watch your step please.

(The doors open and several people get on carrying packages, among them, a teenager with a boom-box, and two children. Three women go over to Diane and begin working on her. The men who have just entered start a card game.)

Betty:	Oh, look, there she is. Let's get to work. We don't have too much time. Miriam, you start her hair. I will start her makeup. Then you can start getting her clothes ready.

Miriam: (unpacking a brush, curling iron and hairspray)
            I'm going to try and put it up, but I don't know,
            she's always had such thin, limp hair.
Betty: Just do your best, Miriam. That's all any of us can
            do. Can you hand me the mascara? And the eye
            shadow? I don't know why she ran around
            without any makeup on. I told her a thousand
            times she just didn't have the kind of face that
            could go around without a lot of help. Oh, look,
            the lipstick is all wrong for her!
Miriam: Oh, who cares? It's not like she can pop up and
            do any of her usual complaining.
Betty: Watch what you are doing with that curling iron,
            Miriam, you nearly burnt the dress just now.

(turning towards the opposite end of the subway car)

Betty: Hey, you kids, knock it off. I told you already,
            you need to be behaving in a respectful manner
            at a time like this...Shamus, did you finish writing
            your portion of the eulogy?
Shamus: I don't wanna' do it. She was a *bitch*. I don't
            have anything nice to say about her.

(Gasps can be heard.)

Betty: Shamus! You should be ashamed of yourself.
            She is your *mother.*
Shamus: Oh, and because she was my mother, I am not
            supposed to recognize she was a *bitch*?

(More gasps.)

| Miriam: | You sit down there, young man, and think of something nice to say about her. If you can't think of something nice...then, make something up! And turn down that boom-box. It's disrespectful at a time like this. |

(The two children play chase up and down the aisle of the subway car.)

Betty:	(turning to the men who came aboard with them) It would be nice if you could watch the children instead of playing cards.
Bob:	You talking to us, Betty?
Betty:	Yes. Of course I am. Can't you see we have our hands full here?

(turning to children)

Betty:	Children! Stop writing on the seats! Sit down over here and play nice!
Homeless Man:	(doing crossword puzzle) What's a five-letter word for insane?
Elliot:	CRAZY
Bob:	WACKY
Elliot:	NUTTY
Shamus:	DIANE
Betty:	Shamus!

Bob:	The boy has a point, Betty. (chuckling)
Miriam:	DAFFY
Elliot:	GOOFY
Betty:	LOONY
Bob:	BUGGY, BEANY, BATTY
Elliot:	KOOKY
Miriam:	Will one of you guys please help Shamus out?

(The men look over to where Shamus is sitting.)

Bob:	Come on over here, Shamus. Have a seat. (pats the seat next to him) How's it going? Why so glum?
Shamus:	I'm going to have to stay with my dad now until I graduate high school.
Elliot:	That's not so bad, is it?
Shamus:	It sucks!
Bob:	What's so bad about it?
Shamus:	I don't know what's worse. Living with a crazy mother or an alcoholic father. She was a raving maniac. Always getting us kicked out of places, always starting trouble with the neighbors wherever we went. The police called us by our first names. They knew us because so many neighbors called the cops because of all the crap she pulled. I hated living with her. She was making *me* crazy. But going to live with my dad is going to be just as bad.
Elliot:	Ah, it couldn't be that bad, could it?
Shamus:	He's a juicer. Even when he's not drinking the shrink says he's always "acting alcoholicly." Dry drunk they're called. He's vicious. Every time I'm with him he's taking a swing at me with

something. And everyday he spews his venom. Always yelling at me that I'm a loser and a moron and how I'm gonna' end up living on the streets because I don't have enough brains to even take care of myself.

Homeless Man: Hey! I resent that. You have to have a lot of brains to live on the streets.

Shamus: (giving the homeless man a dirty look) Anyway, he's been saying these things to me since I was a little kid.

Bob: Now, Shamus, you know those things aren't true. Can't you just ignore those things when he says them?

Shamus: I guess. But it's pretty hard when he just keeps riding on me. Sometimes he's relentless. The other thing is that he can't hold a job. I'm scared if I go stay with him, I won't even have food to eat. He keeps getting pissed off at his bosses and then he either quits or gets fired. This year he got this really good job. It was a miracle because he doesn't have a whole lot of good references. Anyway, he gets it in his head that his boss is doing something wrong. Like all of the rest of them, I guess. And so he tells his boss in front of a bunch of people that he's "too self-absorbed." Can you believe it? I mean, I'm just a kid and even /have enough sense to know you shouldn't talk to your boss that way. Even / know it's not a good idea to offend someone who has power over you.

Barry: Look kid, if he had a history of good ideas, he wouldn't be an alcoholic.

(Shamus looks over towards Barry as if noticing him for the first time.)

Bob: Well, Shamus, it's just one year. Don't you think you can hang in there and tough it out for just one year?

Shamus: (beginning to cry) It's not just that. He's...violent. He goes into these uncontrollable violent rages. I'm afraid sometime that I...I might have to defend myself, you know...(long pause)...It's all *your* fault! (Stands up and points his finger towards Barry. Barry looks away, out the window.)

(The two children start running up and down the aisle, blowing bubbles and laughing. The women continue to dress Diane.)

Betty: Looks like she had put on a few pounds recently. I can't get this dress zipped. Miriam, can you pull it tight around the waist and hold it right here? (the women grunt and struggle.) There! Got it. Just the veil left. Miriam, can you help me pin this on?

Miriam: It's not going to hold very well. I told you, her hair is thin and stringy. Here, let me pin it over here, while you hold it in place. (the two women struggle for several seconds.) Okay. Done. We're ready, aren't we?

Betty: Let's give her a once-over.

(The women look Diane over, fixing her up here and there.)

Betty: Yeah. She looks better than she ever did when
                  she was alive. (turning to one of the men) Okay,
                  Pastor, we're ready to begin. Children, come on
                  over here and sit down. Shamus, did you finish
                  that eulogy?
Miriam: (looks at the men) Come on, let's all sit together
                  now. We're ready to begin.

(The men, with the exception of Barry, all get up and move near
the women and children.)

Pastor: (stands and shuffles through some papers)
                  We're gathered together today... (clears throat) to
                  um...we're gathered together today to say
                  goodbye to Diane. She leaves behind friends,
                  relatives, and her beloved son, Shamus.

(Sounds of wailing as the women begin sobbing. Tissues are
passed from one to another. The two children begin kicking the
seat in front of them.)

Pastor: Diane was a wonderful person who always gave of
                  herself to others.
Homeless Man: Yeah, rumor has it, she was real generous
                  spreading her neurotic, vindictive impulses with
                  whoever came within spitting range.
Pastor: (clears throat) And, um, Diane was, uh, (shuffles
                  papers) a person who cared deeply...
Barry: (mumbling) about herself.

| Pastor: | ...who cared deeply about her son, Shamus. Shamus will now say a few words about his mother. |
| Shamus: | (stands) Um, well, my therapist says that thanks to growing up in a chaotic home with my mother, I now have what he calls a "high tolerance for ambiguity." I guess that means I have her to thank for the fact that I can survive even in the most fucked-up situation. |

(The women gasp and begin sobbing again.)

Shamus:	And, uh, I guess it was real good of her after she decided to have me, to go ahead and feed me and give me somewhere to live and all. Um, I guess that's all I have to say. (sits down)
Pastor:	All right then. Diane did not have any religious affiliation, so she left no special instructions. We do know that she has left this earthly life and is now in a more peaceful place.
Homeless Man:	Or is it that we know *this* is a more peaceful place *because* she has left this earthly life?
Pastor:	I will now turn it over to her loved ones. Does anyone have any final words?
Child:	(kicking the back of the seat) When are we going to *eat?* I'm hungry!

(The women turn towards the children.)

| Betty: | *Shhh!* Be quiet. We're almost done here. We'll eat in a few minutes. |

Child:	Is she *dead*, mommy?
Miriam:	Yes.
Child:	If she's dead, why does she have on a wedding dress?
Miriam:	Because she makes a beautiful bride. Don't you think so?
Child:	I wanna' *eat*.
Pastor:	Well, as I was saying. We'll now turn the services over to the loved ones who wish to say their final words to Diane.
Child:	Wait a minute. If she's dead, how can she hear anyone's final words?
Betty:	Be quiet!

(Children begin whining and fidgeting.)

Miriam: I'll say a few words. First of all, I will not be held responsible for how Diane's hair looks now that the veil is on her head. Secondly, I just want to say that Diane was my best friend and when I was in a serious depression because I couldn't get my writing published, it was Diane who convinced me I should just give up my dream of ever being a writer. She convinced me I really didn't have any talent and that I should just stop trying and causing myself heartbreak. I have Diane to thank for saving me. She was relentless in her efforts to get me to see I was really talentless and that I was just living in a dream world. I'm going to miss having her to help me see the truth of things...(begins to sob as she returns to her seat)

Betty:	(standing) I would like to say that Diane was very good at being able to read people. If something was bothering you, she had a knack for zeroing right in on it. Ever since we were kids she could tell if I was worried about something, or sad, or whatever. She would just pop up and start talking about whatever it was that was bothering you.
	There was this one time when I was younger and I had just had a miscarriage. I had been so excited that I was pregnant. Ran out and bought baby things and maternity clothes before I was even showing. Anyway, I was just devastated when I lost it. I couldn't talk to anyone about it for months. Then one day Diane comes over and she's only in the house a few minutes and she starts going on about how some women are never meant to have children, and all the things that could be wrong physically that prevents some women from ever having a full-term pregnancy, and all the problems some women have after they have had miscarriages. Boy, she just went on and on. I'll tell you, I had one hard cry after she left that day. Got it all out of my system. Yep. She really had a knack for reading other people.
Pastor:	Is there anyone else who would like to say something?
Child:	Are we going to have a wedding now?
Miriam:	Hush up. No. We are *not* going to have a wedding.
Pastor:	All right then. Well, uh, we'll conclude then. If you'll all follow me in a silent prayer.

(The men and women bow their heads. The children start smacking one another.)

71

Pastor:	Thank you. Uh, before you leave folks, I have been asked to let everyone know that there will be uh, food and beverages served for the friends and family of the deceased.
Child:	Yeah! Food! I'm starving! Where's the food at?
Betty:	Well, thank you very much, Pastor. It was a lovely service. And just in time, too. Your exit is coming up next.
Pastor:	Oh, uh, yes. I'll be getting off here. Good-bye.

(Doors open and the Pastor exits.)

Bob:	All right. Shamus, what do you say you turn that boom-box of yours up and let's have a little music.

(Shamus turns up the volume and alternative music blares from the portable stereo.)

Bob:	Who wants a drink?
Elliot:	I'll take some. I could use it.

(Bob pours champagne into several paper cups.)

Elliot:	What about that food, ladies?
Miriam:	Coming up. We're just dishing it out.
Bob:	All right everybody. Let's lighten up. It's time to enjoy ourselves! (reaching over and turns

72

volume up on boom-box)　Drinks and food for everyone! Come on, Betty, let's dance.

(Several people begin dancing in the aisle.　Laughter permeates the subway car.)

Elliot:　　　　Come on over here, Barry.　No hard feelings, man. Have a glass of champagne.　These sandwiches here are really good, too.　Help yourself to whatever you want.

(Barry hesitantly gets up and walks to the other end of the car towards the celebration.)

Elliot:　　　　That a boy!　(slaps Barry on the back) Here. Have a drink.　Miriam...get Barry a plate.
Barry:　　　　I didn't mean for her to *actually die*. I just wanted her to die for *me*.
Elliot:　　　　Well, now, you never know the power of a thought, do you?　(chuckles)　Drink up, boy. (pats him on the back)　Miriam, you ready to dance with me again?

(The men and women start dancing.　The children throw food at one another.　Shamus drinks heavily and bobs his head to the music.　Loud laughter permeates.)

Elliot: Come on. We've got to get Barry a dance partner!
                 Give me a hand, boys.

(The men go over to Diane and lift her body up, dragging her over towards Barry.)

Bob: There you go. Dance with your bride, Barry.

(Laughter from everyone. Barry holds on to Diane's body and moves around in a mock waltz for several minutes.)

Homeless Man: A real Hallmark moment, Barry. What's that?
                 Tears in your eyes? You never made a very good
                 victim, did you, Barry?
Barry: Shut up.

(Barry carries Diane's corpse back to the seat and props it up. Laughter, dancing, drinking and eating continue.)

Conductor: (From   somewhere   off-stage,   something
                 unintelligible is heard)...reminding you of the
                 "No food or drinks" rule while on the train.
                 Thank you.

(Moaning can be heard.)

Betty:	Well, I guess that's it. The party is over. Let's get this stuff packed up.
Child:	Aw, I don't want to go. We're having fun.
Miriam:	Now, you kids just sit down and wait for a couple of minutes and you'll get your packets. Do you remember what you are supposed to do with them?
Child:	I remember! I know what to do!

(Women gather up and pack everything.)

Miriam:	Okay. We're all packed up. Everybody ready? We're almost at the next stop.
Child:	Yeah. We're ready.
Conductor:	(From somewhere off-stage, an unintelligible announcement)
Elliot:	All right. Let's go.

(Children are handed packets. Men and women and teenager from the funeral gather in front of the exit door.)

Conductor:	(From somewhere off-stage) Watch your step please.
Betty:	Okay, kids. Go ahead. Open your packets.

(Children reach into small mesh bags and begin throwing rice at Diane's corpse and laughing.)

Elliot:	All right, then. Good job. Let's go now before the doors close.

(The funeral participants all step out onto the platform. The lights flicker on the train. Barry walks across the car and returns to his original seat. Sarah and Doug enter the train. Sarah walks over and sits in the seat facing Barry, and Doug sits behind Barry.)

Sarah:	You know, Barry, I'm really worried about you.
Barry:	Why? Worried about what?
Sarah:	You are acting weird lately.
Barry:	No weirder than usual. (chuckles)
Sarah:	I'm serious, Barry. I'm really worried about you.
Barry:	Could you give me an example?
Sarah:	Well, for one thing, you seem to be pulling away from everyone.
Barry:	Pulling away?
Sarah:	Yes. You know, you seem distant. Far away. Detached. You never return my phone calls. Doug says you don't return his phone calls anymore either. (She motions towards Doug, who is sitting behind Barry)
Barry:	Oh. I see. You have been *discussing* my social etiquette behaviors. (turning to look at Doug) Is this some sort of *intervention*?
Sarah:	*Barry.* We're talking to you about this because we care about you. We are worried about you.
Barry:	I see. And just what is it you are proposing that I do?
Sarah:	Be like everyone else...
Barry:	Hmm. That seems to be a recurring theme lately.
Sarah:	See what I mean? Why can't you just act normal?

Barry:	Normalcy has always been seriously over-rated in my opinion. Anyway, are you suggesting that I'm *abnormal*?
Sarah:	No. Well...no. Not exactly. I'm saying we are worried about you because you don't act like...
Barry:	Like everyone else, who, of course, *is* normal.
Sarah:	Do you want to know what I think the problem is?
Barry:	So there *is*, in your assessment, a *problem*?
Sarah:	The problem is that even though you are a genius, you do not know how to relate to other people on the level you need to.
Barry:	I see. I need to learn to dummy-down, in your assessment?
Sarah:	That's not what I meant. There's no need for you to get offended.
Barry:	First of all, people do not *need* reasons to get offended. And secondly, I am not offended. I'm amused.
Homeless Man:	You better hope you are not offending him. He's got a pretty deadly finger, there.
Sarah:	You know, people who do not know you very well think you are arrogant. I know you, so I know that's not the case. I used to though. I mean, when I first met you. But I know now that isn't the case.
Barry:	Sarah, I don't *care* what people think about me. Maybe that's *your* problem. You care too much about what other people think.
Sarah:	Why don't you care, Barry? That's not normal. That's exactly what I'm talking about. I'm worried about you because you don't seem...well, *connected* to other people. You don't care what anyone thinks. Not even me.
Barry:	Sarah, there's a big difference between not caring about what you think about me, and not caring

about you, as a person. You are a great human being. I like you. You have a good mind. You're a loyal friend. I care about you as a person. I do *not* however, give a flying fuck about what you, or anyone else, for that matter, (glances back towards Doug) think about me.

Sarah: And you think that's okay? You think *that's* normal? *Everyone* cares about what other people think. You don't live alone on a desert island, you know.

Homeless Man: Doesn't she mean a *deserted* island? Or, does it really matter what the vegetation is?

Barry: In order to care about what other people think, Sarah, it requires a very, very important element.

Sarah: What's that?

Barry: You have to *value* their opinion. I do not value other people's opinions about me. And, if I don't value their opinion, then I can't very well care about what they think.

Homeless Man: (shaking his change cup) I'm actually *selling* opinions today, Barry. Only ten dollars. Cherish them, keep them to yourself, toss them around, hold on to them...they could go up in value.

Sarah: How can you say those things, Barry? What is happening to you? You didn't used to be like this.

Barry: I've always been this way. All my adult life, at any rate. You just never heard me say the words. The sentiments have always been there, though. Look, Sarah, I don't expect that you'll understand this, but here goes...Whatever this is you are calling "normal" is something you have created in your own mind. It's *your* reality. Not mine. Look, everyone comes to the table with their own personal history, experiences, hang-ups, inner conflicts, and expectations. *Those* are the things that shape their perceptions. Their perceptions of me, you, the headlines on the evening news, the weather, you name it. Everyone creates their own unique version of reality...their own unique version of what the TRUTH is. One person's truth or perception of me is no less, or no more, valid than the next person's. The main point I'm trying to make is, that while I appreciate your perception of me, I cannot value it any more than I value my next door neighbor's perception of me. Or my *own* for that matter.

Homeless Man: Barry, here is *my* perception...I'm worried people might start to think you are selfish. (shakes his cup in front of Barry)

(Barry reaches in his pocket and tosses change into the Homeless Man's cup.)

Barry: I appreciate that you are concerned about me, but you are worried about me on *your* terms.

Sarah: How do you mean?

Barry: You think I should be conducting my life according to *your* perception of what reality should be. If I don't meet the standards of what you think is the "right" way to live one's life, then you get worried. Consider this possibility, however. Suppose my reality has nothing at all to do with what *you* think is important or appropriate. Suppose that in *my* construction of reality I am acting in my own best interest. Perfectly "normal", if you will. (pauses and smirks) How do ya' like me now?

Sarah: Now I *am* worried about you.

(Barry looks to Mosh Pitt for help. Mosh shrugs.)

Barry: (looking out the window) I'm not sure what you
                expect from me.
Sarah: Sometimes the things you say about people are
                so nasty. I mean *really* nasty. That's not healthy.
Barry: The truth is always healthy.
Sarah: The *truth*? Saying nasty things about people is
                not the truth.
Barry: I don't engage in gossip. I don't ever make
                negative remarks about superficial issues like
                someone's physical appearance. The only thing I
                may comment about is someone's behavior.
Homeless Man: (going back to his crossword puzzle) Hey, Barry,
                what's a six-letter word for "nasty"?
Mosh: How about "HONEST"?
Homeless Man: Nah, it starts with a "P"
Barry: "PEOPLE"
Homeless Man: "PEOPLE", that works! Good thing, too...for a
                minute there I was worried it might be "pauper."
Sarah: You seem so intolerant of other people these
                days.
Barry: Sarah, I have always been intolerant of people
                who do not act in their own best interest. I think
                everyone should strive to at the very least, act in
                their own best interest, and, when they can
                control it, the best interest of others.
Sarah: I'm talking about your intolerance for, as you call
                them, "stupid" people.
Barry: Same difference.

Sarah:	Again, I am worried about you. I'm not kidding, Barry. This is leading to some serious problems.
Barry:	What exactly are we talking about again?
Sarah:	(sighs) Your disconnectedness. Indifference. Intolerance.
Homeless Man:	Wait a minute! If he is indifferent, then he can't be intolerant. He'd be *indifferent.*
Sarah:	(rolling her eyes and looking at Doug) Doug, you agree with me. Say something.
Doug:	Uh, look man, Sarah's right. You do seem to be pulling away. Holding back. I don't know. I just figured you have something on your mind. The thing is, dude, my uncle was like you. You know, he didn't want to have anything to do with anyone for the longest time. And then one day my aunt walked in and found him in the bathtub surrounded by a blow dryer, toaster, my cousin Bobby's thirteen-inch television set, and my aunt's electric vibrator. My cousin was really pissed off about his television set, but get this, the blow dryer *still* works. My aunt said she didn't want it in the house so she gave it to me. I've had it for like four years now. Still working.
Barry:	There's no way that's possible.
Doug:	I'm not kidding you, dude. The blow dryer still works. It was submerged in water still running full blast. They're not even sure how long it had been going. But it still works.
Barry:	No. Not that. I mean all of the appliances. How did he get all of the appliances in the tub of water? He couldn't have dropped them in all at one time.
Doug:	Oh, that. I know what you mean. The police said he probably had everything lined up outside of the tub and then just dropped them in one at a

	time until he got it right. He had all these extension cords running all over the bathroom into this multiple outlet plugged into the wall.
Barry:	Which one was the "right" one?
Doug:	Probably the television. It was a good thing too, because I'm telling you man, it was getting really crowded in that tub. Besides, all that was left sitting on the floor was a clock-radio and one of those mini-food-processors. After that, he was out of electrical appliances that would fit in the tub. Anyway, dude, I was just worried because my uncle was doing the same sort of thing you are doing before he off'ed himself. You know, spending all of his time alone, not wanting anything to do with anyone else, getting really frustrated with people, you know. It's your business and all. It's just that if anything would happen to you, I don't know, I'd be bummed.
Barry:	That's how it usually is. When someone dies, the friends and relatives don't feel sorrow and grief for the person him-or herself who no longer will be having a life. Who they feel sorry for is *themselves*. *They* will miss the deceased person, *they* will feel lonely, *they* will miss out on this or that experience with the deceased, etc. It's all about the people living feeling sorry for *themselves*. Funerals and grieving are very narcissistic experiences.
Doug:	Wow. I never looked at it like that before.
Barry:	Besides, you are wrong.
Doug:	About what?
Barry:	About me being like your uncle. I didn't just start acting this way. There's been no sudden change or decline in my behavior. I've *always* been this way. Since high school.

Doug:	Are you sure? Why does it seem like you have changed?
Barry:	Because you *know* me now. Just as soon as people get to know one another, well that's when they start wanting to change them. They find flaws, shortcomings, things they want to change about them so that they'll be the perfect mirror-image of themselves. The illusions start to fall away and all of a sudden you see things about your friends, lovers, coworkers, spouses, or whomever, that disappoint you, so you try to change them. Change their behavior. Their actions, reactions. Their attitudes.
Homeless Man:	Remember, Pip, having Great Expectations for others will always lead to disappointment, and is not recommended. Having Great Expectations for your own personal happiness and inner peace, however, is required.
Conductor:	(From offstage somewhere an unintelligible announcement of a stop)...Watch your step please. Have a nice day.

(The car comes to an abrupt stop. The lights flicker and remain off for several seconds. The doors open and an FBI agent and a prosecutor get on the subway car. The FBI agent walks over and stands next to Barry's seat.)

FBI Agent:	Mr. Barry Yeldray?
Barry:	(looking confused) Yes.
FBI Agent:	(showing his identification) Chief Investigator Frauman, FBI. Mr. Yeldray, you are under arrest on three counts of medical malpractice. You have a right to an attorney. If you cannot afford an

attorney, one will be provided for you. You have the right to remain silent. Anything you say from this point forward can, and will, be used against you. Do you understand these rights, Mr. Yeldray?

Barry: (mumbles) Yes.

FBI Agent: All right. The prosecutor will detain you.

(Prosecutor places handcuffs and leg restraints on Barry.)

FBI Agent: You are entitled to a swift and speedy trial, Mr. Yeldray. This is Mr. Corner. He is the government prosecutor and will be in charge of your case. Is your attorney present, Mr. Yeldray?

Barry: (looking confused) What? No.

Homeless Man: Yes he is. Right here. I'm representing Mr. Yeldray.

(Barry looks toward the Homeless Man, confused.)

Prosecutor: Very well, then. If everything is in order, let's begin.

Homeless Man: Wait a minute...uh, Mr. Corner, we don't have a jury. And where's the judge?

Prosecutor: The judge and jury will be here. They are scheduled to get on at the next stop, along with all of the witnesses for both the prosecution and the defense.

Homeless Man: (looking at Barry) Well, look on the bright side, Barry, given the power of a thought, you're lucky you're not on trial for murder. (laughs)

(Barry turns his head and looks out the window of the subway. The lights dim and the curtain closes.)

End of ACT I

~ ~ ~ ~

"Well now, how about a nice round of applause for Murray?" George asks.

The members of the writing group put down their copies of the play and clap with enthusiasm.

"Do we have any comments or feedback at this point?" George asks.

"Next time, *I* want to play the part of one of the male characters," Janelle pipes in. "I don't like any of the female characters."

"Well now," George begins, "maybe we should explore that further during our next session."

"Ah, that's just because Janelle hates women. It doesn't have anything to do with Murray's characters," says Cameron.

"You don't know what you're talking about!" Janelle shouts, slamming the manuscript down and standing up. "I'm going out for a cigarette," she announces. "*Alone,*" she says emphatically, glaring at Cameron as she stomps out of the room.

"I thought it was very funny. I just don't get it why everyone is so upset with Barry, but I guess I'll have to wait until Act II to find out," Sam says.

"Anyone else?" George asks.

"I *liked* the characters," Michael says earnestly.

"Yeah, me too. I thought they were all very multi-dimensional, just like real-life," Suzanne says.

"Me too," several others join in.

"It certainly is an absurdist play. I rather enjoyed it," Iben says.

"Well Murray, it looks like the reviews are positive. Should we plan on reading through Act II after we take a break?" George asks.

"Actually," Murray says, "I was thinking I'd like to make a few changes to Act II, first. Do you think we could hold off on the reading until the next meeting?"

"Sure. Whatever works out best for you," George replies. "Do keep in mind that we want to get it over to Dolan as soon as possible."

"I know," Murray says. "I'll get to work on the changes right away."

"Okay, then. Why don't we take a break, and when we come back we can pick up on our discussion from the last meeting."

Murray tucks a copy of the stage play under his arm and heads for the door. "I'm going to shove off," he says to the group. "I need to get these ideas down before I forget them."

"All right, Murray. We'll see you next time. I'm looking forward to seeing how Act II is going to turn out," George says.

"See you," Murray waves.

"See ya' Murray. Great job on the play," Mark says.

"Yeah, I really enjoyed it. See you next time," Helen says waving and smiling.

Murray waves one last time and turns to leave.

"Oh, Murray," says Arnold, getting up from his seat, "Don't let anything bad happen to Barry in Act II. I kind of feel like I know him."

"Don't worry," Murray says, "Someone has to stick up for the misfits of the world."

Several people chuckle as Murray heads out the door and down the hallway.

On the subway ride home, Murray sniffles and fights hard, but is unsuccessful at pushing down the flood of tears.

IV

"Mollie, I've got some bad news for you," Murray says, looking down and pulling the label off his beer bottle.

"Oh, Murray, you are always so doom and gloom. What news could possibly be that bad?" Mollie asks, smiling.

A waiter wearing his Lucky's cap in a way that says, "Don't bother me," approaches with fresh drinks. He sits the bottles down on the table, leans over, picks up the ashtray, and dumps the contents onto the drink tray before replacing it on the table.

"Can I get you anything else?" He asks with a tone that says, "I hope not."

Murray looks at Mollie. "Uh, how about some tortilla chips and salsa?" He asks her. Mollie nods and smiles. "Okay."

"Chips and salsa, please," Murray says to the waiter. The waiter nods and walks away.

"So what's this so-called bad news?" Mollie asks.

"I'm probably going to have to be shoving off soon," Murray says, his voice shaking.

"What do you mean, 'shoving off'?" Mollie asks with a worried tone.

"You know," Murray says. "Leaving. Getting out of town."

"Why?" Mollie asks in a tone of disbelief.

"I can't go into it, but, well..." Murray pauses. "Things are heating up. Some things are happening..." Murray's voice chokes up.

"*What* things? What type of things, Murray? Are you in some sort of trouble? *Tell* me. Maybe I can help. That's what friends are for."

"I can't. I just can't," Murray says, shaking his head slowly.

"Why not?" Mollie asks with persistence.

"Because, I don't want to get you involved. I'm only telling you now because I don't want you to be shocked or upset or anything if one day you call and I'm gone." Murray takes a gulp of his beer.

"You're telling me so I won't be *upset*? How did you *think* I'd be? You are one of the best friends I've ever had."

"Thanks," Murray says, smiling broadly.

"And suddenly you up and announce that you are going to be disappearing. Just like that? Poof? Where are you going?"

"Can't say. I don't know."

"Well, when *will* you know?" Mollie asks.

"I'm not sure. But even when I do know, I can't tell you." Murray shakes his head again.

"Murray, I'm not getting this. You can't just up and disappear from everyone's life. From *your* life. This is *your* life, too. You live here. You have friends here."

"Well, I don't know about *that*. I have you, yes. But the rest of them..." Murray's voice trails off.

"What about your roommate?"

"Kirby?" Murray chuckles. "He'll be just fine. He's a risk-taker. He can pick up the Gargoyle and read the Freaks-Wanting-Room-to-Rent ads. He'll have a new roommate within a day."

"He'll never be able to replace *you*," Mollie says with earnest.

"Kirby's a tolerant guy," Murray responds. "In this city, if you're willing to put up with someone's vibrator lying around on the kitchen counter, you can have your rent problems solved within hours."

"Oh, Murray, I meant isn't your roommate going to miss *you*? Aren't *you* going to miss *him*?"

"It's not that sort of relationship, Mollie."

"Murray, please tell me what's bothering you. I can help. You'll feel better if you tell me. *Please.* "

"Mollie, do you remember when you were in the hospital and you were so worried that someone was going to find out where you were? No matter what I did or said, nothing could convince you that it didn't matter. From your perspective, your life was going to be ruined if anyone found out where you were. Remember?"

"Are you saying you're going to check into a psychiatric ward?" Mollie asks.

"No. Well...no. But it's the same sort of situation. I will probably need to go away and I need you to understand that I can't let anyone know where I'm going."

"Or your life will be ruined?"

"Something like that."

"Here you go," the waiter says, sitting a basket of tortilla chips and a bowl of salsa onto the table. "Will there be anything else?"

"I'll take another beer whenever you head back in this direction. No big hurry," Murray says.

The waiter nods and walks away, rolling his eyes.

"Will you at least promise me you'll write to me?" Mollie asks almost begging.

"I'll send you post cards from the edge," Murray says, chuckling.

"Murray, I love you. You're my best friend. But, I swear, why do you have to be such an enigma?"

"*Enema*? Have some of this salsa. It's guaranteed to help."

Mollie sighs.

"What about your play? Aren't you planning to have it performed?" She asks.

"My dream," Murray says. "But I just don't know. What I have to do takes precedence over the play."

"But you worked so hard on it. You have to stay here...you have *connections* here. Do you realize how hard it will be to have a playhouse somewhere else pick it up? Without connections it will be impossible!"

"I know," Murray says sadly. He lowers his eyes and shakes his head.

"Oh, Murray. This is ridiculous. You *can't* go. You just can't. What will I *do* without you? Who will hold me together?"

"You're underestimating your own strength, Mollie. Either that, or you're greatly overestimating *mine*." Murray grabs a handful of chips and dips them into the salsa.

"Well, if you go, what will you *do*? How will you support yourself? What will you *do* all day?"

"You sound like my mother," Murray says grabbing for more tortilla chips. "Nice try, though. Trying to scare me into staying."

Mollie's eyes tear up and her lower lip begins to quiver. Seconds later she is sobbing. "You can't. You just can't leave me," she says in between sobs and gulps for air.

Mollie continues to cry for several minutes. A few patrons turn to see what the problem is.

"Mollie. You've got to stop crying. People are going to think I just told you that you are fat or something."

The sobs continue. Murray runs his hands through his hair over and over again. Mollie's body is trembling. She lowers her head to the table and holds her face in her hands. Her sobs grow more intense.

Murray gets up and begins to pace around the bar. The bartender motions his hand towards Murray's table. "She all right?" He asks.

"Yes," Murray responds. "She just got some bad news, is all."

The bartender gives Murray a dirty look, walks over to the stereo system and turns up the volume.

Murray walks around the pool table, and then to the restroom, and then to the window to look outside. A few minutes later he returns to the table. Mollie is still crying.

"Mollie, listen, it was just a joke. I was just teasing you. It was a *joke*." Murray leans forward in his seat.

"What?" Mollie looks up. Her eyelids are swollen; her face is red and tear-stained.

"I said it was a joke. I was just teasing you. I'm not going anywhere. I'm sorry. I thought you would get the joke. I didn't realize you would take it so hard. I'm sorry."

Mollie's face lightens up. She straightens her shoulders and sits back. "Are you serious? It was just a joke? You're not really leaving?"

"Nah," Murray says, smiling. "I'm not going anywhere. I was just teasing." He finishes off the end of his beer.

Mollie smiles and wipes her tears from her face with a napkin. "You have a really weird sense of humor, do you know that?" Mollie asks, sniffling.

"So I've been told," Murray responds, smiling. "So I've been told."

"We should take a trip together some time, though. A vacation. We could get one of those cross-county bus tickets and we could spend the summer seeing the whole country," Mollie says, finishing her drink.

"On a *bus*?" Murray asks. "You want to ride across the country on a *bus*? I thought you get car sick."

"Yeah. You have a point there," Mollie says disappointedly.

"You ready to go?" Murray asks. "I'll ride with you on the BART."

Mollie nods her head and puts on her sweater. Murray stands up and digs around in his pocket. He lays two crumpled dollar bills and some pennies on the table.

"Let's blow this Popsicle stand," he says, smiling and leading Mollie towards the door. He tips his hat brim at the bartender who nods as they leave.

After Mollie gets off at her exit, Murray rides on to the Montgomery stop and heads toward Mission to the Greyhound Bus station. He walks past a row of people sitting on the sidewalk with battered cardboard signs, begging for money and claiming they have multiple children to feed. Several of them smell of urine and booze, and look as if they have not bathed in years.

Murray nods at each one as he passes. They nod back. One of them wishes Murray a good day, another hopes that God blesses him, and a third screams out that Murray is a Capitalist Pig Bourgeois Nazi. As he turns the corner to enter the station, he hears the man scream what sounds like, "All of you goddamned doctors are all alike." Murray hesitates for just a split second and then enters through the automatic doors.

The station is damp and very noisy. The smell of human seepage permeates the air. Paper bags and plastic grocery sacks substituting for luggage are strewn around the aisles. Children cry and whine, or roam aimlessly, drooling suckers from their mouths. Women speak in every possible language to their children and one another. Students sleep with their heads resting on their knapsacks or else strike their best "I am totally bored by this lecture" pose.

Murray wanders around for quite awhile before heading for the desk marked, "Information." "Yes. Can I help you?" The woman asks in a voice filled equally with boredom and disgust.

"Yes. Where can I get some destination schedules?" Murray asks politely.

"Where to?" The woman asks, this time with more disgust than boredom.

"No place in particular. I'm more interested in finding out where I can go. I mean, what my options are," Murray says.

"General schedules are over there, against the back wall," the woman says, motioning with her forefinger.

"Thank you," Murray says, but the woman is already busy rolling her eyes at another customer.

Murray makes his way through the crowd of people to the display of bus schedules. He takes schedules for Nevada, Arizona, New Mexico, and New York and stuffs them into his backpack, and then looks around for an open seat. He stands for a long time against the wall waiting for someone to leave.

When a seat is finally available, Murray sits down and pulls out his writing pad and pen. After twenty minutes of intensely observing, listening, and writing, he is distracted by a large man in an ill-fitting suit and scuffed loafers who sits down in the seat next to him.

"You some kind of reporter?" The man asks, sitting his briefcase and luggage between his feet.

"What's that?" Murray asks, looking up from his writing.

"I noticed you have been taking notes for about a half an hour, now. I was wondering if you are some kind of reporter."

"Sort of," Murray says dryly. "I'm a writer."

"What do you write?" The man asks with interest.

"For the moment, plays," Murray responds.

"My wife loves going to plays. Myself, I could take 'em or leave 'em. Have you written anything I might have seen?"

Murray looks up at the man. "Probably not," he replies.

There are several moments of silence.

"I am in sales. Aluminum siding. I'm taking courses for real estate, right now," the man announces proudly. Murray nods.

"I used to be in car sales," the man says. "Man, what a racket. That business was breaking my balls. You know what I mean? I was drinking too much. Almost cost me my marriage. My sister-in-law, she's a psychologist, says most of the car business is made up of alcoholics and drug addicts. She also says nearly everyone in the real estate business is neurotic. Personality disorders or some such thing." The man laughs heartily.

"What about writers?" Murray asks. "What's wrong with writers?"

The man laughs again. "Couldn't tell you. We don't have any writers in our family. My sister-in-law only gives running commentary on what the family does for a living." He laughs again.

The man thrusts his hand towards Murray. "Zach Taylor," he says.

"Barry," Murray replies. "Barry Yeldray."

"Glad to meet you, Barry."

Murray smiles and nods.

"Afraid of flying," Zach says.

93

"Come again?" Murray says.

"I'm afraid of getting on a goddamned airplane," Zach says, shaking his head. "I used to be all right with it back in my drinking days. I used to get plastered before I boarded, and then drink straight through the entire trip. Now, though, well...I'm stuck riding the bus."

Murray nods, smiles, and returns to his notepad.

"You know," Zach begins again, "I'm heading out to Santa Fe for a convention. The owner picked me to go and find out what's happening in the field. It's because I've had the highest sales figures for the past seven months. Salesman of the month, seven times in a row," Zach says proudly.

"Sounds like quite an accomplishment," Murray replies.

"You think that's something, my son just graduated with his degree in Chemical Engineering and already has a job as a scientist for some big German-based firm. He's working on some top-secret composite material for the Stealth Bomber. The whole damned thing is held together with *glue*. Can you believe that?

"And my daughter is married to the vice president of one of the top investment banking firms," Zach says.

"That should be useful," Murray says.

"Yeah, well, you know what they say, Barry. You can mess with a man's house, you can even mess with his wife, but don't ever try to come between a man and his money." Zach laughs and slaps his knee. "He's handling all of my investments," Zach continues. "The plan is to have over two million by retirement."

"With that much money you ought to be able to *buy* a captive audience," Murray says dryly.

"*What's* that?" Zach asks.

"Oh, nothing," Murray responds. "Just an inside writer's joke."

"Oh," Zach chuckles. "We have those in sales too. We had a lot of 'em in the car business. Plenty of them in aluminum siding too, though. For instance, we have a

94

secret policy not to ever call and sell to anyone whose name sounds black."

"Interesting choice," Murray says.

"Well, you know, they have a reputation of not paying their bills. The owner says we should skip anyone whose name sounds black, and if you get one by accident, then we should just hang up as soon as we know it."

"That's some system you got there. How exactly are you suppose to know just by talking to people on the telephone?" Murray asks.

Zach laughs heartily. "Oh, come on now, you're pulling my leg, aren't you? You can tell by the way they talk!"

Several people look over at Zach.

"I'm proud to say I have a perfect score. If ever I call one because their names are deceiving, I have a knack for catching it right away. I can usually know it just by the way they answer the phone!" Zach says proudly.

"Again, you really have a line of accomplishments. Far more than me, I must confess," Murray says.

Zach laughs and slaps his right knee. "Well now, Barry, I'm sure if we dug deep enough, we'd find something you have done that would make people stand up and take notice."

"No doubt about that," Murray says, looking down at his notepad.

Several moments go by where neither man speaks. Finally, Zach says, "You ever been to Santa Fe?"

"Can't say as I have," Murray says, not looking up.

"This won't be my first. I've been there a few times before. It's like Berkeley...with better art and jewelry," Zach chuckles. "That's what my wife says. Anyway, same types of people. The women are real ugly there, just like they are in Berkeley. Just as well..." Zach chuckles, "It will help ensure I stay honest, if you know what I mean." Zach winks and slaps Murray on the arm.

Murray smiles and nods.

The woman at the Information Desk announces that the bus to Santa Fe is now boarding.

"Oh, hey, that's me. I guess I've got to take off." Zach stands up and tries to button his suit jacket, but fails. He sticks his hand out to Murray. "Well, Barry, I've got to say, this has been the best conversation I've had in ages. Listen, good luck with your plays."

Murray nods and says, "Thanks. Enjoy New Mexico."

"All right, then," Zach says grunting as he bends to pick up his briefcase and luggage. "Take care, buddy. Oh, I almost forgot. Here's my card. In case you ever need some aluminum siding."

Murray takes the business card. He holds his hand up to wave good-bye as Zach falls into the crowd of people pushing to move through the boarding exit.

Murray returns to his notepad. He writes furiously until Zach and all of the other passengers are long gone from the city. Murray then puts away his notepad and searches through his pockets. With a handful of change he walks over to the bank of payphones. Reading the business card, he dials the number marked, "office."

"Triple A, Aluminum Siding, how may I help you?" A young woman asks.

"Ah, yeah, I need to talk wit de owner 'bout somethin' *real* importin," Murray says.

"Who's calling please?"

"Yeah, dis iz Tyrone Washington. Mista' Tyrone Washington. I need to talk wit de owner right away."

"Hold on, sir," the girl responds with a tone that says, "Okay, I'll do it, but only because I'm getting *paid* to do so."

"Sir?" the girl says, a few seconds later, "Mr. Huffington is busy in a meeting right now. What is your call in regard to?"

"Money," Murray says with a tone of importance. "I just gave cash to one of your salesmen and after he lef' I looked at the receipt and realized I gave him more cash than the receipt shows."

"Hold on, sir. Let me see what I can do."

Several minutes pass. Murray paces as he waits. Finally, a man with a brusque tone gets on. "Gerry Huffington. What seems to be the problem?"

"Well, sir, like I was tellin' your assistan' there, my name iz Mista' Tyrone Washington and one of your salesmen was jus out to da house today and I gave him some money, but the receipt says a differen amount den what I done gave 'em."

"Who is the salesperson?" Huffington asks, perturbed.

"Well, now," Murray continues. "it's Taylor. Zach Taylor. See the problem is dat he gave a receipt for da wrong amount, but da wife says to me, she says, 'Call right away because Mista' Taylor is goin' out-a-town'. I remembered dat he said there would be a delay in processing our order on the cause of he was goin' to Santa Fe, New Mexico. And so I thought I better jus call and get this straightened on out instead a' waitin' 'till Mista' Taylor gets back."

"How much money did you give him?" Huffington asks in an angry tone.

"Well, sir, two thousan' dollars. In cash. I didn't realize 'til he was already gone, but the receipt says here I only gave him two hundred."

"Give me your address and telephone number and I'll have a talk with Mr. Taylor and someone will get back to you within the next day or two," Huffington says in an irate tone.

Murray gives the phone number of Pizza Hut and the address of where he used to live years before.

"All right. Thank you for calling," Huffington says, barely concealing his anger.

"Well, all right den, you have a nice day now, Mista' Huffytin," Murray says and hangs up the receiver.

The grin on Murray's face broadens and soon the smile moves to a full-fledged snicker. He puts the business card in his shirt pocket, sits down, and begins writing again.

After several minutes have passed, Murray returns to the phone bank. This time he dials the number on the business card marked, "home."

"Hello?" A woman says.

"Yes. Hello. Can I talk to...is this *Mrs.* Taylor, by any chance?" Murray says in a gruff tone.

"Yes," she replies.

"You and your husband were just in here about an hour ago? This is Jack Purnin from over at Lollipops."

"I'm sure you must be mistaken...how did you get my name and number?" The woman asks.

"Zach Taylor was in here. He left about an hour ago. He was with...I thought it might be you. Anyway, he forgot his briefcase. I opened it up and called the home number on his business card.

"I wouldn't have bothered except that he said he was taking off for an important business meeting in Santa Fe. I thought he'd need his briefcase. Like I said, I ordinarily would just leave it behind the bar...that's what I usually do when someone forgets somethin' here. But Zach being a regular and one of our best customers and all..."

"I see," the woman says in a perturbed tone.

"I'll just keep it behind the bar here if you're gonna' send someone by to get it. Otherwise, when I get off duty, the boss will put it in the back office and then it's locked up if you don't come when he's here."

"Actually, Mr...uh...I'm sorry, what is your name again?"

"Jack Purnin."

"Mr. Purnin, if you would be kind enough to write down a message for my husband and keep it inside the briefcase?"

"Uh, okay," Murray says.

"Say, 'See you in divorce court'!" Mrs. Taylor shouts just before slamming the phone receiver down.

Murray chuckles and rubs his ear with the palm of his hand a bit before replacing the receiver. He returns to his seat and watches as a new group of people begin to flood into the station.

Murray continues to sit for another half an hour. Then, suddenly, he stands up, grabs his backpack, and heads toward the payphones again. He takes his calling card from his wallet and punches in the numbers. While he waits for the connection, he takes Zach Taylor's business card out of his pocket and begins turning it over and over in his hand.

"Hello?" A woman says.

"Hi, ma', it's Murray."

"Murray, what's wrong?" The woman says in a worried tone.

"Nothing, mother. Why does something always have to be wrong?"

"You never call me otherwise," she laments.

"I just called to say 'hello' and to see how you were doing," Murray says.

"Oh. Well, I'm fine. I'm a little upset because my usual stylist, GiGi, was out sick today and they didn't have the consideration to call and tell me, and so after I schlep all the way downtown to get there, *then* they decide to tell me. So I let this other woman do my hair. They told me she had an excellent reputation. Ha! An excellent reputation for no talent, is what *I* say. You should see what she's done to my hair. I could cry.

"I raised a stink and refused to pay, of course. Oh, I'm glad you called. You'll never guess who I talked to today. Your Aunt Hilda. Ben's mother? Well, imagine how I felt to learn that *her* son bought her a new dress and flowers and took her to the Four Seasons for Mother's Day. That Ben, he's some prize. Of course, she asked me what *I* did for Mother's Day and I had to say that I spent Mother's Day on my hands and knees scrubbing the floors."

"You *had* to say that?"

"Well, why not? I couldn't very well lie and say that *my* son took me to a fancy restaurant."

"I sent you a card, mother...and I called. Besides, I live three thousand miles away."

"And have you ever once flown in to New York for Mother's Day? I don't even remember *when* you've been here last. It's been *years.* Anyway, oh, before I forget, someone called here looking for you. Can you imagine that? You haven't lived at home since before you left for college..."

"Who was it? Did they say what they wanted?" Murray asks.

"No. I don't know who it was. He didn't leave his name. He did try hard to convince me to give him your phone number and address out there in California. You're not in some kind of trouble again, are you?"

"He knew I lived in California, but called *you*?"

"No. I'm not sure if he already knew or not. I told him 'My son lives in the Bay Area now, but if I give you his number, he'll never speak to me again.' Because that's how you are, you know. Always putting me in a fix, scared to death you'll abandon me in my old age."

"Did he say anything else? Did he leave any kind of message?" Murray asks.

"No. Did you know that your cousin Seth is graduating soon with his *fifth* Master's degree? This one's in Geology, I think. Can you imagine? *Five* Master's degrees. Just imagine the opportunities he can have with that!"

"Well, so far, the only opportunity has been to live as a professional student for the last decade and a half. It doesn't pay great, but the hours are okay."

"Is that more sarcasm? Why do you always have to be so embittered? You know, *you* could have been successful if you had wanted to. There's no reason for you to get so nasty just because other people have done well for themselves. Oh, that reminds me, your Uncle Don is reviewing my will this week. I should tell you, if you can start acting like a human being, there will be a little something in there for you."

"And how, exactly, am I suppose to act like a 'human being'?" Murray asks.

"What's that? How come it's so noisy on your end? Are you having some kind of party? Can't you have the decency to wait to call me until it's quiet enough to even hear what I have to say?"

"I've got to go, ma'. Bye."

"Murray?"

"Good-bye, mother. I'll talk to you later."

Murray hangs up the receiver, puts his hands in his pockets and paces around the Greyhound station several times. Every so often he stops, runs his hands through his hair, mutters something, and then puts his hands back into his pockets and resumes pacing.

After half an hour of this, Murray grabs a "See the country on Greyhound" brochure and walks into the men's room, using the brochure to open the door and then dropping it to the floor. Once inside, he takes several paper towels from the dispenser and uses them to open, shut, and then lock the stall door, again letting them drop to the floor when he is finished.

Murray digs around inside his backpack and pulls out a thick, black indelible marker. On the wall behind the toilet seat he writes the words, " WE ARE ALL IMPOSTERS!! " He replaces the cap on the marker and opens his backpack, reconsiders, and then on the stall door writes, " VIS VITALIS, I AM LOSING IT! "

He puts the marker back into his backpack, grabs a fistful of toilet paper, and unlocks the stall door, throwing the toilet paper on the floor on his way out. Once outside the restroom, Murray heads through the station and out the automatic doors.

On his way down the street, Murray sees the homeless man who had screamed at him earlier. As he passes him, Murray reaches into his pocket, bends down and puts the aluminum siding salesman's card into the man's begging cup. Murray is several feet away before the man starts screaming. "Hey! What the fuck is *this*? You goddamn Nazi Capitalist Pig!"

Murray snickers and keeps on walking. He meanders through filthy streets lined with addicts, beggars and hustlers, until he reaches the edge of the Tenderloin. A couple of blocks later, Murray stands in front of a loft with a ten foot high painting of a strange looking woman with naked breasts. As Murray nears the building he can see that the lower half of the woman's body is a fish tail. She is holding a man up between her thumb and forefinger. Above the painting of the woman, the lettering reads, "The Abyss Theatre."

"This is it," Murray mumbles. He walks up closer to study the playbills posted on either side of the mermaid's breasts. Murray begins reading. One of the playbills announces a play entitled, "N.I.M.B.Y.," co-written by Dolan Aiello and Cathleen Krimerstanz. The play promises to give a realistic portrayal of the bizarre and twisted relationships between neighbors in the New Millennium.

The other playbill announces not a play, but a film short entitled, "John Wayne's Revenge." The producer and director is Dolan Aiello, and it stars Cathleen Krimerstanz. Both show times are scheduled to play this evening.

Murray looks at his watch and notices it has stopped. He walks over and asks one of the people standing nearby what time it is. Then he walks toward the corner and lights up a cigarette. He paces around awhile looking in the storefront windows before returning to the playhouse. He sees that more people have now gathered outside of the theatre. Instead of proceeding, however, he hangs back and sits down on the stoop of a nearby apartment building. When most of the people have entered the theatre, Murray walks over to the window, pays his money, walks into the theatre, and takes a seat near the back.

Five minutes later, a man introducing himself only as "Dolan," greets the audience and explains the impetus for creating the tongue-in-check, socio-political film short entitled, "John Wayne's Revenge."

"Up until this point, I had assumed it was a modern-day spaghetti-western," chortles a man sitting in the seat next to Murray.

Murray nods.

Next, Dolan gives the backdrop and setting for the play that will be performed, N.I.M.B.Y. (Not In *My* Back Yard), and reveals that it is based in part, on his and his co-writer's personal experiences with neighbors in the Bay Area. Many people in the audience chuckle and fidget a bit in their seats.

Dolan then announces that everyone is invited to remain after the play for a wine and cheese party to meet and greet the actors and authors of the play. He hints that there will be some sort of special treat by way of entertainment.

Finally, the lights dim, and a screen in the front of the stage is illuminated. What follows is a macabre and bizarre sequence of events beginning with someone named John who hacks off his wife's vagina. The dismembered part is then thrown out the window of a speeding car and makes its journey through the streets of San Francisco. It is found lying in a park by a homeless man, who trades it in for drugs. The drug dealer dresses it up and uses it as some sort of receptacle to display his wares, until it is stolen by a drug addict, mistakenly, thrown in the begging hat of a panhandler, shows up in a Noe Valley Feminist Art showing, is hurled from the Golden Gate Bridge, retrieved again, and mysteriously discovered in the Castro district, bought by an anonymous collector, where it is then showcased at a Transvestite Fashion Show, and finally, ends up back with its owner, who has had the foresight to land a book deal *and* a movie contract prior to her restoration surgery. In the end, however, the audience is informed that the man named John is vindicated. He has sought and tasted revenge.

Many of the audience members laugh throughout the film. Murray remains silent but fidgets in his seat a good deal. When the film ends, Dolan leads a question and answer session on the social and political ramifications of sexual mutilation.

Murray gets up quietly, walks outside the playhouse, lights a cigarette, and paces the sidewalk in front of the theatre. Every so often he stops, checks that his fly is closed, and resumes pacing. When he finishes his cigarette, he starts to walk back into the darkened theatre. Just as he opens the door to the theatre, he spots the car that had been parked outside of his house on and off for the past week. There is a man sitting in the driver's seat. Murray panics and rushes inside the theatre. The curtains are just ready to open.

The stage is set up to mimic San Francisco row houses: pink, green, blue, orange, and yellow. They are lined up, one after another, each one touching, and split into 2- and 3-flats, crammed with people. Everyone appears to be home. Bizarre conversations and mean-spirited remarks can be heard coming from the windows, balconies, and backyards of each unit.

Murray shifts in his seat and surreptitiously eyes the people sitting around him in the theatre. On the stage, a man and a woman are outside the pink house, talking on their balcony. Below them, an attractive blond woman is watering her flowers.

"Just look at her out there, Tim. Slut. She's out there everyday washing her car, or watering, or some damn thing, always without a bra. *Slut*."

"Why is she a slut, Ann? Your sister doesn't wear a bra. Is *she* a slut?"

"The reason my sister doesn't wear a bra is political." Ann points to the blonde watering flowers. "Does *she* look political to you?"

Tim leans over the balcony and takes a good, hard look at the woman. "No, I'll give you that. She sure isn't political."

The audience chuckles at the remark. Murray smirks and then looks around nervously. On stage there are sounds of shouting and objects being thrown against a wall. The commotion is coming from the green house.

"Git ow! I hate you, David!"
"Ah, come on, Wen-Chian. I didn't mean anything by it."

There are more crashing sounds. The downstairs neighbors look out their window.

"Tina, are they at it again?"
"Yep. Don't worry, though. Within an hour, the two of them will be up in that bedroom screwing like rabbits again. This is just their warped idea of foreplay."

On stage there are more crashing sounds. Items start flying out of the second floor window of the green house.

"Git ow! "
"Come on, baby. Let's talk. Just calm down."
"Don't tell me to calm down! Git ow of my fucking owse!"

Piles of clothing, books, shoes, and papers come flying out of the second floor window of the green house. David is standing on the ground, gathering up his belongings as they fall.

"I never wanna' see you agin! You asshole!" Wen-Chian shouts, as she throws more of David's things out the window.

The third floor neighbor steps out onto his balcony and looks down at the commotion.

"Hey! Will you two nuts keep it down! We're trying to have a life here!"
"Fuck off, Joe!" Wen-Chian shouts.

"Mind your own goddamn business, Joe," David yells. "Everyone knows you don't *have* a goddamned life."

"Yeah, Joe," Wen-Chian yells. "Mind your own fucking biznez!"

David looks up at Wen-Chian. "Oh, honey, can I come up? Can we talk, please?"

Wen-Chian looks lovingly down at David. "Umm...Okay...Oh, one of your shoes is in the bush there."

Murray gets up quietly, picks up his backpack, and ducks into the restroom. Once inside, he lights up a cigarette and begins pacing. Every few minutes he walks over to the door, shuts the restroom light off, opens the door an inch, and peeks through to look for the man from the mysterious car.

Murray continues like this for over a half an hour. Pacing, smoking, checking, pacing, smoking, more checking. Just as he is running his forth cigarette butt under the water faucet, he hears footsteps approaching the restroom. He grabs his backpack and ducks into a stall.

From the bottom of the stall he can see shiny, polished, black dress shoes and the bottoms of dark dress pants. Murray's heart begins to pound wildly. He puts his hand over his mouth to quiet the sounds of his heavy breathing. There is the sound of the man using the urinal and then of running water, and then the paper towel dispenser.

Murray remains completely still. Several minutes pass with no noise. Murray takes a risk and moves his head slightly to the left, to peek through the slit next to the stall door. The man is reading something from a small notebook. He places the notebook in the breast pocket of his jacket. As he opens the restroom door to leave, the sound of audience laughter echoes throughout the restroom.

Murray exhales and shifts his weight. He waits several more minutes inside the stall before coming out. He walks to the sink and splashes cold water on his face, and then holds the inside of his wrists under the stream of cold water. When he has dried himself off, he grabs his backpack and walks outside of the restroom, taking a seat only a couple of feet away from the men's room door.

The audience is laughing and some audience members are yelling things at the actors on the stage. Murray notices that the stage seems to be in utter chaos. All of the windows, yards, and balconies have activity going on at the same time. Music is playing from one of the units in the yellow house. There is a man picking lemons from a tree hanging over into his yard. Nearby, there is a woman looking out the window of the blue house.

"That bastard is stealing our lemons off of our tree! Did you hear me, Eddie?"

"What are you talking about, Linda?"

"That guy next door. He just took lemons off of our tree. Can you believe what balls he has?"

"You aren't talking about Kurt, are you?"

"Kurt who?"

"Kurt. The guy who lives next door. I saw him outside this morning and I told him to help himself to all the lemons hanging over the fence on his side."

"You *what*? I can't believe you did that, Eddie!"

"Why not? They are hanging over onto his property. He has the legal right to cut the damn branches completely off that are hanging over, if he wants to. What's wrong with letting him have the lemons?"

"Because, they are *our* lemons. That's why!"

Linda takes out a stepladder.

"Where are you going with that ladder?"

"I'm going out to take the rest of our lemons!"

"Why? You don't even eat lemons, Linda. You get canker sores! Why do you even care about the damn lemons?"

"You had no right to tell someone else they could help themselves to our lemons. The lemons belong to us. They are *ours*. I'd rather see them rot out there than let the *neighbors* have them!"

She leaves with the ladder, slamming the door. One of the third-floor tenants in the orange house steps out onto his balcony.

"I told you...turn that goddamned music down!" The man shouts.
The music becomes louder.
"Yeah!" Eddie yells, leaning out of the window of the blue house. "Listen to Paul. Turn the fucking music down!"

Murray gets up again and ducks into the men's room. He shuts the light off and peeks through a one-inch crack in the door. He surveys each row, person by person. Next, he closes the door, turns on the light, and shuts himself up in the same stall he had been in earlier. For the next twenty-five minutes he sits on the toilet seat and writes furiously in his notepad, stopping only to listen whenever the sound of footsteps near the restroom door.
When he finishes writing, Murray shoves his notepad inside of his backpack and returns to his seat outside the restroom door. He turns his attention back towards the stage.
A man on the second floor of the green house opens his window and shouts.
"Hey! I don't know who's doing it, but turn that goddamned music off!"
The music gets louder. In the pink house, a man is sitting on his balcony reading the newspaper. He shouts from his balcony to his upstairs neighbor.

"Hey, Nathan. Look here. It's advertising right here in the Gargoyle for Nude Grandmas. That ought to be right up your alley!"
Nathan walks to the edge of his balcony and looks down. "What is your problem, Ronny?"

"Me? There's nothing wrong with *me,* Nathan. *You're* the one with the problem, aren't you? Didn't you tell my wife last week that she looked hot in her shorts and tank top, and that older women turn you on?

"Well, right here's the answer to your problems." Ronny pokes his finger at the advertisement. "It says, 'Nude Grandmas--80 years old, *plus*!   Videos, pictures, and personal contacts.' You want the number, Nathan?" Ronny laughs heartily.

A man takes an empty seat directly behind Murray. Murray freezes with fear. A couple of minutes later, the man taps Murray on his shoulder. Murray jerks his head towards the man.

"Sorry to startle you. Do you know when this breaks for intermission?" The man asks.

Murray shakes his head and faces forward. His heart is still pounding wildly. Again, he tries to focus on the play.

Paul steps outside onto his balcony of the orange house again and yells, "What the hell is wrong with you? You're not playing with a full deck. I told you to turn that music down or I'm gonna' come over there and personally do it for you!"

The music blares even louder. A woman in the yellow house leans out her window and yells across to the neighbor in the adjoining orange house.

"Burt, would you mind keeping your windows open if you are going to smoke inside your house?"

"What are you, some kind of a *nut*, Donna? Don't tell me what to do in my own house."

"My house has cigarette smoke in it from you. The least you could do is keep your windows open."

"Oh, really? Your house has cigarette smoke in it from *me*? What is it, Donna? Traveling through the *walls*?"

"It must be, Burt. My house smells of cigarettes and *I* don't smoke."

"Well, you better call the media, Donna. That's some kind of phenomenon happening there, cigarette smoke traveling through the walls of two houses. Hey, Donna, can you smell the bread Betty is baking?"

"No! Just cigarette smoke. It reeks in here!"

"That's real interesting, Donna. The fact that odor molecules can pass across the walls of two houses for cigarettes, and yet the ones for bread know enough to stay right where they belong...Hey, Donna, can you smell my farts, too? Are they special enough to pass through the walls of two houses? Here, let me send you one right now."

"Fuck off, Burt!" Donna slams her window shut.

Paul walks back out onto his balcony of the orange house and shouts, "This is my last warning. If someone doesn't make him turn that music down, I'm gonna' go over there and kill that son-of-a-bitch."

The music continues to blare from somewhere inside the yellow house. Neighbors continue to chat. Then the music goes off. Silence. Suddenly, there is the sound of a gunshot, followed by screams and gasps. The curtain closes.

The house lights go on. The intermission is announced. People begin to stir from their seats. Murray stands up and makes a beeline for the exit door. He hangs around near the vestibule for a few minutes, and then goes outside with a small group of other theatre-goers. Once outside, he moves just to the right of the marquee, and stands between a couple of other people and the building. After a few minutes, he strains to see if the dark car is still parked nearby. The car is there. It is still empty. Murray lights a cigarette and inhales deeply.

"Can I get a light?" Asks a small-framed Asian-looking man in his late forties or early fifties. He is wearing a cap and round glasses.

"Oh, sure," Murray replies, fumbling for his lighter.

"How do you like it so far?" The man asks, his eyes twinkling.

"What's that?" Murray asks in a distracted way.

"The play. How do you like it so far?" Asks the man.

"Oh. Interesting. Very interesting." Murray replies.

"Abstract Realism," the man says chuckling.

"How's that?" Murray asks, trying to remain hidden within the small group gathered around him.

"Abstract Realism. Like the subway, you might say. My name is Juno." The man says, putting his hand out.

Murray shakes the man's hand. "Mosh," Murray says.

"Mosh. Is that short for anything?" The man asks, smiling.

"No," Murray says, "just Mosh."

"What do you do?" Asks Juno.

Murray is distracted. He strains his neck to see the car. Juno turns to see what Murray is looking at.

"I'm sorry," Murray says, realizing Juno is waiting for some reply.

"What is it you do?" Juno asks again, smiling.

"Oh, this and that," Murray replies.

"I'm a jewel thief," Juno says.

"What?" Murray asks, looking confused.

"A jewel thief," Juno says. "Officially, I'm a gem collector and appraiser, but really, I'm a jewel thief." He laughs.

Just then a tall woman with long, straight, black hair walks up. Her face is pale white and she has dark eye makeup and lipstick on. She has on a tight-fitting black dress, black fishnet stockings and black boots. Her outfit is adorned with a black leather dog collar on both her neck and right wrist. She is smoking a cigar.

"Hi, Juno," she says.

"Hi. How's it going?" He asks. "Hey, Raven, do you know Mosh?"

The woman looks at Murray, shakes her head and extends her hand towards Murray. Murray shakes her hand gently.

"How do you know Dolan and Catherine?" She asks. "Do you swing?"

Murray fights to keep from jolting.

"No," he responds. "Does everyone here know them?"

Raven looks around at the people gathered outside. Murray follows her gaze and notices that everyone except himself is dressed in black.

"Just about," she says. "Are you into Wicca?"

Murray shakes his head.

There is an uncomfortable pause. Finally, she asks, "Oh, do you know them from the club?"

Murray smiles.

"Oh, okay," Raven says, relaxing a bit. She flips her hair back off of her shoulders, revealing that the snake tattoo that is running above the top of her breasts, curls around her neck. "That's how *I* know him. Well, sort of. My roommate Darly works there as a dominatrix."

Murray tries hard not to react.

"I'm trying to become an S-and-M performance artist-slash-Goth-exotic dancer. Well, I actually am already, but I only have Sunday nights at the club, so far. Until I can bring in a clientele, Mike says. Then I can add on more nights. Until then, I work days at the cafeteria at the high school." Raven points her thumb in the direction behind her.

"Hmm," Murray says. "I can see that."

Just then, two women and a man, all dressed in black, catch Murray's attention. All three have the kind of pale, white skin that has moved from chic to the I-don't-have-enough-oxygen look. One of the women has straight, long, purple hair, the other has a shaved head with a tuft of red and green running down the center.

"Did you read the last issue of 'Death Becomes You'?" Purple Hair asks.

"What's that?" Asks the shaved-headed woman, blowing smoke from her nostrils.

"*You* don't know what *it is*?" Asks the emaciated male standing with them. "It's a 'zine that features stuff like electrocution and cremation. Oh, and autoerotic strangulation...a *personal favorite*," he says, smiling.

The two women laugh.

"*And* necrophilia," Purple Hair says, running her tongue around her lips and making a 'mmm' sound. "You should read it," she adds, turning to the woman with the shaved head.

"The Gargoyle just ran a list of their twenty favorite 'Death Becomes You' pix," the male says. "I can't remember all of them, but there was, like, 'Please Be Gentle When You Cut Me', and, oh damn, what else? I know them. A couple were my favorites...oh, oh...'Tasting Death Without Gagging on Blood' was one, and, 'Embalming 101: Mortuary Science for the Absolute Beginner'. That one was good. A little dense, but very enlightening. The best one though, I *must* say, was, 'Funerals That Have Turned Me On'."

Purple Hair nods. "I have my copy back at the apartment. I'll loan it to you when we get back," Purple Hair says to the other woman.

"Cool," Shaved Head replies.

"Are you staying for the party afterwards?" Juno asks Murray.

"What?" Murray asks, turning his attention to the man. "Oh, oh, I'm afraid I can't," Murray says, finally gathering his thoughts.

"Oh, no. You'll miss Juno's card tricks," Raven says.

"Card tricks?" Murray asks, looking at Juno.

"Tarot cards. I'm the entertainment tonight."

"You don't say," Murray says, amused.

"He's *really* good," Raven says, "He predicted my boyfriend would get in a motorcycle accident last year, two days before it happened."

"Impressive," Murray says.

"Say," Juno offers, "I could do you right now, Mosh." Juno sits down on the sidewalk cross-legged, and begins cutting the cards. "I warn you though, I have my own unique way of doing it."

"Okay by me," Murray says, squatting down beside him. Juno makes three piles, shuffles the remaining cards, and asks Murray periodically to tap a card or to tell him when to stop. Some cards are placed face up, others are placed face down. Juno shuffles some more, taps a few cards himself, which he places face up, spread out on top of the previous piles.

Finally, he stops shuffling and says, "Ah-ha. Hmm," then pauses. "This is strange. The cards tell me you are a healer. Or, at least, *were* a healer in an earlier part of your life."

Murray jerks slightly but says nothing.

"Well," Juno goes on, "that would explain the softness of your hands I sensed when we shook earlier."

Murray remains silent.

"Okay," Juno says, after a few more rearrangements of the card piles. "Ask your question."

"Do I have to say it aloud?" Murray asks.

Juno laughs. "No. You can keep it to yourself. Just say when."

"Now," Murray says and taps a card. Juno turns over three cards.

"Ah," he says, "Sticks. Well, Mosh my friend, you are going to get exactly what you asked for."

"Great. How about that," Murray says, smiling.

"Now, for your future," Juno says, shuffling. He places one card face up, then another, then a third. He quickly turns the third card face down.

Just as he does though, Raven gasps. "The Death card," she mutters.

"That doesn't sound good," Murray says.

"Oh, not to worry," Juno says reassuringly. "Because it appeared with the other two cards, it means it won't be *you* who is going to die. Possibly someone close to you though."

Murray flinches a little. Just then the theatre whistle sounds to announce the start of Act II.

"Well, we'll have to finish this some other time," Juno says, gathering his cards.

Murray and Juno stand up. The crowd is gathering around them, pushing toward the door.

Just as Murray falls in line to enter, he stops and looks back at the street. The car is gone. He steps to the side and turns around.

"Anything wrong?" Juno asks.

"No. I just remembered I was supposed to make an important phone call during the intermission. I guess I'll have to miss the first couple of minutes."

"Okay, then," Juno says. "I'll look for you inside. I'll save you a seat."

Murray turns right, walks past the theatre, and heads for the drugstore on the corner, picking up his pace as he goes. Just outside the drugstore is a payphone. Murray walks over to the payphone, cleans the receiver with his handkerchief, and dials.

"Hello."

"Hi, Mollie?"

"Uh-huh, Murray?"

"Yeah. It's me. Did I wake you? It didn't sound like you."

"Hold on." There is a pause of several seconds.

"Gummy Bears," Mollie says finally. "I wasn't asleep. I was eating Gummy Bears."

"Oh. That's not a good sign."

"Yeah. You're right. I was talking to my mother tonight. What's up?"

"Oh. Yeah. I was wondering if I could crash on your sofa tonight. It's a long story."

"Yeah, sure. No problem. In fact, Mary is staying at Todd's apartment tonight. I'm sure she wouldn't mind if you crashed in her room."

"Thanks. The sofa will do just fine. I'm on my way. See you in a little bit."

"Okay. Bye."

Murray pushes the hook down, waits for a dial tone, and punches in his own number.

"Hello."

"Kirby? It's Murray."

"Oh. Hi. Everything all right?"

"Yeah. It's a long story, but I'm going to be crashing over here at a friend's place for the night. I'm just calling to check in and to ask you if you wouldn't mind leaving some food and water for Shadow. I might not get back until late tomorrow morning or early afternoon."

"Yeah. No problem. His food bowl is still pretty full though. Guess he didn't feel much like eating today."

"That's a first," Murray says, chuckling.

"He finished nearly all of his water though."

"That *is* unusual."

"Well, anyway, I'll take care of everything as soon as we hang up."

"Thanks a lot. Oh, hey, any messages for me?"

"Sack called. He said for you to call him when you get a chance. It's about the rally for Meals-Not-Militia."

"Okay. Thanks. Is that it?"

"Well, that's it for the phone messages, but there are a couple of other things. Strange, actually," Kirby says. "First off, I don't know if you have noticed, but there has been this car hanging around here. Black. Always clean and waxed. Official looking. Anyway, there's always this guy just sitting in it. Sometimes he's on the phone. I don't know that it has anything at all to do with *this* place, but there's definitely something going on.

"Karen said she has seen the guy inside the car taking notes on some little pad. And yesterday she said when she was coming up the walk, this guy got out of his car. But then he just stood there beside the car. Then, after she came inside, he got back in his car and made a phone call. When we left to go to the gym about fifteen minutes later though, the car was gone."

"Is there anyone out there now?" Murray asks.

"No. I don't think so. He was out there earlier, but he took off a few hours ago. I didn't see anyone when I came back a little while ago," Kirby says.

"What's the other thing?" Murray asks casually.

"Other thing?" Kirby asks, sounding confused.

"You seemed to indicate there was more than one strange thing going on," Murray says.

"Oh. Oh, yeah. Well, just one more. I think. Maybe it's not strange to you. Anyway, when I got back from class this afternoon there was a card...another business card, stuck in the door. You know? The way we sometimes have flyers from pizza parlors and whatnot stuck in the door? So I read it and it's from a...hold on, I laid it on the kitchen counter here, let me get it."

There is a slight pause. "Okay," Kirby says finally. "Yeah. This time it's from a Dr. Kenneth Caldwell. Says here, he's a *psychiatrist*. It's a San Francisco address and phone number. The other thing though, is that he wrote something on the back of the card. It says, 'Dr. Yardley, I knew it was you at our chance meeting in the subway. Please call me.' And then he scribbled what looks like his initials. What do you make of it?"

"Well," Murray starts to speak, then pauses for a couple seconds to gather his thoughts. "My guess is this Dr. Yardley must be about to win the Nobel Prize and now all his old friends are coming out of the woodwork to be close to him." Murray chuckles.

"Whatever it is, it's really strange how people are intent on believing this doctor actually lives here," Kirby offers.

"Well, look at it this way," Murray says, "it keeps things interesting. Anything else to report?"

"No. That's it," Kirby replies.

"All right then, I'll see you sometime tomorrow. Thanks for taking care of Shadow's food and water."

"No problem," Kirby says. "Later, then."

"Bye."

The two men disconnect. Murray starts walking towards the BART station, stopping every few yards to look around for the man in the black car. It is not until he climbs the stairs out of the subway exit near Mollie's house, that he takes a deep breath and starts to relax.

When he gets within a couple of blocks of Mollie's apartment, Murray stops in at the corner liquor store and buys two six-packs of beer and a bag of Gummy Bears. He walks the rest of the way to Mollie's place in a slump, and breaths a sigh of relief when he finally sees her building.

"Hi, Murray," Mollie says, after looking through the peephole and unlocking the four locks on her front door. "What did you bring?"

"Oh, a little sustenance for us, is all," Murray says, allowing Mollie to relieve him of the package.

"You look beat," Mollie says, heading towards the kitchen.

"You don't look so great yourself," Murray says, chuckling.

"Yeah. It's been quite a day," Mollie says, sighing and unpacking the bag. "You want a beer? What's this...Gummy bears! Oh, Murray, you're the best. Thank you."

Murray chuckles and takes the beer from the counter, grabs one for himself and one for Mollie, and puts the rest in the refrigerator.

Murray walks into the living room and sits down on the sofa. He groans softly as he does. Mollie curls up in the chair across from him.

"So," Murray says.

"You first," Mollie says.

"Okay. Where do I begin? Well, a lot has happened today. But let me tell you what happened tonight. I went over to the playhouse. You know, the one Dolan owns?"

"That's the guy who may take your play, right?"

"Well, I don't know. We'll see," Murray says, chuckling. Mollie nods.

"Anyway," Murray continues, "As it turns out, nearly everyone who was in the audience tonight were friends or colleagues, or somehow otherwise connected with Dolan and Catherine."

"Who's Catherine?"

"I'm not sure if she's his wife, girlfriend, or just business partner. Somehow she's connected, though."

"Okay. Go ahead," Mollie says. "How was the play?"

"Well, before the play, there was this film short produced by Dolan and Catherine. It was...well, you would have found it very disturbing. It was, let's say, a political exposé about female castration."

"You're right. I probably wouldn't have liked it," Mollie says, making a face.

"The play was all right." Murray continues. "It was all about neighbor relations in San Francisco row houses. Juno called it, 'Abstract Realism'."

"Wait...Who's Juno?"

"This guy I met there that's hooked up somehow with Dolan."

"So what happened?" Mollie asks, digging into the bag of Gummy Bears.

"To begin with," Murray says, pausing to take a drink, "all right, let me preface it with this, it was nothing in particular that anyone *said* or *did*. It was more just my read on things."

Mollie nods in understanding.

"Well," Murray continues, "you know the kids who hang around the Haight and the clubs on Folsom who wear black, but they don't really mean it?"

"Yeah." Mollie nods her head and pops another Gummy Bear into her mouth.

"Well, the people at the theatre tonight all *mean* it."

"*Ewh*. Dark, huh?"

"Yep. Really dark. The type who are..." Murray pauses for just the right words.

"Over the edge?" Mollie offers.

"Well, if not over it, close enough to see it."

"Hmm," Mollie responds.

"There were a lot of dark souls. Dark spirits. Dark intent," Murray says.

"I swear, I'll never understand those people," Mollie says. "Those ones who are intent on putting their toes right up to the line. If they ever really felt what the third rail was like, they would not be so hot on always testing limits. I can tell you this, once you've actually gone over the edge, for real, I mean, there's nothing glamorous about it. Ask anyone inside a Psych ward how glamorous it is. It's not."

"I suppose," Murray says, "the only thing they find glamorous is the risk. It's the *possibility* of pushing things too far or too hard that turns them on. Or, maybe it's the illusion of the whole thing. You know, the illusion that they are living on the edge." Murray pauses to take another drink.

"Maybe," he continues, "they are just so depressed that it's a way to have a slow, safe suicide...with lots of company. I don't know," Murray says, shaking his head and rubbing his beer can.

After several minutes of silence, Mollie asks, "So did anything bad actually happen to you, or was it just more of a bad-vibe experience?"

Murray sits back, lights up a cigarette, and says, "I had my fortune told by a jewel thief. Tarot cards."

Mollie rolls her eyes and takes a drink of beer. "A *jewel thief* who reads Tarot cards?" She asks.

Murray nods. "By Juno, who I was telling you about earlier. That's not the half of it, though," Murray pauses. "The death card came up."

Mollie sits up straight in her chair.

"Not for me. For someone close to me," Murray says dryly and inhales his cigarette.

"Well, I don't know how much stock you should put in a jewel thief's reading. Kind of creepy, I'll give you that, but I wouldn't think too much about it," Mollie says, biting down on a fresh Gummy Bear and shaking her head. "A *jewel thief?*" She mutters and shakes her head again.

Murray clears his throat and begins. "Actually, uh, the problem I'm having with it is that lately I've, uh...lately, the past few weeks, I've been having those knowings again."

Mollie sits bolt upright in her chair.

"They've been coming stronger and stronger lately," Murray says.

"Oh, God. You mean the same kind of feelings or intuitions you were having before Michael died?"

"Yep," Murray says, slowly nodding his head.

"Who is it? Do you know?" Mollie asks with desperation in her voice.

"No. I've just felt it wasn't me. Someone close to me though. As the knowings got stronger, I listened more carefully to see if I could get a clue, but...nothing. And now, with the Tarot card reading..." Murray's voice trails off.

"Forget the Tarot cards," Mollie says. "Your knowings, though, *that* has me worried. Do you think it's *me*?"

Murray shrugs. "Maybe it's my mother," he says.

"Maybe it's *my* mother," Mollie says, and then mumbles something underneath her breath.

"Speaking of your mother," Murray says, changing the subject, "Didn't you mention on the phone tonight that you spoke with her? How did *that* go?"

Mollie curls up in the chair again. "Oh," she sighs, "I can't believe it. I mean, I can't believe I keep letting her upset me like this again and again." Mollie's eyes tear up. She reaches for a tissue on the end table next to her, blows her nose, and wipes her eyes.

"For years now," Mollie begins, "I mean years and years now, she's been telling me that I don't open up enough. That I keep my feelings buried. Both she and my therapist say that's the root of all my problems...why I got...sick...before. So for all this time, she's been telling me, 'You need to open up, let your feelings out. Say how you really feel about things'. So..." Mollie begins to sob.

After several minutes, she calms herself down, takes a big gulp of beer, puts her head back against the back of the easy chair, and sighs. "So, anyway, I manage to get her attention long enough to actually tell her how I've been doing and how I've been feeling about things...In between her beeper, and call-waiting, and cell phone going off, that is. And you know what she says to me?"

Mollie bites her lower lip as tears fall from her eyes onto the bag of Gummy Bears lying in her lap. Murray reaches over, grabs some tissues from the box, and hands them to her.

"Thanks." Mollie manages a soft smile. "She says to me that I had better do a reality check and that I'm...I'm...I'm held together with *paperclips and rubber bands*!" Mollie blurts this last part out and then falls into deep sobs.

Murray walks over and pats her on the back a few times. "And Gummy Bears," he says, smiling. "Don't forget about the Gummy Bears."

"What?" Mollie asks in between sobs.

"You're also held together with Gummy Bears," Murray says. "That's a pretty strong adhesive, I'd say."

"Oh, Murray." Mollie smiles broadly and throws two bears at Murray. "I can always depend on you to make me feel better."

Mollie dabs her face with the tissue, blows her nose, and covers her legs with the wool throw hanging over the back of her chair.

The two of them share the silence for nearly twenty minutes. When Mollie looks over at Murray again, she sees that he is starting to doze off.

"Oh, Murray," she says urgently.

"Hmm?" He asks without opening his eyes or stirring.

"That's what all that talk was about earlier today, wasn't it?" Mollie asks.

"Hmm?" He responds.

"Today, when you started talking all that stuff about things were happening that you didn't want to talk about, and that you might have to leave and go away. It's all because you've been having those precognitions about death, isn't it? Isn't it, Murray?"

Murray does not answer. In a few more seconds, he begins to snore. Mollie stands up, walks over to the hall closet, pulls down a blanket, and covers Murray with it. Then she picks up her bag of Gummy Bears, turns off the living room lights, and softly tiptoes into her bedroom.

V

"*Ewh!* That cat threw up in the hallway!" Karen screeches, as she enters Kirby's bedroom.

"Huh? Well, clean it up," Kirby says, keeping his eyes on the computer screen.

"You want *me* to clean it up? Are you kidding? *I'm* not cleaning up puke. He's not *my* responsibility. Besides, that cat creeps me out."

"Then don't clean it up," Kirby says, scrolling down his screen, "but then stop complaining about it."

"You don't think I should complain? I have to jump over the puke to get to the bathroom!" Karen says with disgust.

"All right," Kirby says, shoving the keyboard away. "Where is it? *I'll* do it."

"In the hallway, outside of the bathroom door. I thought cats were supposed to be *clean,* anyway."

"He was *sick*, Karen. Are you worried about being clean when *you* are sick?" Kirby says, getting up from his desk. "Probably," he mutters to himself as he walks out of the bedroom.

Kirby grabs a roll of generic paper towels from the kitchen counter and heads down the hallway. He cleans up the mess, washes his hands, and walks around the apartment calling Shadow's name. On the third call, Shadow comes out from Murray's bedroom and stands looking up at Kirby. Kirby bends down and pets Shadow's head.

"Are you all right, guy? That's the third time you threw up in the last few days." Shadow stands looking up at Kirby. "Come on, let's see what's happening with your food and water. Your buddy won't be back until tomorrow."

Kirby walks into the kitchen and bends down at Shadow's bowls. "Shadow," Kirby says disappointedly. "You've hardly touched your food again. And you have polished off nearly all the water. I'll get you some fresh water."

Kirby takes the bowl to the sink and fills it up. Shadow is standing by the food bowl when Kirby returns with the water. "You're not becoming bulimic because I teased you about being overweight, are you guy?" Kirby sets the water bowl down and rubs Shadow's head.

"Now *you're* talking to that cat?" Karen says, standing in the doorway of the kitchen with her hands on her hips. "Unbelievable," she says, rolling her eyes.

"Lighten up, Karen," Kirby says, giving Shadow a final pet. "I don't know what you are so bent out of shape about. Is it that time of the month?" He says, walking past her and heading back into the bedroom.

"Ugh! Don't *even* start that crap with me," Karen says, following him into the bedroom.

"It's just a cat, for God's sake," Kirby says, guiding the mouse on his computer. "I can't believe you talk about actually having kids some day. How are you going to have kids if you are allergic to puke?" Kirby says, reading the screen.

"I won't have to worry about cleaning up puke. I'll have help," Karen announces matter-of-factly.

"Oh. I see," Kirby replies, returning to the computer screen.

Kirby sits busily typing at the keyboard for several minutes. Karen is sitting cross-legged on his futon, picking fuzz off of his flannel comforter.

"What's with those two, anyway?" She asks finally.

"What two?" Kirby responds absent-mindedly, hitting the space bar.

"You know. Murray and that cat," Karen answers. "He's always talking with that cat like he's a *person*. Sometimes I get the feeling he likes that cat better than he likes people."

"Don't see as I'd blame him," Kirby mutters.

"What? You know, I think this place is having a bad effect on you. I feel like I don't even know you sometimes."

Kirby remains silent and intent on his work.

"Seriously, Kirby, there's something weird going on between Murray and that cat. Did you ever notice how they *communicate*?"

"Yeah," Kirby says, turning away from the computer screen. "I think it's amazingly cool."

"Well, *I* think it's creepy. You know what else is creepy? Murray's weird ability to *know* things."

"I don't know what you're talking about," Kirby says, reaching over and hitting the printer's "on" button.

"No? Come on, Kirby. That guy...it's like he has some weird sixth sense or something. It's almost like he can read your mind, like he knows what you are thinking."

"If that were true," Kirby says, smirking, "then he would have probably banned you from this house long ago."

"Shut up," Karen says, sulking. "I'm serious. Last week you were sleeping and I went into the kitchen to get some milk and he comes in and says, 'You're worried about your mother?' and I say 'yeah', and of course I was in shock that he knew anything about my mother, and he says, 'Everything is going to work out. She's going to be just fine'. Can you believe it?"

"Well, everything *did* work out. The tumor was benign. Why are you so upset?" Kirby asks, flipping through the pages that have just come off the printer.

"*Because*...how did he *know* anything about my mother? Did *you* say something? I asked you not to say anything about it to anyone."

"No. Maybe he overheard us talking about her."

"That's impossible. I never discussed her while I was here. Besides, how did he know how everything was going to turn out?" Karen asks with a troubled look on her face.

"Come on, Karen. He just saw that you were upset and was trying to say something comforting. He was just trying to be nice. Give it a break."

Karen leans her back against the wall, stretches her legs out on the futon, and crosses her arms across her chest. "Well, what about all the other weird stuff he does?" she asks defiantly.

"Like what?" Kirby asks, returning to the computer screen.

"Like when he suddenly jumps up and runs out of the house sometimes, for no reason. He does it a lot at five or five-thirty in the morning sometimes."

"How do *you* know? You don't stay over that often."

"Well...the times I *do*. I know because he wakes me up doing it. It's really weird. Where do you think he goes?"

"I don't know. Maybe he's having a secret affair," Kirby says, chuckling. Karen rolls her eyes.

"And what about the *main* thing he does? That plunging. Two o'clock in the morning I hear him plunging and plunging the toilet. What's *that* all about?" Karen does a fake shivering.

"I don't know. Maybe he's well-endowed in the digestive department," Kirby says, typing something on the keyboard.

"*Gross,*" Karen responds. Just then, the telephone rings. "I'll get it," Karen says. "Hello? *Hello*?" She hangs up the receiver. "And that's another thing about this place. All of these creepy phone calls."

"No one there again?" Kirby asks.

"No. And where does he get his money?"

"What? Who are we talking about *now*?" Kirby asks, typing.

"Murray. Who do you think? Where does he get his money? What does he *do*? He doesn't seem to have a job."

"I don't know, Karen. It's not the sort of thing you should go around asking people. He doesn't talk about it, and I don't pry. I don't care. He pays his half of the rent and the bills on time. That's all I care."

There is a pause as Kirby considers the question further. "Maybe he has an inheritance," he continues, "maybe he has some money from a lawsuit, a car accident or something. Maybe he's on disability. I don't know."

"And that's another thing," Karen says, picking up her Emory board off of the dresser. "He doesn't drive. He

127

doesn't even use a *computer*. I hear him in his room typing all of the time. God knows *what* he's working on. But he's using this really old *typewriter*. I didn't even know you could buy those things anymore."

Kirby laughs. "Well, I've offered him a couple of times to use my computer, but he says he prefers to use the typewriter." Kirby pauses and scrolls the computer screen.

"You know," Kirby says, "there's actually a lot of people out there who don't care to use computers. Believe it or not, that does not make them weird, or social misfits or anything. In fact...for all the times I've lost things because computers have crashed on me, I've been tempted to do things the old way myself."

Karen gives a "*tssh*" sound and rolls her eyes.

The two are silent for several minutes. Kirby types on the keyboard. Karen files her well-manicured nails.

"And what about his friends?" She asks.

"Are we back to *this* again? For someone you don't like, you sure spend enough time thinking and talking about him," Kirby responds, looking over at Karen.

Karen is unaffected by Kirby's comment. "What about that strange girl that I've seen here a couple of times? Polly or Mollie, or *whatever* her name is. She gives me the creeps. She looks like some kind of mental case."

"Why?" Kirby asks, turning towards Karen. "Because she doesn't look or act like one of your sorority sisters?" Kirby smirks and returns to the computer screen.

Karen remains silent for quite awhile. Finally, she says, "No. Forget it. I don't see why you insist on living in this city, anyhow. Why can't you just live in Berkeley? It's such a hassle to keep driving out here. Besides, wouldn't it be nicer to be closer to school instead of making that drive everyday?"

"We're not going to get into that again, Karen. I've already told you. I'm not going to live in Berkeley. Nine months was more than enough for me."

"But *why not*? I don't get it."

Kirby pushes the keyboard back and turns his chair to face Karen. "Look," he begins, "I've told you already, I don't know how many times...I can't stand that place. I don't even like to have to drive out there to go to class. If you want to know creepy, now *that place* is creepy."

"I don't understand why it bothers you so much," Karen says.

"If you lived in other places...that is, if you ever bothered to leave the state, you'd understand why," Kirby says. "That place is filled with a bunch of hypocrites. A lot of people masquerading as free-thinkers and liberal-minded do-gooders and intellectuals. In reality, they are the most intolerant group of people gathered together in one place I've ever seen."

"I don't agree. Berkeley is the one place in the world you can go to be however you want," Karen says emphatically.

"Yeah," Kirby snickers, "as long as the way you want to be is exactly how the majority of people there already are. They're liberal and tolerant all right, just as long as the only thing they have to tolerate is something that does not disrupt their version of reality.

"That place," Kirby continues, "is filled with a bunch of angry, humorless people who want to change everyone to think and be just like themselves." Kirby pauses for a couple of seconds.

"Besides...Berkeley is one giant magnet for nuts," he says, shaking his head. "All those people steeped in their so-called political causes. Instead of working through their unresolved personal, psychological issues, they turn all their energy onto some inane cause...Even the ones involved in relevant causes are really just fueled by their own personal muck and anger."

Kirby is silent for several minutes and then adds, "Besides, there's too much whining."

He finishes what he is working on and then reaches over and turns his screen-saver on.

"Oh, like there are no nuts or whiners in San Francisco," Karen says, making one last attempt at her argument.

"Oh, they're here all right," Kirby says. "It's just that in San Francisco at least, if someone gets in your face with their crap, you can tell them to fuck off without worrying that there will be a petition and a rally the next week to run you out of town."

Kirby gets up and pushes his chair away. "Enough of all this meaningless talk about things we can't change. Let's talk about something we *can* do something about." Kirby kneels down on the futon next to Karen, leans in and kisses her.

"Hey! I thought you said you wanted to *talk,* " she says, lying down.

"Oh. Forget that," Kirby says, lying down next to her. "We've talked too much already."

* * * *

"All right. Then we are all set for the big day," Sack says, standing in the middle of the living room, looking around him. "Todd, you and John will be in charge of bringing the soup over. Shirley will bring the cups and the literature. Oh, don't forget the ladles this time." Shirley nods.

"Murray, you're bringing fresh bread and muffins, right?" Sack asks.

"Homemade," Murray says proudly.

"The rest of you, then," Sack continues, "you know what your primary responsibilities are." Sack gestures to various people as he speaks. "You'll be relief for giving out the soup and bread and muffins." He points again. "You'll be in charge of spreading the word to anyone who hasn't heard we're there handing out free food." Sack gestures around the living room and dining room areas. "And the rest of you, your jobs are to hand out the literature to everyone you can.

130

"Remember, don't stray too far from where the food is set up, because your primary job is to run interference when the cops arrive. They're probably going to try and seize the food stand again. We want a lot of media attention, so do whatever you have to. Anyone who gets arrested, make a commotion. Especially if the television cameras are nearby. And don't worry. Leventhal has agreed to take care of everything for us. You'll only be in jail overnight, at the most. Are there any more questions?"

Sack looks around the room, and then walks over towards the dining room area. "Any questions?" He asks in that direction. There is silence. "All right then. Murray, you've got the interviews and play-by-play covered for the radio station?"

"Yep," Murray replies.

"Just a few final words, then," Sack says, standing up straight and shoving his hands in the pockets of his faded, torn blue jeans. "First of all, I'd like to thank everyone for coming tonight. Your support is really appreciated. Especially those people who came in from Berkeley and are not official members of Meals-Not-Militia. Those of you who have come in from the East Bay, we want you to know you can count on all of us from Meals-Not-Militia for what you've got planned for People's Park and Livermore over the next few months."

Sack pauses and walks around the living room. "As you know, you're all invited to hang around and enjoy the party tonight. Murray and Kate put together some food, and Todd claims to have a mean bag of weed for dessert."

Several people chuckle.

"One last word of caution, though," Sack says, lowering his eyes and looking very serious. "The heat is on around here."

Sack pauses. Everyone is silent and looking directly at him. "Both Van and Gary from the station have had visitors poking around asking questions, and Todd and John have seen some guy that looks like a Fed parked outside of here off and on for the past couple of weeks. Gary is concerned about someone trying to shut down the radio station, so he's moving the location for now. We're not sure if it's the station, or Meals-Not-Militia they're after. It might be something else entirely. We just can't be sure. So it's very important that everyone keep your mouth shut about what's going down. Don't even talk to your closest friends about anything we are doing. You just never know who they'll get to."

Several people nod their heads in agreement.

"And keep your eyes and ears open. If anyone sees or hears anything that might be relevant, even if it's just a hunch, be sure to let either Gary or me know. You can always leave a message for me here at the house." Sack pauses. "Well, I guess that's about it. We'll see all of you at ten o'clock, day after tomorrow. Enjoy the party."

There is a round of applause and a couple of hoots and hollers, and then Todd turns on the CD player. People get up from their seats and stretch, mill around, and chat. Some people head for the kitchen.

Murray gets up and follows Sack into the kitchen. "Say, I was wondering," Murray begins hesitantly, "would it be all right if I stayed here tonight after the party? I don't want to be taking the BART back that late, and the buses will already have stopped running."

"Yeah. No problem. You can crash upstairs on the cot in the office. You okay for getting back tomorrow?" Sack asks.

"Oh, sure. No problem there. Thanks a lot." Murray says.

Sack nods and walks toward the back porch. In a few minutes he backs his car out of the driveway.

Murray helps himself to a paper plate and heaps it full with food from the spread on the kitchen table. He reaches into the cooler sitting on a crate beside the kitchen sink and gets himself a beer, and then heads back into the living room. The reggae singer on the CD player is imploring the listener to "legalize it." Murray takes a seat on a folding chair near three other people who are in the middle of a conversation.

"I'll tell you how to deal with the contract on America," one of the men says angrily, "We need to go out and *organize* our communities, that's how. We need to brainstorm on how to do that. We must have *unified*, progressive organizations. We need roundtables to unify the best activists."

The man turns to Murray. "Chad. People United." The man says, sticking out his hand towards Murray.

Murray shakes his hand and motions that his mouth is full. After a couple of seconds, he says, "Murray."

"Well, Murray," Chad says, "I don't know where you stand on this, but I was just saying that if we can just organize, we can grow all the food we need for the homeless. We can make sure that no kid goes ignorant. We can get them tutors, and we can make sure we get enough votes so that we never lose an election."

"I'm glad someone is finally talking seriously about organizing. The main problem with overcoming the strangle-hold of the current administration," a long-haired, middle-aged man named Bill says, resting his paper plate on his knee, "is just that. We *really* need to organize! We must register people to vote, yes, but we must *teach* them to vote in the *right* way."

"The real question is," a plain-faced, overweight woman named Sharon says, leaning forward, "why are so many people nowadays working for next to nothing? Is it because they love their jobs so much? No. It's the taxes that's keeping them down." Sharon pauses to take a drink of her bottled water. "Right now in the Bay Area, we have 220 volunteers signed up so far for social action," she continues, "I think we can all agree. We must all go forward to be *one solid* group."

Murray clears his throat, stands up with his plate and beer, and announces, "Well, if you'll excuse me, I have to go mingle a bit."

"Sure thing, Murray. Nice talking with you," Chad says.

Sharon gives Murray a smile.

Murray walks around to another small group gathered on folding chairs. "Mind if I join you?" He asks, sitting down on one of the empty chairs.

"Hey, Murray," a bearded man named Gene says. "We were just talking about the fact that the homeless themselves should have a say in what happens to them."

"If you're going to outlaw panhandling on the streets," a twenty-something girl with short hair, named Sandy adds, "then those people actually *doing* the panhandling should get to vote on it, at least."

A dark-skinned, young man named Alanti pipes in, "Yeah, one of the council members at the city council meeting last week was a real hard-liner. She's trying to outlaw panhandling within twenty-feet of ATM machines. She's even proposing not allowing panhandling after 11:00 PM. Can you believe that? Our basic concern is the *Rights of the Homeless*. We don't care about other's *inconvenience*. I don't even know why they are so concerned about safety issues. If you don't want to give anything, just say so." He pauses for a few seconds then adds, "The homeless really need to be able to speak for themselves."

"What's your take on all of this Murray?" A smallish, balding man in his thirties named Brad, asks. Then, without waiting for a response, "Did you read that crap in the newspaper by one of the people from the Board of Supervisors? Unbelievable! This guy writes that Meals-Not-Militia is guilty of committing a conspiracy. Yeah. A conspiracy to *feed* people."

Several people shake their heads.

"So anyway," Brad continues, "he goes on about how many people fear the homeless...of course, he doesn't mention anything about the *police.* And he says there is all this misconduct by street people, and that it's a cancer that must be prevented from spreading because the homeless are on drugs and alcohol, and therefore their misconduct is *volitional.*

Can you believe that? Volitional? Now, I take issue with that because, as everyone here probably knows, when you take alcohol or drugs, your behavior is most definitely NOT volitional! I don't know what this guy's education is, but this is really dangerous because people will read this crap and *think* this is correct."

Brad pauses, shakes his head, and says, "Maybe better times are ahead. Maybe I'm a dreamer."

Gene adds, "Ultimately, there is no fault to that end."

The group falls silent. Murray shakes his beer can and says, "Time for a fresh one." He stands up, picks up his paper plate, nods to the group, and heads back towards the kitchen.

As Murray approaches the foyer, two white males are standing just to the side. As he passes them, one of the men says in an angry tone, "Since the Civil War, African Americans have been scapegoated in the eyes of the American Working Class. Since the 1960's, *women* have been scapegoated in the eyes of the working class. Gender and race are NOT a fringe benefit of the Revolutionary days. *I'm sorry.* Clarence Thomas isn't doing working blacks any good. Sandra Day O'Connor didn't do women any good during her tenure. It's all about gender and race at the expense of *class*...which is *the* unifying force of human beings. Class wars. Our job is to WIN that WAR! I just want to bring to your attention that *this* is what we're talking about here."

Murray makes his way past the two men and into the kitchen. Several people are standing around the kitchen table.

"Murray," Todd says, "did you try this potato salad? It's great."

"I was just making my way for seconds," Murray says, reaching for the make-shift serving spoon.

"Did you catch the Bee Babe this week?" Todd asks.

"No," Murray says disappointedly. "I wasn't home. Did you see it?"

"Yeah," Todd says, smiling. "You missed a great one. She did this entire Shakespeare play in the bathtub with these little hand puppets and paper bags with faces drawn on them. And, get this, her cat was dressed up in this stupid King costume. He was supposed to be King Richard, I think. Anyway, it was really great because she kept dropping the puppets and the head kept coming off of one of the dolls, and so she kept having to bend way over to pick them up."

Murray chuckles. "Sorry I missed that."

"At the end, the King gets killed, so she took this diner squeeze-bottle and squeezed ketchup all over the cat."

Todd and Murray laugh.

"I can't believe you guys watch that bimbo," Miriam says, dipping a potato chip into the bowl of onion dip.

Todd and Murray give each other a private look.

"So, Miriam," Murray says, "what have you been up to?"

"I've been working everyday on helping to fight this anti-panhandling resolution they're trying to pass," Miriam says, shaking her head.

"How's it coming along?" Murray asks.

"Well, it's not over yet. The city council felt so intimidated by all of us protesters that they pushed it back. It's anti-human, I tell you. There should be no ordinances against BEHAVIOR of the homeless." Miriam pauses to take a drink of her non-pasteurized carrot juice.

Murray shifts his weight from his left foot to his right.

"Everyone looks to us, you know. All of the U.S. looks to California, well, the Bay Area at least, to see how things should be done," she goes on. "If it passes here, it can pass anywhere. The whole country is looking to us now to see whether we will decide to allow panhandling, or will squash the constitutional rights of homeless American citizens."

Murray notices that Miriam's face and throat are red and her hands are clinched into little balls.

"If a person sits on the streets, or lies there, this should not be punishable. Most homeless have been thrown out of jobs and have as much right to be on the streets as anyone," she says.

Miriam takes a breath and then continues. "Everyone has a right to live by virtue of the fact that they are alive. Everyone has a constitutional right to food, shelter, and clothing. Our legislators need to know this. To deprive people of a job is INSANE. A person has a right to exist, you know."

Miriam takes two steps back towards the kitchen wall and leans against it. She looks physically exhausted from her own words.

"Yeah, well," an elfin, dark-haired young man named Rani jumps in, "You know, San Francisco, Berkeley, this whole Bay Area, in fact, likes to cling to the appearance that all is well. They use the excuse that there is this element of fear because some of the people have been homeless for so long that they no longer exhibit human qualities. They *claim* that fear dominates in John Q. Public, but you know, we *all* know, the *real* reason."

Several people in the kitchen nod knowingly.

Rani continues, "The Bourgeois wants the Proletariat to stay hungry, to stay in the hole and dirty, which is precisely the reason they refuse us and try to shut down Meals-Not-Militia's efforts."

Several more people have now gathered in the kitchen and are saying things like, "That's right," and "You got it," after each of Rani's statements.

After several minutes, Rani's voice raises to a fevered pitch. "City Hall is against us feeding the homeless because feeding the homeless would *keep* them here and they want the homeless to go away. And why? Because they like to pretend they have this beautiful city. They need the tax-revenue. The tourists. And the homeless are an eyesore."

Someone shouts, "Yeah! You got it."

"The merchants want the homeless gone and they put pressure on the politicians. The whole damn thing is driven by money. By filthy capitalism. They don't want to feed the homeless," Rani concludes, "but they spend billions on weapons!"

People are now pushing inside the kitchen from the rest of the house.

"Actually," Teri, a large woman, wearing a drab-colored dress over brown corduroy pants breaks in, "The solution is very simple. The group I'm working with *has* the answer."

All heads turn to listen.

"If we could acquire properties with no money down, we could get *all* the homeless off the street."

Several people nod in agreement.

"There are properties all over the Bay Area. Just sitting there. Vacant. The government is choosing to throw billions on a defense system, and this is keeping the homes away from the homeless. The main problem though, is how can you teach a population to gain a conscience? As a society, we must have a collective conscience, rather than just allowing some realtor to *sit* on the property for a tax write-off, or whatever."

Murray finishes off his second plate of food, tosses the paper plate into the recycling box, and opens another beer, just as tempers begin to heat up. The activists, having worked themselves up into a frenzied-state, are now shouting. "A police state mentality does not work in San Francisco and Berkeley, because here, WE FIGHT BACK!" One of them screams.

A young man Murray does not know yells, "Yeah!" and bangs the back of his head against the kitchen wall several times.

Someone named Kris, from a group called 'People United' shouts, "This Super-Police-Mode mentality the city governments have adopted to crush protesters does not inspire a peaceful compromise."

Daryl, a young man Murray knew to have joined Meals-Not-Militia a year ago, stands up on one of the kitchen chairs and addresses the crowd gathered in the kitchen and adjoining dining room.

"Non-violent marches and rallies do not work. There are too many police now, and more importantly, the media simply does not pay attention to non-violent protests. You have all this nuclear testing and waste dumping going on at Indian Reservations and the radioactive waste being dumped in Needles. They don't give a fuck about what's happening to the *turtles!*"

Several women hold their hands to their mouths and shake their heads from side to side. One young woman in bib-overalls says, "It's a hypocrisy."

Daryl continues, "We need to rally to get the government to convert the nuclear weapons into peaceful products. We need to get people to write to the House of Representatives for nuclear disarmament...The University is behind Livermore Labs. We're not fighting a government, we're fighting ORGANIZED CRIME!"

"Yeah!" Several people yell out.

Daryl steps down off of the kitchen chair. Two people slap him on the back. "Right on," one of them says. There is much chatter and head shaking. Many people are standing with their bodies held in a rigid manner as if they are ready for attack at any moment.

Murray moves forward and squeezes between groups of people. He reaches in and lifts the bowls of chips and onion dip off of the kitchen table. Next, he walks back behind the group of people and sits the bowls down on a crate at the edge of the kitchen, near the back porch. He is standing there munching on chips and watching the crowd when a young man with long hair tied back with a hemp Scrungy and a tie-dyed shirt comes up.

"See, this is exactly why we started our paper," the young man says. "I'm Bill Garland, Free Speech Express."

Murray nods as he plops a chip with a large dollop of onion dip into his mouth.

"Our advertisers are all merchants that can't get access in the Mainstream Media. Our focus is the modern day police state. It's a voice for the disenfranchised segment of society. It also covers world politics and economics. It highlights the Fascist Nature of the New World Order."

Murray leans against the doorway and puts his left foot on the crate. He keeps his eye on the people gathering around a new speaker in the center of the kitchen.

"I think so many people throw around the word 'Fascism'," Murray says without taking his eyes away from the crowd. "I think we have to be careful about using the word 'fascism,' Bill. What do you mean when you say that?"

"You know," Bill begins, "back in 1975, Fascism was discredited as a viable ideology. People said it had been conquered in 1945. That's WRONG. It DOES exist today. Even in Italy...and in Germany too."

Bill pauses to gather his thoughts. "Essentially," he says, "it is BIG Business in bed with the State. In this country, that amounts to BIG Industrialists in alignment with the police powers of the state who are oppressing the masses." And then, as an after-thought he says, "A person has a right to exist!"

"Can't disagree with that," Murray says, reaching for more chips and dip. "Good luck with your paper," he adds. The young man nods and moves through the crowd in the kitchen. In a few minutes, Murray notices the young man is talking to someone else in a corner of the dining room area.

The crowd in the kitchen grows tighter. A man in the center of the crowd has everyone's attention. Murray can see the man has a crew cut and thick, black-rimmed glasses. Murray notices he is wearing a T-shirt that looks like it says, "Technology Suds." From where he is standing, Murray can just barely make out what the man is saying.

"...so basically," the man says, "the City Council has stepped up repression of the masses of people, and this is just one component of political repression. People aren't even free to hand out flyers to spread the word anymore.

It's fundamental...it's economically rooted. We are talking HUGE marginalization here."

The people on the inside of the circle appear to be mesmerized by the speaker. Some of those on the outside of the circle are straining, moving to and fro, and muttering, "What's he saying?" "What did he say?" and "I can't hear him."

"Could you speak up? We can't hear you back here," someone yells out.

"Yeah. We can't hear you over here either," someone else says.

The man starts to stand up on one of the kitchen chairs. As he steps up, however, the chair tips, the man loses his balance, and starts to fall. Several people break his fall and steady him, while a couple of others grab a hold of the chair and keep it still.

Finally, the man stands up on the chair. Murray can now see that the shirt actually reads, "Technology sucks."

"So, as I was saying," the man continues, "people are homeless and living in the streets because the market place simply DOES *NOT* WORK! Look around." The man gestures with both of his hands. "There are huge vacant places throughout the entire Bay Area. All this hoopla for the FREE Market, but you can plainly see it does not work at the most fundamental level. There are over *6 million* people living on the streets in this country," the man says, his face growing red and his voice growing louder. "The Free Market isolates! It's divisive!"

Just then, Murray hears Sack's late model Mercedes pulling into the driveway. Murray walks over to the back porch and cups his hands around his eyes, as he presses his face up against the screen door. Sack gets out of the car, opens the trunk, and lifts out two large boxes of Meals-Not-Militia literature. Murray looks over at the man standing on the chair and smirks.

"Fundamentally," he is saying, "we must re-distribute the wealth in this country so that not one person is left living on the street. The New World Order of Capitalism is what caused this!"

Several people clap and others yell comments in support of the speaker.

"The Roosevelt Mythology is unlikely for one fundamental reason...Privatization is the current movement in this country. So it is NOT a solution..."

Murray holds the screen door open as Sack carries the boxes in and drops them down on the floor of the porch.

"We need a *Redistribution of the Wealth* in order to solve the problem. Capitalism has outlived its usefulness in its ability to give food and clothing to the masses!" The man continues.

Sack stands in the doorway of the kitchen, hands tucked inside the front pockets of his jeans, and looks on, taking the entire scenario in.

"One-third of humanity in the world is out of a job because of the Technological Revolution!" The man shouts.

Several people yell, "Yeah!" and "Right on!"

"Therefore," the man continues, "we must all have a reduction of human labor. Need versus Capital for the Redistribution of Wealth in this country is *the* answer!" The man's neck and face are crimson. Veins are bulging from the sides of his neck; his fists are clenched. The crowd of activists looks on, mesmerized.

Murray stands in the back of the room, one hand in the pocket of his beat up cotton pants, the other holding a beer can. He is watching Sack and smirking.

"People already *know* this," the man standing on the chair shouts, "but they see the government as so powerful and omnipotent, they don't see a way to change things."

Sack calls out John's name and motions for him to come over. John makes his way around the back of the crowd in the kitchen and heads towards Sack. Sack whispers something to John and motions towards Todd, who is leaning up against the kitchen sink, munching on pretzels.

John makes his way over to Todd. He says something to him, and the two of them head out into the living room.

"And so," the man standing on the chair is shouting, "in Berkeley, for instance, there are thousands of pieces of property owned by realtors who make more money by writing it off on their taxes rather than renting it, *and* all the land owned by the university regents. These properties could house *all* of the homeless in the Bay Area!" Several people begin to clap. A few more hold up their fists and say, "Right on!"

Just then, Todd appears at the kitchen doorway. He motions to Sack, holds up a bag, and points to it.

"May I have everyone's attention?" Sack says in a booming voice.

Everyone looks his way. The young man who had been ranting grows silent.

"I promised you some dessert. If you will all follow Todd into the living room, he is going to fire up some bowls right now," Sack says.

Several people cheer. The crowd breaks up, leaving the man standing alone to find his own way down from the kitchen chair. Murray watches him struggle from the corner of his eye. People start to herd into the living room. "All right," they are saying, "Bring on some of that *evil weed.*"

Murray crushes his beer can and throws it into the recycling bin. He looks over at Sack, who is watching the last of the people head out into the living room.

"Crowd control, eh?" Murray says to Sack.

"Yeah, well," Sack replies, "can't let them use up their energy now. I need them to store it up until Saturday."

Murray starts to clean up the kitchen, separating plastic, aluminum, and paper for the appropriate recycling bins.

"I'm gonna' head up to the office for a bit," Sack says. "I've got a couple of important phone calls to make."

Murray nods and continues to clean up. When he has finished cleaning up the kitchen, he takes a paper bag and walks out into the living room. He walks around the dimly lit room gathering paper plates, aluminum cans, and plastic forks as Crosby, Stills, Nash, and Young croon from the CD player. Everyone is relaxed now, heads resting back against the sofa and chairs, or sitting cross-legged on the floor. A few people sit on folding chairs silently passing a joint. Several people are speaking to those sitting nearby. Their tone is considerably milder than some thirty minutes earlier.

Murray finishes collecting the garbage, separates it into the appropriate bins, then washes his hands and begins to carry the food from the kitchen table out into the living room. "Ah, Munchies! Good!" Someone says, as Murray sits the bowls down on the coffee table. Several people quickly head for the food.

When he finishes carrying out all of the bowls of munchies, Murray opens a new can of beer and leans against the doorway separating the kitchen from the living room and dining room areas. John is nearby. He is sitting cross-legged on the floor, sharing a pipe with two other young men.

After he exhales and passes the bowl he says, "My grandmother is suffering and in a good deal of pain, but she refuses to consider the medical use of marijuana. She grew up in a time in which clothing was made from hemp and so she's aware of the clothing aspect, but she's old-fashioned. I'm doing everything I can to convince her that she should use marijuana to help her."

"What is she suffering from?" Asks one of the young men.

John exhales. "Emphysema and bronchitis," he says.

There is silence. The other two young men nod.

"Pass the lighter. It's out," one of the young men says.

The other young man passes the lighter and says, "I think people should be able to have the legal right for the pursuit of happiness to...like, after a hard day's work or of protesting, or whatever, to go home and light up a bowl."

He takes the pipe, inhales, passes the pipe to John, exhales, closes his eyes, opens them, and continues speaking. "I'd rather be around a lot of potheads, than around a bunch of drunks that get stupid and fight and puke on people."

"Cool," the other young man says, nodding in agreement.

"I mean, come on," the first young man continues, "the only fight I ever got into with a stoner was where the pot originated from!"

Murray smirks, turns, and heads back into the kitchen. He turns the light off, heads out the back door, and sits down on the back steps. Then he lights up a cigarette, rests his head against the banister, and watches the fog roll over the night sky.

* * * *

Murray awakens to the sound of kitchen noises. He groans as he hoists himself up from the tiny cot. He reaches for his pair of pants and shirt hanging on the doorknob, and with his eyes still partially closed, he gets dressed and heads downstairs. As Murray descends the stairs, he can hear John and Todd in the kitchen talking. As he turns the corner, John is speaking.

"...so then I'm on this airplane with all of these Corporate-types. Only no one can tell us apart because instead of their Armani suits, they're all wearing their jumping gear. And me too. We all have on jumpsuits, helmets, goggles, and parachutes. All of a sudden someone yells, "Jump!" and everyone starts jumping out of the plane. I look out to see where we're suppose to land, and I see that all these guys are jumping into this *gigantic* bowl of mashed potatoes."

"*Cool*," Todd responds. "So did you jump too?"

"Yeah, but wait. See, I keep looking down at the mashed potatoes from the airplane, and I notice that a few seconds after these guys land, they turn into these things that look like giant peas, and they start floating in the mashed potatoes...just bobbing up and down, up and down."

"Weird," Todd is saying as Murray enters the kitchen. "Hi, Doc," Todd says when he sees Murray. "You've *got* to hear John's dream."

"Hmm," Murray says, as he reaches for the coffee carafe and begins filling it with water. He catches a glance at John who is looking towards Sack and grinning.

"Sack will want to hear about it too," John says, a bit too cheerfully, as Sack enters the kitchen.

Sack pulls a chair back and sits down at the table. "To begin with," Sack says, opening the newspaper, "I don't even remember any of my *own* dreams, so I don't have interest in hearing about other people's dreams. And secondly, it just seems like an insipid topic for conversation."

"Sack doesn't think I should discuss my dreams with other people," John says, smirking.

"No, actually, I'm glad you have Todd to share them with," Sack says, as he flips the pages of the newspaper. "It saves *me* from having to hear about them."

"So what happened after the Corporate guys turned into giant peas?" Todd asks with interest.

"Okay," John begins. "So, I'm the last one left on the plane, and I'm really nervous about jumping. But then I see that everyone else is okay because they are all afloat in the mashed potatoes. So I hold my breath and I jump."

"Did you turn into a giant pea like the rest of them?" Todd asks.

"No," John says, grinning. "I didn't turn into a pea. I just stayed myself."

There is a long pause.

"So what happened?" Murray asks.

John slowly finishes chewing a mouthful of cereal, swallows, and says solemnly, "I sank and drowned."

Todd lets out a loud groan. "What a downer."

"You know, John," Murray says, pouring a cup of coffee, "Freud would have a field day with that one."

"Yeah, I know," John says, smirking.

Murray sits down at the table with his coffee mug.

Todd looks over at Sack. "So you don't ever like to hear about people's dreams?" He asks, getting up to put his dishes in the sink.

"That's not entirely true," Sack says. "I would *love* to hear about *your* dreams, ever since your new friend Mary started spending the night."

"Very funny," Todd says, rinsing water over his breakfast dishes. "Well...I'm out of here."

"Say, are you going downtown?" Murray asks.

"Yeah. You need a lift?" Todd asks.

"Is Mission out of your way?"

"No problem. I can cut over from Army. I've got to leave now, though," Todd says, digging his keys out of his pocket.

"Okay," Murray says, taking a big gulp of coffee. He pours the rest down the drain and rinses out his cup. "Well, I guess I'll see you guys tomorrow," he says to Sack and John.

"Later," John says, giving a wave.

"Don't forget the tapes for tomorrow," Sack says, still looking through the newspaper.

Todd and Murray walk out to where the car is parked.

"Hey Murray?" Todd says, as he starts the car. "Mary said something to me yesterday...It made me think about things, you know, psychologically-speaking. Anyway, my question is, how do you know if you're normal?"

Murray stays silent for several seconds before answering. He clears his throat and says, "Normal? By whose definition? There's no such thing, Todd. So you don't ever have to worry about it again."

"Cool," Todd says, as he checks his side mirror and careens his way into the morning traffic.

Murray asks to be dropped off at Mission and Army. He walks down Mission to the Safeway, turns left for two blocks, cuts right, and comes through the back way, squeezing between an opening in his neighbor's fence. The neighbor's dog Jake watches Murray's every move, but remains silent.

Murray enters through the back door. Shadow is there to greet him.

"Hey, Shadow! What a surprise! Now, how did you know I would be coming in the back way?" Murray says, bending down to rub Shadow's head and face. "Hey, hold on there a minute. You've lost weight. Look at how loose your collar is...Shadow, how did you lose so much weight in just a couple of days?"

Shadow meows and holds his face up towards Murray.

"You know what I brought for you, little buddy? A surprise. Your favorite. Look!"

Murray digs into his pocket and brings out a fistful of rubber bands. He drops them and they bounce across the floor. Shadow remains motionless.

"Hey, is something wrong, buddy? You love rubber bands, remember?"

Shadow takes his right paw and pushes a couple of the rubber bands around on the tile for a few seconds, then meows and lies down on the floor.

"I don't know, Shadow. Now I *am* worried about you," Murray says, walking towards the kitchen. "The day you're not interested in rubber bands..."

Murray looks around the kitchen and living room. "Anybody home?" He calls out. Silence. "Looks like it's just you and I, Shadow. I'm going to be baking today. Maybe I can get you interested in a muffin. It looks like you're no longer much interested in your regular food," Murray says, walking over and checking out Shadow's bowls.

"Well, we will see what we're going to do about this," Murray says as Shadow comes over and sits beside his feet. "Let me check the mail, here."

Murray flips through half a dozen envelopes. On the bottom of the pile is a note from Kirby. Murray reads it.

"Hey, Shadow," Murray says, reading the note. "Kirby says here that you have not been eating your food and that you've thrown up a few times." Murray bends down and pets Shadow. "You have the flu or some nasty virus, little buddy?"

Murray walks to the recorder to check for messages. Shadow trots alongside him, talking the whole while.

"All right, buddy, let me wash up here, then you and me will bake up a bunch of bread and muffins, and then we'll see if you'll eat *that*."

Back in the kitchen, Murray measures and mixes and bakes and cools, and then starts the process all over again. Despite a good deal of coaxing, Shadow refuses to eat even Murray's most tempting of muffins. About two hours after Murray has started baking, Shadow disappears. When Murray calls him, Shadow does not come. Murray searches for him and finds him curled up at the foot of the bed.

"Okay, buddy," Murray says, "you're obviously not feeling well. You rest in here and when I finish, I'll come in and hang out with you."

Shadow lowers his head and closes his eyes.

When Murray finishes the last batch of baked goods, he goes into his bedroom, turns on Cable Public Access, and sets up his typewriter. For the next several hours, he types his rewrites to Act II of his stage play, while bizarre images of naked women with freakishly enlarged breasts dance across the television screen. When Murray stops typing to change the ribbon, Shadow jumps off of the bed and crawls underneath it.

"Shadow! What are you doing underneath of there? What is wrong with you?" Murray asks with concern in his voice. "Is this my punishment for being away so much lately?"

Murray gets down on his hands and knees and pulls Shadow out from underneath the bed.

"You are so light now," he says, cradling Shadow in his arms. "I said you needed to lose weight, but not *that* much, buddy."

Shadow does not speak, and he does not do his usual struggling to get out of Murray's arms.

Murray pushes the typewriter out of the way, grabs the remote, and sits down in his leather chair, holding Shadow. The two of them sit like this for over three hours, interrupted only twice by phantom telephone calls with no one at the other end.

When Murray starts to get sleepy, he stands up and gently places Shadow at the foot of his bed.

"By Monday if you're not back to your old self, little buddy, I'm afraid you are going to have to visit the vet."

* * * *

The next morning, Murray has just started showering when he hears the phone ring. "Damn it," he says. "Ah, the hell with it. Probably just another phantom caller."

He showers, shaves, combs his hair, and is about to start packing up the baked goods when he remembers the phone call and checks the recorder.

"Murray? This is George Pelton. I've spoken with Dolan. I need you to bring over your final version of Act II of your play just as soon as possible. I wouldn't delay...Dolan is willing to read it now. He's in the process of making a decision for next season's line up. Hope you can drop it by my office within the next couple of days. So long."

Murray's heart pounds. He plays the message over two more times, and then goes into his bedroom to tell Shadow the good news. Shadow is underneath the bed again. Murray gets down on his hands and knees to talk to him.

"Shadow. Good news. I am going to have my play read. Now it will get picked up soon, and then we can get out of this place, and on to our new home. How do you like that?"

No response. Murray strokes Shadow's head for several moments.

"All right, buddy, I'm going out for a few hours, and then I'll be back to take care of you. Try to eat something while I'm gone."

Murray packs the recorder, mike and tapes into his knapsack. Next, he packs all of the food into three cloth tote bags. As he closes the front door, he looks up and down the street for the black car. "*Hmph.* Guess it's too early in the morning for 'em," he mutters, and he locks the door and heads west, towards the BART station.

* * * *

Unlike typical Saturday mornings, today BART is crowded with people. Murray walks downstairs to the subway. He must set his bags on the ground and lean up against a pillar because all of the benches are taken. When the train pulls in, many of the seats are already filled. Murray struggles with his bags of food, and makes his way to a seat in the back of the car. With his three bags and knapsack, he must take up the entire seat. Several people give him a dirty look.

The train is filled with several small groups of people who are traveling together. They laugh and talk about what they expect to do at today's festivities, and reminisce about what they did during previous years. When they arrive downtown, nearly the entire train empties out at Murray's stop. He struggles with his load as he climbs the stairs with the crowd of pushing and laughing tourists and Bay Area residents.

When Murray climbs out of the subway he follows the crowd in the direction of City Hall. The streets have been cordoned off and there are police directing traffic to the appropriate detours. Two clowns are walking down the middle of the street, occasionally waving at passing children. One of them is carrying a lemon icy. As they pass him, Murray hears one of the clowns say, "I hope it does happen, man. Just because we're on General Assistance they expect us to just keep coming and working without a contract? Where's the benefits and job security in that?"

As Murray nears City Hall he sees a gigantic banner stretching across the entire street. "Beautiful City by the Bay Day" it says. Murray smirks. As he walks down the street, the aroma of some fifty different types of food fills the air. Everywhere vendors are setting up umbrellas and tables. Some are already open and have small crowds of people waiting in line. There are three mimes warming up a juggling act with hoops and balls, and a street band is tuning up their instruments.

As Murray crosses the street, he sees a tall, thin, middle-aged man with a gray ponytail down the middle of his back. He is spinning around and around on roller blades. He has on gold sunglasses, gold lame` tights, and a gold knit top and helmet that resembles something from Flash Gordon. The man has two dogs on leashes with matching gold sunglasses and gold Flash Gordon outfits. "Space Dogs," Murray mutters to himself. "There wouldn't be an event in this city if they didn't show up."

Murray crosses the next street, hangs a right, and walks in the opposite direction of the festivities. He stops, sets his bags down on the sidewalk, rubs his hands, and stretches his arms out a couple of times. He picks up his load again and ducks over to a side street. He walks another two blocks and finally spots John's old, beat up VW van with the decal of the jumping fish between the headlights. Murray sighs and picks up his pace.

When Murray arrives at the van there is a lot of activity going on.

"Murray. I'm glad you're here," John says, lifting a large metal container from the back of the van. "We've got all the food here. Oh, did you bring the bread and stuff?"

Murray nods.

"All right then," John continues. "Stay here and wait for Peter and the rest of them to show up. Todd and me are going to take the van over to the park and fill it up with as many of the homeless as we can fit in here and bring them over. That way we're guaranteed a showing right from the start. I don't want to depend on there being enough people when we first set up."

Todd pulls the last box out of the van and shuts the doors.

"The mayor makes his big 'This is the best city in the world' speech in about half an hour," John says, getting behind the wheel. He leans out the window. "We want to be already set up and serving food by then because there'll be a lot of media around. Besides, there will be too much going on for the cops to bother with us while the speech is happening."

Murray nods and says, "Okay by me."

"Okay," John says, starting the engine. "We'll see you over there in a little while. Peter should be here any minute."

Forty-five minutes later, the streets are crowded with people. The stage where the mayor is to make his speech is filled with brightly costumed and feathered men-posing-as-women-posing-as-blue-flamingos. They are dancing around in perfect unison to the live band, just to the left of the stage.

On the sidewalk to the right of the audience, separated by a row of Porta-potties, and just a couple hundred yards away, is a small crowd of people gathered around two card tables. One of the tables holds a large metal container filled with soup that someone is emptying into Styrofoam cups. The other is heaped with bread and muffins. A banner is stretched across both the tables with the words "Meals Not Militia" printed on it.

There are about seventy-five activists present. Twenty or so are walking around several feet from the card tables holding up protest signs that say things like, "Feed the Homeless: They are a part of this beautiful city too!" and "The City Council think the homeless in S.F. are an eyesore" and "Billions wasted on defense could feed and house the homeless!"

Several activists are holding leaflets, passing them out to the people walking by. There is a box to the right of the tables, filled with literature on the plight of organizations trying to assist the homeless. Standing next to the box, is a coffee can with a piece of masking tape on it that says, "Donations."

There are homeless people everywhere, standing in line, and sitting on the sidewalk, drinking soup from cups, and eating pieces of bread and muffins. Some sit on the pavement, others lie down on their sleeping bags. Two homeless people do a bizarre dance to the salsa-like music being played by the band. Many of those seated have cups or hats set out, collecting donations of their own.

In a few moments, the mayor gives his speech, reminding all of the residents and informing all of the visitors and anyone else who might not know, that San Francisco is, in fact, the greatest city in the world. When the speech ends, the crowd cheers, and hundreds of balloons are launched from just behind the stage. The band begins playing a jazzed-up version of "I left my heart in San Francisco," and the audience gets up and begins to mill about. People holding media cameras leave the focus of the stage and begin to move out, scanning the various activities. Murray spots Sack standing on the curb, just to the left of the card tables. He has a tattered card clipped onto his shirt pocket that says "PRESS" and he is holding a video-cam.

Murray gets his recorder and microphone out of his backpack, and prepares to start interviewing people. He heads towards a group of activists near the steps.

"Liberation Radio,' Murray says. "Would you like to say a few words about what's happening here?"

He holds the microphone near one of the young women.

"Yes. Well, uh, we are here to do the job the city refuses to do, and that is to give food to those people who need it."

"I see," Murray says. "Would anyone else like to say a few words?"

"Yeah," says a young man with a ring in his left nostril and two more above his eyebrows. "We are activists for the homeless and we are proposing...No, wait. We are *demanding* that the city give up Treasure Island in its entirety. The old military buildings that are standing there now can be used to provide *thousands* of units for the homeless within a *month*. We should shelter the people in this area because we have the power to do it. We will *all* benefit because homelessness is connected to everything!"

"Thank you," Murray says. He walks over to some people who have gathered on the sidewalk.

"Liberation Radio. Would you like to say a few words?"

"Yes!" A man shouts. "This rally for the homeless is wonderful! It's so unifying. It actually is electrifying our movement!"

"Thank you," Murray says.

Murray moves down the sidewalk and asks a gathering of people if they would like to say something. A serious-looking middle-age man with long hair and a faded T-shirt with a peace sign on it, says, "This is all about free speech. The government in the Bay Area is trying to destroy that concept in Gestapo-like fashion."

Murray is temporarily distracted, as he notices that a crowd of passersby is gathering nearby. One of the homeless men has his panhandling cup out and is trying, unsuccessfully, to do a handstand.

"Anything else?" Murray asks the speaker.

"Yes. They did the same thing in Berkeley. They are trying to destroy the concept of People's Park. It was a complete Fascist-tactic to rip out the 'free box' used to give handouts to the homeless. They are trying to destroy free speech and prevent the distribution of free clothing and free food. They wanted to tear out all the grass and the public restrooms and build yuppie volleyball courts. This is a direct attack on the First Amendment!"

The man's face has become bright red, and his voice is strained. "They wanted to build public restrooms over the very place where it all occurred. They wanted to let the yuppies urinate and defecate where the First Annual Free Speech occurred!

"And now, what are they doing? Now they are suing penniless protesters. The fascists will not allow people to distribute free-speech literature. It's outrageous!" The man screams, shaking his fist into the air. "The suppression of opposition is the definition of Fascism!"

"Thank you," Murray says. "I'm sure our listeners will appreciate that."

A young man with a shaved head standing next to Murray suddenly grabs a hold of the microphone, pulls it towards him and yells, "Play the Game! Play to Win!"

Murray takes control of the microphone and walks over to where the card tables are set up. Just behind where the food is, and to the right, there is a large gathering of homeless people. One of them is playing a guitar, and several others are singing. Murray bends down with the microphone and asks, "Are you one of the people who came to get food today?"

"Yeah," the man says.

"Our listeners would be interested in anything you have to say," Murray responds.

"Well," the man says, "Meals-Not-Militia always feeds me with *dignity*, man. Your listeners should learn...they should *know,* the efforts of these people here. We're all people, man, and that's what it's all about. It's all very encouraging."

"Thank you," Murray says, standing up.

He walks over beyond the card tables to where the activists with the protest signs are milling about. "Liberation Radio. Would you like to say something to our listeners? How do you feel about this...uh, what's going on here today...feeding the homeless?" Murray asks.

"Well, it is the *only* thing that shows this is the beautiful city by the Bay. I hope the mayor and City Council members hear this," a young woman smelling of jasmine, says.

"I'd like to say something," the man standing next to her responds. "This is a great celebration. It's a modern version of Woodstock. You know what I mean? Let's keep it going for another eternity! Giving out free food like this is a good place to start.

"Myself, I'm working on a documentary on activists causes and social injustice and environmental causes. It's really about overcoming the element of Fascism that permeates. America is being run by Mega-Corporations. I mean...look around you...just look at this city." The man motions with his arms outstretched.

"There is a narrowly-focused agenda to make a lot of money for people at the top and stockholders. It's happening though...People are coming together on their own. It's not the Summer of Love again, but eventually, the Beast *will* die and we will all dance and sing!"

"Well, uh, thank you," Murray says. "I'm sure our listeners will enjoy hearing that positive perspective."

The man nods and picks up his protest sign again.

Murray turns and notices that a man dressed in a clown outfit is at one of the tables helping himself to muffins. Murray walks over to him with the microphone.

"Sir, Liberation Radio. Would you like to say anything to our listeners?"

The man looks up, gives Murray a dirty look, and in a perturbed voice says, "I'm a *clown*, man." He walks away shaking his head and eating a muffin.

"Well," Murray says into the microphone, "you know what Wavy Gravy used to say, 'Clowns are safe. Let's hear it for the clowns'."

Murray turns and walks over to one of the activists serving food. "Would you like to say something for Liberation Radio?" He asks.

"Sure. Yeah," a young man says. "This is a necessary proactive attempt to take on the Captains of Industry who are planning daily to take over this country and loot from the masses. That's you and me!"

The young man puts down the soup ladle and takes a hold of the microphone. "We're living in a country that is dominated by *soulless* corporations whose job is to loot the country and rule the world," he says, appearing physically distressed.

"And they get permission to do it by buying both parties and the media...That's why I am working for Meals-Not-Militia," he says, his hand shaking. "Someone has to take these Captains of Industry on!"

"Our listeners will appreciate that," Murray says. "Thank you."

Murray starts to walk towards the portable restrooms where some of the activists are carrying protest signs. As he starts to cross the small plaza, he is stopped by one of the homeless people.

"Hey," the man says, "You tell the people listening...wait...you got listeners?"

"Yes," Murray says.

"Well, you tell 'em that it's *wrong* to try and get rid of the homeless. It's wrong to say that anyone who can't go shopping should be removed...Don't let old-what's-his-name take the cable car up Powell. He'd have to rewrite the song."

"Thank you," Murray says. "Our listeners will appreciate your comments. Are you enjoying the food?"

"Well, uh...I'd *like* to have something to drink. I used to drink Old-fashions, back in the days when I was Chairman of the Board..." The man begins muttering something unintelligible and wanders off.

Murray approaches a young woman with a T-shirt that reads, "Sun Mad Raisins." The shirt has a picture of a dead woman wearing a red bonnet and picking raisins. Underneath the picture, the shirt says something about the food being unnaturally grown with insecticides and fungicides.

"Would you like to say a few words to our listeners about the event here today...specifically, the event feeding the homeless?" Murray asks.

"Yes. It's a wonder there is any decent food left in this country to feed *anyone*, " the woman says. "The chemical additives, preservatives, and colorings they are putting in our food are poisoning us all today. It's nothing short of genocide. Chemicals known to be carcinogenic, and the FDA allow our food supply to be tainted with it!" The woman shakes her head as she speaks.

"These chemicals are not only damaging the immune systems of children...they are directly affecting the physical and emotional well-being of everyone. Everyone!"

"I see. Well, thank you," Murray says.

"Hotdogs are the worst!" The woman shouts, taking a hold of the microphone. "People should be made aware. It's a Crime Against Humanity! There are all the nitrites and nitrates, and known carcinogens in them. Your listeners should know! Hotdogs are the worst. They're not fit for public consumption!"

"Thank you," Murray says, taking a step back. "That was a very valuable piece of information."

The woman nods, stiffens her back, and walks away.

Murray walks several more yards and approaches a young man and woman. Both are holding signs that say, "Alliance Against Psychiatric Rape. Stop the forceful coercion of Thorizine and other psychiatric drugs! Stop electric shock therapy!"

Murray asks the young woman if she would like to say anything for Liberation Radio. "Yes," she says. "On behalf of everyone who has ever suffered at the hands of the mental health industry, I would like your listeners to know we have filed a class-action suit against coerced treatment, including anti-psychotic drugs and electric shock. Also, we have support groups that meet weekly at St. John's church every Tuesday at 8:00 p.m. I would just like your listeners to know that a person has a right to exist."

"Thanks for that," Murray says. He turns to the young man. "You're holding a sign here, I'll read it for the benefit of our listeners. It says, 'Alliance Against Psychiatric Rape.' So how did you get involved in this organization?" Murray asks.

"Uh, actually, this is the first I've ever heard about it. I'll tell you what, though, these so-called, quote-on-quote, 'crazy' people...just give them a couple of joints. They'll be fine. It's a lot less harmful.

"My neighbor, she has what's called manic-depressive? She was pregnant and so she stopped taking her medication because it can cause, like, birth defects. It's pretty bogus stuff. Anyway, so she started smoking pot because she had got off the dangerous medication in order to protect the baby. The pot helped to keep her leveled out...*you* know.

"Anyway, so she just smokes a joint whenever she's feeling like things might get bad. And, anyhow, then the baby was due to come. She goes into labor and she was in all of this pain, and so she smokes a half a joint so she doesn't flip out or anything."

The young man shifts the sign he is holding from his left hand to his right. He pushes his hair out of his eyes and continues. "So she goes to the hospital because the baby's coming, right? And she's in all of this pain, and screaming and crying, and all. And the nurse asks her, 'has she taken anything in the past 24 hours?' And she's screaming in pain and all, and she says, 'Yeah, just a half a joint.' So then she goes on and has the baby, and it's healthy and all. Everything was fine. But then the next morning, this woman from Child and Family Services, and this guy from the health department, come into my neighbor's room while she's lying there in the hospital bed resting. So they ask her about what she told the nurse about smoking half a joint, and she says, 'yeah she said that,' and then they tell her they're gonna' test the kid for drugs, and if the tests come back positive, she's gonna' have her baby taken away from her.

"So, of course, she's an absolute mess. She's all alone with no family. Anyway, she gets all upset and is crying. The baby had this plastic bag taped on and they tested the urine, and sure enough it comes back positive for cannabis. So they come back the next day, and tell her the baby is going with Child Welfare Services, and she's got to go to drug treatment, and then she can get a lawyer, and then go to court, to try and convince the judge she's not an unfit mother. Is this unbelievable, or what?"

Murray shakes his head. "So how did it all turn out?" Murray asks.

"Well, she starts crying and begging the woman from Child Welfare to listen to her, and then she confides that she is a manic-depressive, and that the only reason she smoked pot was because her prescription medicine would most probably cause horrible birth defects or even have killed the baby. Finally, the woman decides to let my neighbor go home with the baby and be on what they call a 'watch.' That's when they give you some material to educate you, and then come by your house for a year on unannounced visits to make sure you're not an unfit parent."

The young man shakes his head. "Ridiculous," he says. "Anyway," he continues, "pot is a lot less harmful than other drugs. It's also *great* for quitting smoking. Every time you feel like smoking just light up a couple of fat ones, and you'll be fine. Or *whatever* is wrong with you, whether you're so-called crazy or whatever, just get yourself a big bag of leaf and light up one of them. It's less harm on the lungs. It breaks up the phlegm, you know, and lets you cough it up...That's all I have to say, I guess."

"Well, that was very enlightening," Murray says. "I'm sure many of our listeners will be very interested in what you've had to say."

Murray turns to walk back towards the food tables. As he gets within ten feet or so of them, he sees a police car pull up just in front of the tables.

"Uh, there appears to be some police activity about to occur," he says into the microphone. "A squad car has just pulled up, and two officers are approaching the food tables...They are talking with the food servers. Some other activists have approached...The officers are going back to their squad car...They are just sitting there now. We'll have to wait and see what is going to happen."

Murray looks around and spots a homeless man alone near the steps, lying down in a sleeping bag. He walks over and bends down near the man. "Do you have anything to say about what appears to be happening here? It looks as if the police may stop the food from being served to the homeless," Murray says.

"They're out of their cotton-pickin' minds. If I could have some kind of coat, but uh...some boy come and took it. 'Xcept I have a sleeping bag here so uh...I'm doing just fine. I do have a place to stay. That's why I'm stayin' *here*. Because I have my mother and father's house and my brother's place. But I live *here* 'cuz I want to live with the PEOPLE. Because I don't like to be locked up behind closed doors. I am not homeless. Because I can think and walk and pray and am ABSOLUTELY FREE and then I'm never homeless."

Murray is distracted by the sound of a scuffle. He looks up and discovers six police cars have pulled up. Some of the activists are shouting.

"So, uh, you *choose* to be living here?" Murray asks.

"I'm independent because I am that way. Because I feel that way. I admit I'm kind a' stupid but they ask me all kinds of questions so I try my best to answer 'em. People bring me blankets, sheets, sleeping bags. Everything I need. One guy a little bit ago...just right before you came here, I never saw him in my life, just gave me a *twenty dollar bill.* The hospital though...the doctor woke me up in the *middle of the night* and just kicked me out *before daylight* and threw me out of the hospital because there is nothing wrong with me. Nothing at *all.* I want to be out here because I can't stand to be locked up inside the walls of any house or any place. Here, I am absolutely free...I don't like the slick way of life."

"Well, uh, thank you very much for this interview. Our listeners will really appreciate hearing what you have said," Murray says.

The man is lying down with his eyes closed now. Murray looks around. Everything is chaotic. He speaks into the microphone.

"It appears that the police are shutting down the serving of food to the homeless. There are...let's see...I can count nine squad cars here at this time. The police are taking away the soup kettle and the tables. The activists are arguing with the police. Some of the police are holding batons...there is a sizable crowd gathering in the cordoned off area of the street...there is some media filming...one of the activists just fell to the ground. It is unclear whether he was pushed or just fell...there is a lot of shouting and scuffling going on...I'm going closer to see if someone will talk to me."

Murray moves several yards closer to the activity. "Here is someone. Sir...are you from Meals-Not-Militia?"

"Yeah," the man says.

"Can you tell me what's happening here now?" Murray asks.

"This is just like what happened at the Civic Center," the man says. "Fifty-seven people were arrested that time. It's government harassment. After that time, they resumed their court order prohibiting M.N.M. from serving food to the homeless. They claim we are in violation of the codes of Parks and Recreation and the Health Department. They said we were not to serve food any time, any place, in the city of San Francisco."

The man pauses to listen to an argument between two activists and the police. "So anyway," he continues, "the political reality is that the city wants to outlaw and banish an entire class of people from San Francisco by staging a protracted series of arrests. It's all part of a much larger plan to eliminate poverty in this city by *outlawing the poor*."

The man shouts towards the police, "Hey! Leave her alone. She's not doing anything!"

He turns back towards Murray. "Anyway," he continues, "the real story is that the homeless and the panhandlers scare away the tourists. It's an *image* problem."

The police are now handcuffing the food servers and taking the food away. A police wagon pulls up alongside the curb.

"I've got to go see if I can help, dude," the man says.

Murray nods.

"There should be *no* laws against serving food," he shouts to Murray as he walks away. "We all have the right to eat!"

Murray talks into the microphone. "A large crowd has gathered...It looks as if a good many people have been arrested at this point...There is a lot of shouting and a lot of shoving...Some activists have sat down on the ground and the police are forcibly lifting them up and putting them into the wagon...One woman is waving a loaf of bread at the police and shouting something about 'Bread is the only weapon we need in the war against Fascism and hunger!'...She has just hurled the loaf of bread at the police officers and has hit one of them in the head...they are struggling to subdue her...Several activists continue to shout from the steps and hold their signs up...I'll go over and see if we can get any final words."

Murray heads towards the steps. He spots Sack on the opposite side of the street, alongside other people with cameras, filming everything.

"Excuse me," Murray says approaching the activists. "Liberation radio. Would anyone care to summarize what has happened here?"

"The way things are going right now," one of them says, "there is a Wave of Terrorism against us. Every generation of politicians produces new harassment. This has been a problem since 1976. They want us to get kitchen facilities in order to serve food. But that would *never* work because the people *we* help get claustrophobic in buildings of any kind. They aren't used to being cooped up indoors. They can't handle waiting in lines. Unless we can adopt these people and get them into families, they cannot ever get off the streets. They have become non-persons except to their own circle of friends. They have no addresses...That's what we'd have to do. To start adopting them. Then we'd get fifteen thousand people off the streets. Until then...we will be here getting arrested because we believe they have a right to eat."

"Well, thanks for those final comments," Murray says.

The man nods, picks up his protest sign and heads toward the commotion. The police wagon and several police cars are filled with activists. Several police have formed a barricade and are holding their batons in a threatening manner. A few activists continue to shout at the police, but they are keeping their distance. Most of the homeless people have left. A few remain, watching from a safe distance. The police order the activists to disperse. After two more warnings, the remaining activists walk away, shouting something about Fascism. The police wagon and squad cars pull away, one by one.

The police officer with the megaphone addresses the crowd of on-lookers gathered on the street. "Okay, folks. Show's over. You can all move along now," he says.

Within fifteen minutes, everyone who could pose a threat has gone, and the remaining police cars pull away.

Murray leaves his hiding place from beside the portable restrooms. As he steps around the corner, he sees Sack about a half a block down, swinging his video camera as he walks.

Murray turns the recorder back on and speaks into the microphone. "Tony Bennett must have traveled in very different circles while he was here," he says. There is a pause. "This is Pierre Salinger for Liberation Radio, signing off."

He clicks the button, packs up his gear, and heads for the subway.

* * * *

It is late afternoon when Murray returns home, cutting across his neighbor's garden, and through the break in the fence, to get to the back entrance. Again, the dog is outside watching, and again he remains silent.

When Murray unlocks the back door, Shadow is not there to greet him. By the time Murray has shut and secured the locks, however, Shadow has made his way halfway down the hallway leading to the back door. He walks unsteadily and seems weak.

"Shadow," Murray says a bit alarmed, "Oh, come here, little guy."

Murray bends down and gently scoops him up into his arms. Shadow looks into Murray's eyes.

"Oh, Shadow. You really are sick, aren't you? You don't seem to be licking whatever this is on your own. Well...that's it, little buddy. Monday morning I'm calling the vet. I'll see if Kirby or Todd is free to give us a lift."

Shadow looks up at Murray and answers weakly.

Murray walks into his bedroom and gently sits Shadow down on the bed.

"Stay here, now, I'm just going to make myself something to eat, and check the messages, then I'll be back in here to be with you. I've got to work as long as it takes on those changes to Act II tonight, so I can get the play into George's office Monday."

Murray takes off his backpack and goes into the kitchen to start some hotdogs and pork and beans. He checks the messages. There's just one, from Kirby, saying he won't be back until Tuesday.

Murray eats, makes a pot of coffee, and then heads into the bedroom to type the changes to his play.

He turns the television on, sets up his typewriter, and gets to work. He types for hours, stopping only occasionally to talk to Shadow, refill his coffee, or to light a cigarette. Sometime around three o'clock, he notices that Shadow is no longer on the bed. In between typing, he gets down on his hands and knees and talks to Shadow, trying to coax him out from underneath the bed.

Around five-thirty in the morning, Murray finishes typing the final changes to Act II. He stands up, stretches, gathers all of the pages of Act I and Act II together, and places them inside an empty box. As he rolls the typewriter over near the wall, he hears Shadow whimper.

"Shadow?" Murray says in an alarmed tone. "Shadow, come on out of there and let me have a look at you."

Murray bends down, sticks his hand under the bed, and reaches for him. Shadow is just out of reach. He does not budge, but lets out another whimper.

"Shadow? *Shadow*?" Murray says frantically. "Are you all right...God...Come out of there."

Again, he tries unsuccessfully to grab a hold of him and bring him out. Murray stands up and paces, running his hands through his hair.

"What am I going to do?" He says, and paces some more.

Suddenly, he hears Shadow groan. Murray bends down again to see where Shadow is. While still on his knees, he lifts the entire bed frame up and rests the weight of the bed on the back of his neck and shoulders. With half of the bed in the air and resting on his back, Murray reaches his arms as far as they will go, and grabs a hold of Shadow by the scruff of the neck. Slowly, he brings him out. When Shadow has cleared the bed, Murray grunts and pulls his own head and body out from underneath the bed. The frame crashes to the floor with a thud.

Murray picks Shadow up and carries him into the kitchen. "Let's take you into where the light is better and have a look at you," he says.

Murray sits Shadow onto the kitchen counter and looks at his eyes and into his ears. Next, he tips Shadow's head back, and with one hand on either side of his jaw, gently pries Shadow's mouth open.

Murray gasps. "Oh, God...jaundice," he says. "Oh, God, Shadow. You're all yellow...Oh God." Murray picks Shadow up and cradles him. He carries him to the phone, and with his hand shaking, dials.

Several rings. Murray paces with Shadow in his right arm and the telephone receiver in his left hand. Finally, a sleepy "Hello?"

"Mollie?" He asks.

"Yes...Murray? What's wrong?" She asks alarmed.

"Mollie. It's Shadow." Murray says, and then begins crying.

"He's...he's dying."

"Oh no!" Mollie says.

"I've got to get him in right away to see the vet at the Emergency Clinic."

"Okay," Mollie says in a panic. "Okay. I'll wake up Mary. She can drive us. We'll be there just as quick as we can."

"Thanks," Murray says sobbing, and he hangs up the phone and cradles Shadow.

VI

Murray paces the floor with Shadow in his arms, stopping occasionally to stroke Shadow's head, and to peek through the blinds. "Hang in there, little buddy," he says every so often.

Within half an hour, Mary's car pulls up. Mollie gets out and runs up to Murray's house. He is closing and locking the door, just as she makes the turn around the hedges.

"Let me see him," she says, rubbing Shadow's head. "Oh, poor little guy. He got so skinny so fast!" Mollie says, walking towards the car. "Do you have the address, Murray?" She asks.

"Yep. Right here," he says, sounding like he has something caught in his throat. The two of them get into the car with Shadow, and Mary speeds off to the Emergency Clinic.

The streets are relatively empty, so the drive is an easy one. Murray remains silent and rocks Shadow back and forth in his arms. Mollie turns around toward the back seat and faces Murray.

"He's going to be all right," she says. Murray nods and his eyes fill with tears. "You look a wreck," she says to him. "When was the last time you got some sleep?"

Murray clears his throat. "I didn't go to sleep last night. I was up all night in a rush typing the changes on my play. George Pelton called and left a message that he needs it right away for Dolan to read. I was going to have it in his office in the morning, but now..." Murray's voice trails off as he looks down at Shadow and shakes his head. "*This* is all that matters now," he says, as he begins to cry softly.

"Where is the play supposed to go? His office at the hospital?" Mary asks, making a left-hand turn.

"Yeah," Murray says.

"Don't worry about it. I'll take it over there for you on my way to work," Mary offers.

"Thanks, Mary," Murray says. He is silent for the rest of the drive.

When they reach the Emergency Clinic, Murray takes Shadow to the front desk and explains his symptoms. Mollie takes the clipboard and fills out the required information as Murray dictates to her.

Within ten minutes, the assistant calls for Shadow. Mary says she will stay in the waiting area while Murray and Mollie take Shadow into the examination room. Within a few minutes, the veterinarian enters the examination room reading over Shadow's information on the clipboard.

"Hello. I'm Dr. Noah," he says with a caring smile. "So we have a pretty sick kitty here."

Murray nods.

"When did he eat last?" The doctor asks.

"He hasn't been eating all that well during the past couple of weeks, but a few days ago he started throwing up, and I don't think he has eaten much of anything for the past two days," Murray says in a worried tone.

"Hmm," the doctor says. He gently pushes and prods on Shadow's belly and sides, looks in his ears and eyes, and then opens Shadow's mouth and looks inside. "Oh, poor little guy," he says, stroking Shadow.

"Well," he says, looking up at Murray. "I'm going to run some tests to see what we come up with, but at this point, I can tell you he has Feline Hepatic Lipidosis...fatty liver disease."

Murray nods solemnly.

"It used to be said, 'A yellow kitty is a dead kitty,' but we've had some pretty good luck with beating this," the vet says with a tone of reserved optimism.

"What could have caused this?" Mollie asks.

"Not eating," Dr. Noah says. "When cats stop eating, their liver starts converting the stored fat, and eventually, often in a very short period of time, the liver ceases to be able to function."

"But what would cause him to quit eating?" Murray asks in a distressed tone.

"Hard to say. It could be that he ate something poisonous. Perhaps it was a viral infection. It could be stress. Has there been any major changes in the household lately?"

"Well," Murray responds, "sort of."

"There's no way to really say. It could be a blockage in the path leading to the gallbladder. There's a slight possibility it's a tumor, but really, there's no way to tell until we do a biopsy and run some tests."

"So you mean," Mollie says, "that if a kitty doesn't feel well and he stops eating, he can get liver disease just like *that*?" She snaps her fingers.

"Some cats can get liver disease from missing only one meal," the veterinarian says gravely. "What we need to do at this point is to get him hooked up to an IV and get him on antibiotics and some glucose right away. The only way he is going to make it is to get some food into his system. The sooner we can get that started, the better."

"Okay," Murray says, stroking Shadow's head, "whatever it takes."

"All right. I'll take him and get him what he needs. If you'll go back into the waiting area, they will give you some literature and some forms to fill out," Dr. Noah says, and then he gently picks Shadow up and takes him away.

Murray stands in the examination room and begins to weep. "We've never been separated like this before," he says, shaking his head. "I don't know how he's going to get through this without me...locked up in some cage with tubes in him and strangers taking care of him...I should have *known*," he says, sobbing. "Why didn't I *know*?"

Mollie puts her arm around him. "Whatever it takes, Murray, remember? This is his only chance. We can't do anything for him, only they can," she says. She reaches across the metal table and pulls several tissues from a box on the counter. "Here," she says, handing the tissues to Murray.

After several minutes, Murray composes himself, and he and Mollie return to the waiting room.

"They just called your name," Mary tells Murray.

Murray nods and walks over to the front desk. The receptionist hands him two brochures about liver disease, and a card with the clinic's phone number on it. She slides a release form towards him and asks him to read and sign it. Murray's hand shakes as he writes. The veterinary assistant informs him they will monitor Shadow, and will be in touch over the next couple of days. Murray nods his head and returns to where Mollie and Mary are seated.

"Are you through here?" Mollie asks him. Murray nods. The two women stand up. "I'm going to stay with you today," Mollie says to Murray. "I asked Mary to stop off at Safeway on the way back. I'm sure you don't have any decent food at your place," Mollie says, smiling.

Murray laughs softly. "Thanks," he says.

Before leaving Murray's apartment, Mary picks up the play to drop off at George Pelton's office. Mollie unpacks the groceries she has bought, and makes some tomato soup, grilled cheese sandwiches, and coffee for she and Murray.

After they eat, Mollie convinces Murray to come with her to the top of Bernal Hill. The fresh air would do him good, she says. Murray is so distracted and worried about Shadow that he doesn't even take notice of his surroundings. As a result, he misses the fact that as he and Mollie leave for the hill, there are now two black cars parked on either side of his house.

On their way back from the hill, Mollie spots a sign for a garage sale and begs Murray to come with her. Maybe they would get lucky, she tells him. She buys a small, antique, hand-carved box. After several more minutes of looking around, the two head toward the main path. Mollie runs her fingers over and over the box as they walk. She tells Murray that she isn't sure why, but that she just knows it is somehow very special, and that she will paint it just as soon as she gets back home. Murray tells her that if it doesn't have money or a genie in it, he can't imagine how it could be special, but suggests that she could use it to hide her Gummy Bears in.

After the garage sale, they spend the rest of the day browsing the bookstore, drinking coffee on Cortland Avenue, and walking around Bernal Heights. Then they head back to Murray's place, where they play Scrabble and gin rummy until dark. Mollie makes a supper of stir-fried Cashew Chicken with fresh apricots and mushrooms. Murray jokes with her that he ought to have traumas more often.

After they eat, they rent a movie about women who can't stop obsessing about food. Mollie falls asleep on the sofa half way through it, and Murray turns the VCR off and brings her a blanket. He spends the rest of the night in his room, pacing and crying. When he finally does sit down, he smokes a cigarette, rocks his body back and forth, and prays out loud that Shadow does not die.

The next morning Murray walks Mollie to the BART station, and then returns to the empty apartment. For the next two days he is like a zombie. He does not eat or sleep. At one point, Murray drops to his knees beside the bed and begs God out loud to not let Shadow die while he is away with strangers in the veterinary hospital. If he has to die, better that Shadow is at home and they are together, Murray tells God. Though he is not convinced, he says aloud, that anyone is listening.

On the afternoon of the second day, Murray finally falls asleep from pure exhaustion. He sleeps so soundly he does not even hear the phone ringing, at first. By the time he gets up, the call has transferred to the recorder. Murray turns the volume up. It is George Pelton saying that he is sending the manuscript of the play via messenger over to Dolan today. Murray shakes his head. "After all this time waiting for this to happen," he mutters, "and now that it finally has, it hardly matters at all."

＊ ＊ ＊ ＊

Dolan's assistant Lara looks at her watch, sighs and rolls her eyes.   "I thought Dolan and Catherine were suppose to be back a half an hour ago," she says.

Juno is sitting on a wooden stool doing origami. "Maybe they are over at the club having a little afternoon delight," he says, chuckling.

"Well, I'm *hungry*.   Plus, I have to stop by the bank. I want to take my lunch," she says whining.

"Go," Juno says, hopping off the stool.   "I'll man the battle station."

"Are you sure?" Lara asks, already getting up from the desk.

"Oh, yeah. I'm an old hand at this...or is that 'old hat'?" He says chuckling.   "Anyway...go...go to lunch.   Chop, Chop."

"Thanks, Juno," Lara says, throwing her bag over her shoulder.   "I'll probably be a little over an hour. Is that okay?"

"Take as long as you need.   I'll try to resist the temptation to sell this joint while you're gone."

"I don't care," Lara says, swinging her hips on her way out. "Just as long as *I* get my paycheck, I don't care *what* happens to this place."

"So long," Juno says laughing.

"Bye...Later," Lara says.   "I'll leave the outside door propped open," she says, bending over to drop the doorstop.   There is the sound of her high-heels click-clicking on the sidewalk, and then she is gone.

Juno flips through the appointment book on the desk, and then opens the desk drawers and riffles through them. He looks through the accounting book and the balance sheet, snickers, and places them back in the drawer. As he is looking through the "in" box, the phone rings.

174

"The Abyss Theatre. How may I *help* you?" He says in an exaggerated voice. "No," he says after a few moments. "We are not interested in a subscription to the Number One San Francisco newspaper." There is a pause, and then, "We are not interested...Why not? Because, I already changed my oil for the year," he says and drops the receiver down, chuckling.

He picks up a stack of bound plays lying on the corner of the desk and flips through them one by one, shaking his head as he does.

Just then, a messenger pulls up, stops, and parks his bike just inside the door. The messenger looks at the ticket and then takes a package from the metal carrier on his bike.

"Abyss Playhouse?" He asks.

"Yep," Juno says.

"I have a package for Mr. Dolan Aiello."

"Yep," Juno says, "that's me."

The messenger brings the package over and lays it on the desk. "Sign here," he says, handing Juno the ticket.

After the messenger has gone, Juno takes a letter opener out of Lara's desk and carefully bends back the prongs of the staples holding the package together. He gently slides the contents out and looks it over. The title page says, "*The Paradox of Illusions*, by Murray Y. Bardos." Juno turns to the next page. As he scans the cast of characters something catches his eye. He goes back through the list again and stops when he sees the name, "Mosh Pitt."

"Mosh," he says softly. He flips to the play and begins reading, stopping every so often, his eyes twinkling.

* * * *

On Wednesday, Murray receives a call from the veterinarian's office. An hour later, Mary and Mollie arrive at Murray's apartment to pick him up. Murray climbs into the backseat. When Mollie turns to talk with him, she tells him he has the appearance of a ten-year old who has just been told he is getting a pony for his birthday. Murray chuckles.

When they arrive at the animal clinic, Mollie goes in with Murray to speak with the vet. The doctor warns Murray that while Shadow is now much stronger, he is still very sick. The vet says Shadow must be fed through a tube every two hours, and given several different types of medication throughout the day. He asks Murray if he is up for the challenge.

After a few minutes, the internist on-duty comes in to speak with Murray. No, there is no sign of a blockage or tumor, nor any abnormality. The specialist speculates vaguely about stress or schedule changes, but offers no definitive explanation for the sudden mysterious affliction.

The specialist then gives Murray instructions for medication and feedings. He gives a demonstration for how to give an injection, and then asks Murray to try it. He is astounded at Murray's attempt, and tells Murray so...he has never had someone "Get it on the first try."

Next, he says he must impress upon Murray that Shadow was very close to death, and that he is not out of the woods yet. And, above all, "the food is the medicine"...Shadow must be fed the prescribed amount at regular intervals. Oh, he adds before leaving, and incidentally, in all his years of practice, he has never seen an animal so gravely ill with so much "psychological...what is it? How to put it? ...*Spirit.*"

Murray looks at Mollie. They share a knowing smile.

Finally, the big moment arrives, and the veterinarian's assistant brings Shadow to Murray. He is frail looking and his right front leg, neck, and stomach have been shaved. There are bandages covering the place where the biopsy was, and where the IV's were placed. There is also a tube leading into Shadow's nose and down his throat. Murray holds out his arms and cradles him like he is a newborn baby.

"Did you hear me talking to you, Shadow?" Murray asks when the assistant has left the examination room. "I was praying and talking like crazy to you the whole time we were apart."

Shadow offers a faint response.

"Oh," Murray says, "I'm so glad you're going to be all right, buddy. I'm so glad we're back together."

"From the looks of things, I think the feeling is mutual," Mollie says, rubbing Shadow's head.

"Come on," Mollie says. "I'm sure he's eager to get back home to familiar surroundings."

By the time Mollie and Mary leave his apartment, Murray has set up a system to measure and mix the food and medications, and has made an hour-by-hour chart to keep track of all that must be done. With Mollie and Kirby's help, the first three feedings are tricky, but go well. Murray mixes and mixes the thick pudding-like food to get it smooth enough to be pulled through the syringe, and then oh-so-slowly squeezes it through the tiny tube entering Shadow's nose and down his throat. Between the necessary preparations before the feedings, and the clean up afterward, Murray has only a few minutes to rest in between feedings, but he does not mind, he tells Kirby. And he means it.

At eleven that night, Murray cuddles and talks to Shadow as he slowly squeezes the food through the tube in his nose. At eleven-fifty, Kirby yells out in an alarmed voice that Shadow is sick. Murray runs from the bathroom, pants undone, to discover that Shadow is not only vomiting, but has bitten down on the feeding tube and broken it in two.

Shortly after midnight, Murray and Kirby stand in the examination room of the Emergency Clinic. Murray's heart is pounding and his head is whirling. The broken tube is removed, there is a discussion about the problems with putting in another tube, the possibility of a surgical insertion of a tube into Shadow's stomach, concern that Shadow will not make it through the surgery, a call to the internist, another call, and some sort of disagreement and apparent power struggle between the attending vet and the specialist on-call. Forty-five minutes pass. All the while Murray paces.

In the end, Murray asks if he can just forget the tubes and feed the food with the syringe, directly into Shadow's mouth. Like you do a baby, he says. The attending vet mutters something about it not normally being done that way, and Murray says, "Whatever it takes."

In another twenty-five minutes, Kirby and Murray are in their living room drinking a beer, and Shadow is curled up sleeping at Murray's feet. It's funny, Kirby says, how Shadow became "just like a regular cat" when he was at the vet, and not at all like the way he is when he is at home with Murray. Long after Kirby goes to bed, Murray stays up just watching Shadow sleep, occasionally bending down next to him to make sure he is still breathing.

Murray's days move on in two-hour intervals, preparing, feeding, cleaning up the mess, giving medications and injections, and starting the whole process over again, until it all finally blends together, and Murray has difficulty remembering what day it is. If not for Shadow's schedule hanging on the refrigerator door with a magnet, Murray tells Mollie on the phone one day, he would be completely disoriented.

After a week of this, Murray falls into a routine, and his stress and worry begin to feel familiar, like the normal order of business. One evening, during Shadow's regular feeding, Murray tells him, "You've got to get better and stronger soon, buddy. I have a feeling that my play is going to be bought and then we can move you to a better place...a place where you will have a yard and you can play outside in the sunshine." Shadow looks up into Murray's eyes, but says nothing.

After the feeding, Murray gets busy with his paper towels and dishcloths, doing the usual clean up. He is mumbling something as he washes the food from Shadow, the floor, his clothes, hair, and everywhere else it has managed to get, when the phone rings.

"Hello," Murray says, sounding worn out.

"Hello. What's wrong with you? You sound like you just lost your best friend," his mother says, her voice sounding impatient.

"Huh...I almost did," Murray says sadly.

"What are you talking about?" His mother asks.

"Shadow came pretty close to dying. He's still not out of the woods yet. I have to feed him with a syringe every two hours like a baby and give him medication in between that. I'm very...stressed, I guess. I'm pretty worried about him." Murray's voice crackles at the end.

"*Who's* Shadow? Is that that *cat* of yours?" His mother asks with a tone of disbelief.

"Yes," Murray says.

"Oh, for God's sake, Murray. Grow up. It's just a cat," his mother says in a perturbed tone.

Murray begins to pace and run his hands through his hair as he holds the receiver.

"I can't believe you, getting so emotionally involved over a *cat,*" she continues. "*Tsk Tsk.* You know, it's just like when you were a little boy. You still have not changed.

"Remember when you were younger? You must have been no more than seven or eight. Your Aunt Ginny...well, actually, she was your *second* aunt. She was actually *my* aunt...she gave you a puppy? You kept it outside in that box on that heating pad and it would cry and cry. It would go all night long so that I got so nervous what the neighbors would say.

"And then your father, God bless his soul, may he rest in peace, he got the idea to put a wind-up alarm clock in the box with the puppy because you got so upset." She laughs. "You wouldn't stop crying and carrying on and were refusing to go to school because you were worrying so much about that *dog.*" She laughs again. "So your father thought the ticking of the clock would soothe the puppy. He said it would remind the puppy of his mother's heartbeat, or some such nonsense. We finally decided to take the puppy back to your Aunt Ginny because it was just too miserable being with us."

She laughs again. There is a pause.

"And then," she continues, "a few years later, you had that gerbil you kept in a cage in the garage. Do you remember that? You kept insisting that the gerbil was *lonesome* in there by itself." She laughs. "Can you imagine that? *Lonesome!* You were always a bit of a strange child, I must admit." She laughs heartily.

"What was I saying...oh, yes, so your father bought another one for you and wouldn't you know it, within a little bit, one of them pops up pregnant. Oh, I'll tell you, I'll never forget it." She laughs again. "That mother had those babies and you got so tickled, you would have thought they were *human* babies." She laughs and then pauses. "Hold on a minute, I have to wipe my eyes, I've been laughing so hard..."

"Anyway, then the mother gerbil, or the father gerbil, I don't remember which, starts eating the little babies. You came home from school one day and saw it eating the babies and you went absolutely crazy. Do you remember that? There were only four or five left. One of them, I clearly remember this, had it's two back legs eaten off already when you rescued it. Do you remember?

"And then, there you were. Out in that garage, every morning, and right after school every day, holding them and giving them some pep talk, and feeding them milk with an *eyedropper*!" She laughs. "Can you imagine that? Keeping them all night on a heating pad...all *that,* even though the vet you begged your father to call clearly said they were gonna' die. But *you* wouldn't have any of it. *No*

Siree. I really did worry that you weren't right in the head during those days." She chuckles and then pauses.

"So how *are* you mother?" Murray asks when she has stopped laughing. "How's your health been?"

"Why do you ask?" She responds in a suspicious tone. "I hope you don't have in your head that there's going to be any money in my will when I go. The way the prices of things are going up, I'll be lucky if I have enough to live on."

"It was just a question, mother," Murray says.

There is another pause.

"Oh, you almost made me forget the reason I called," she says. "I wanted to tell you about your cousin, Dennis. You remember I told you he was made President of that big corporation of his?"

"I thought it was *Vice*-president," Murray says.

"Well, whatever it is. It's some big executive position, anyhow. Why are you always trying to short-change others their due, Murray?"

There is no response.

"Anyway, there's no sense in raining on other people's parade. I was going to tell you some *good* news, unlike what you had to tell *me*. You know, Murray, you don't have to blow out *other* people's candles in order for your *own* to shine. At any rate...what was I saying before I was interrupted?

"Oh, yes. Well, your cousin Dennis and his brother, Jacob. Do you remember Jacob? He's a few years younger than you. He went to Cornell? Anyway, the two of them have a sort of side business going, making these special kind of...now what do they call them? Wouldn't you know, I'd forget the name?...Oh, now I remember. Jet-skis, they're called.

"Anyway, last month they went public with their company. It started just a few years ago in Jacob's garage. It's amazing! And, anyway, to celebrate, Dennis rented a yacht! Can you believe it? And he invited the entire family and some of their friends for a big party last Saturday. Oh! It was magnificent!

"Well, I've never had a better time in my entire life! There was a band and catered food, and everything. I'll tell you, those two boys really have made the most wonderful life for themselves!"

"That's nice, mother. Well, I've got to go. I've got something I have to do."

"Oh, it figures, Murray. You just can't stand to hear that other people are doing better than you," she says in an irritated tone.

"Good-bye, mother. I have to go now. I'll talk to you later."

Murray hangs up the phone and paces the floor for several minutes. He picks the phone receiver back up and starts to dial, but then hangs the receiver up again. He heads into the kitchen, looks at the clock, checks the chart on the refrigerator door, and begins preparing Shadow's medication.

Murray gives Shadow his injection and then begins pacing around the apartment again, muttering something to himself. He stops every couple of minutes and runs his hands through his hair. After twenty minutes or so, he stops pacing, walks to the phone and dials.

"Hello?"

"Hello, mother. It's Murray."

"Murray, what do *you* want? Not to apologize, I suppose?" She asks.

"No. I'm calling to ask you a very important question," he says.

"What's that?" She asks.

"I would like to know why it is, that throughout my entire life, you have insisted on rewriting family history?" Murray asks.

"*What?* I don't know *what* you are talking about," she responds.

"Well," Murray begins, "let me refresh your memory...To begin with, mother, *I* didn't keep Milkshake outside. He was outside because *you* refused to let him come inside the house. *I* didn't want him to have to stay outside, and neither did dad. It was *your* rule. Since you have obviously forgotten, it was your rule. 'No animals in the house.' Because you didn't want your perfect little world to get dirtied."

"Wait a minute! *Who* is Milkshake?"

"He was my *dog*, mother. You remember, the one who cried and cried because he was forced to stay outside day and night, and was cold and lonely...yes, *lonely*, mother. But I don't suppose you would know anything about the feelings of anything or anyone except yourself..."

Is *that* what this is all about, Murray? A *dog*, some *God knows*, how many years ago?"

"No. It's about your rewriting of history to suit your own warped perceptions of reality. The dog was *not* too miserable being with 'us.' He was miserable not being free to come in and be with dad and me. He was miserable because he was cold, and because he was kept up in that box you made him stay in, with nothing to do but lie there!"

"Murray, you make it sound like that dog was being tortured."

"And then," Murray continues, "you made me keep the gerbil in an aquarium *inside the garage. I* didn't keep it there, *you* did. Even the gerbil was too much of a threat to mess up your perfect little world."

"That's simply not true, Murray," she says.

"And, as long as we are on the topic of rewriting history, let's talk about Dennis. Dennis, Mr. Vice-President. Mr. Success. Who cheated on his first wife, right through both of her pregnancies...who had more girlfriends while he was married to Gina, than a pro basketball player."

"Murray! How can you *say* those things?"

"Very easily, mother. Because it is the *truth*. And Jacob, his now oh-so-successful brother," Murray continues. "You forgot to mention that all through his teens he was a juvenile delinquent, or that he got caught and was suspended from Cornell for cheating on a calculus exam...and wasn't it less than five years ago that I heard he was fired because the company suspected him of embezzlement?"

"Oh, Murray. The *things* you say! They never *proved* that!"

"So the two of them have made the most wonderful lives for themselves, have they? I'm sure if you put them to the test, they wouldn't have the slightest idea of what happiness is."

"Murray, what have I done to deserve you talking to me like this?"

"*Done*, mother? I've told you. You have rewritten history at every turn in the road, to fuel your own private version of reality. Why is it that *everyone* in the family is so successful and so wonderful except *me*? Why is that mother? Why do you need to have that fantasy?"

"I don't have any fantasies," she replies flatly.

"Oh, no? If everyone else is so perfect in the family, then what happened to Carl? Did he go off and adopt a *different* family?"

"I don't know what you are talking about, Murray."

"Well, then let me remind you. Carl is my cousin. Your *nephew*? Your *brother's* child? Don't you remember your brother's own child? The child your brother ran off and *left* after Aunt Carol died? You remember, don't you mother? Carl, your brother's child, was shipped off to live with grandma? Funny how your memory slips like that from time to time..."

"Carl...let's see," Murray continues. "Carl got involved heavily with drugs...both the buying and the selling end, if I remember. There were a couple of armed robberies of grocery and convenient stores early on, and oh, there was the grand theft charge when he climbed up on the roof of that stereo store and then crawled through the air shaft and emptied out the entire contents of that place. Are you remembering yet?

"Because if *that* hasn't jogged your memory, maybe *this* will...There was that nasty little business about him dating that seventeen-year old, remember? And all that talk that he was the one who got her to start taking drugs?"

"Murray, *you* are the one making up family history. I don't know anything about this. It is simply not true."

"And then one day," Murray continues, "while the girl's parents were away vacationing in Jamaica, Carl spent the night at her home...and they were doing heroin..."

"Oh, Murray. I'm glad your father isn't around to hear the filthy things you are saying right now. *Lies.* All lies!"

"And the girl took too much and she died. And then Carl panicked, *probably* because he was on parole...and so he shot her body up with speed to try and revive her and get her heart beating again..."

"Murray! I *won't* listen to this..."

"And it didn't work, so he freaked out and stuffed her naked body into her clothes closet for her parents to come home and find her that way..."

"Murray!"

"You don't remember Carl, mother? Really? Because if you *do* allow yourself to remember Carl, mother, then you will be forced to also remember that the reason he no longer comes to the family barbecues is because he is serving a twenty-five-year-to-life prison sentence."

"Murray, I *will* not listen to this. I *will* not..."

"All right, mother, I'll change the topic, then. What about daddy? What about the time he had a nervous breakdown and got locked up in the psychiatric hospital and *you* told everyone he just took a vacation because he needed a *rest*? For years after that, every time he did or said anything you didn't approve of, you taunted him and threatened to tell everyone about him having had his 'little episode.' Do you remember *that* family history?"

"Murray, you should be *ashamed* of yourself, talking about your father like that..."

"Ashamed, mother? Ashamed of *what*? *I'm* not the one who is ashamed of the *truth*. I have a clear perspective, mother. I'm not the one who has been walking around for twenty years telling people my husband died because he had *heart* problems..."

Murray's mother gasps. "Oh dear God...", she says.

Murray's face and neck are bright red. He is pacing furiously. His left hand is tightly gripping the telephone receiver. His right is clenched into a fist.

"I've got to go," he says suddenly, and hangs up the telephone.

Murray walks around the apartment, bumping into furniture and muttering to himself. After several minutes, he stops, picks up the telephone again and dials.

"Hello?"

"Hello, Mollie? It's Murray," he says. "Say," he pauses, "do you happen to have any more of those Gummy Bears?"

VII

Kirby had just left for a required fieldtrip to the tide-pools, when Sack pulls up unannounced. Murray hears his car, peeks out the blinds, and goes outside to meet him. Sack is wearing faded blue jeans with large holes on both knees, and a horizontal tear across the left thigh. His once-black T-shirt is now that special sort of charcoal gray that comes only after years of laundering. He is barefooted, and wearing black wrap-around sunglasses. His hair swings defiantly in his face as he walks.

"Hey," he says when he sees Murray. "I'm glad I caught you at home. I've got to talk to you about something important."

Murray looks surprised. "What's up?" He asks.

Sack motions for them to move away from the car. The two walk to the steps leading to the upstairs flat and sit down.

"Listen," Sack says in a serious tone. "I've got bad news."

"Oh?" Murray says.

"Yeah. Things are heating up. We're pretty sure at this point that it *is* the Feds who have been around," Sack says. Murray fidgets uneasily.

"They've had surveillance around the house for the past few days and Todd says that one of them followed him to his girlfriend's house Friday night. There has also been some people, other activists, talking about some guys asking a lot of questions. Surprisingly," he says, rubbing his chin, "many of the questions being asked are about you."

Murray's body jerks.

"Me?" He says.

"Yeah," Sack says. "I don't know what to make of it...Maybe they're after the radio station. That's what Gary thinks...I don't know," he says, brushing his hair from his face. "Everyone is so paranoid right now, it's hard to say.

I'll tell you one thing, though, I warned Gary about getting involved with outsiders. Like all of those activists from the East Bay; we don't know anything about most of them...or what else they're involved with." Sack pauses and shakes his head.

"All of those people over at the house that night before the rally," Sack continues. "I warned Gary. There's no way to know who might have been infiltrating."

Sack stops talking and rubs his chin again.

"At any rate," he continues, "Gary is worried that the phones might have been tapped. We're moving the location of the radio station again, and we're going to lay low for awhile."

Murray nods. "Okay," he says.

"Any ideas why they would be asking questions about you, in particular?" Sack asks.

Murray shrugs. "You got me," he says, "but it sure doesn't feel good."

Sack nods his head. He pulls a small twig off the bush next to him and bites down on it with his front teeth. "All right," he says. "For now, we're just going to stay cool. Keep your eyes and ears open. If you hear anything, don't call. Get word to Todd, and I'll get over here when I can."

"Okay," Murray says solemnly.

Sack stands up, and smoothes his jeans down over his legs.

"I'll walk you to your car," Murray says, standing up. When they get a few feet from the car, Murray notices that two children about age five and seven are inside. "Oh. You got the boys with you today," Murray says.

"Yeah. I have them for the weekend. We're going to the beach."

Murray looks over again and notices for the first time the surfboard and two boogie boards strapped to the roof of Sack's faded black, late-model Mercedes. The rusted, bent coat-hanger used for a radio antenna is still sticking out of the back, just as Murray remembered it, but there have been some new additions to the slew of political bumper stickers pasted on the rear end.

Murray shades his eyes with his hand and sees that the two boys are bouncing up and down inside the car. "They're so excited, they are *bouncing*, " Murray says, laughing. "When was the last time *you* remember bouncing?"

"Me?" Sack says. "I *never* bounced. Never in my life."

Sack starts walking closer to the car. "I've got to get these guys to the beach," he says. "What are *you* up to for the day?" He asks Murray.

"Oh, uh, I have to stick around here...I need to take care of Shadow."

"Oh, yeah. That's right," Sack says. "Todd told me about what happened. I guess his girlfriend drove you over to the animal hospital?"

Murray nods.

"How's he doing?" Sack asks, opening his car door.

"He's really improving," Murray says, smiling. "He went from needing to be fed every two hours, to every four hours, but I still have to stick close to home. He's starting to actually eat a little of the food on his own now, so I'm hoping he won't have to be force-fed for much longer."

"All right, then," Sack says, getting inside his car. "Take care. I'll be in touch."

"See ya'," Murray says, smiling.

As Sack pulls away, Murray spots the black car on the opposite side of the street, just at the bottom of the hill. He goes inside, locks the door, and opens a beer.

* * * *

As the days pass, Shadow gets stronger and healthier. Eventually, Murray begins to anticipate what each new day's sign of improvement will be. Slowly but surely,

Shadow begins to lick more and more food from the syringe on his own.

One day, while talking with Mollie, Murray says, "Shadow is actually struggling and fighting now to resist the forced-feedings. It's really a healthy sign."

"*Hmph*," Mollie responds. "I wished they would have seen it that way when *I* was in the hospital."

Murray chuckles, and Mollie tells Murray it is great to hear him finally laugh again.

By the fourth week, Shadow's coat is starting to get shiny again, and his eyes are beginning to become clear. His checkup is a good one. Dr. Noah informs Murray that Shadow's liver cell count has gone down dramatically and that he has gained a pound.

By week six, Shadow has begun eating on his own, requiring only one supplemental forced-feeding a day. His strength is returning, as is his voice, and he follows Murray from room to room, chattering away nonstop.

Within just another couple of weeks, Shadow has gained another pound and is eating completely on his own, summoning Murray to get him his breakfast each morning with loud, demanding chatter.

Wanting to entice him to eat on his own, Murray throws out all of the dry, nutritionally balanced food from the health food store, and replaces it with moist, commercial food that comes in cans with names like, "Royal Prime Feast in Gravy" and "Sea Captain's Special Choice." Shadow gobbles it up, as Murray stands by, looking on like a proud parent.

By the ninth week, Murray believes the suspicions he has been having for the past couple of weeks are confirmed. Even Kirby notices it. Shadow has clearly become a different cat. Murray can't quite put his finger on it, he tells Mollie one day on the phone, but Shadow is definitely different. The two of them have become bonded in a way that Murray had never imagined, he tells Mollie. They are now far more than inseparable.

And, Murray tells her, Shadow has now started acting differently, doing strange things he has never done before. There is his new habit of jumping up on Murray's lap to be near him as he types, or sitting on the lid of the toilet seat each morning and watching Murray as he shaves.

The most interesting change, Murray tells Mollie, is Shadow's new habit of standing on the edge of the bathtub in the mornings, to be with Murray as he showers. "Shadow!" Murray had exclaimed when it happened the first time. "You're getting sprayed with water. You know you hate water!"

Not a minute goes by, Murray says, in which Shadow is not at his side. In fact, he tells her, Kirby is complaining that he can't get a moment of silence for all the talking Shadow is doing now. Maybe, Murray speculates, it is like when *people* have a near-death experience, and then after they pull through it, their entire lives change.

* * * *

With Shadow improving, Murray begins to relax and to shift his focus onto other things. He pays close attention to the messages on the recorder now, and jumps to answer the phone when it rings. Each time it happens, he tells Shadow, "Maybe *that's* Dolan calling about my play."

On Thursday morning, Murray leaves early to check his post office box. When he arrives at the subway, it is crowded with the tail end of the morning rush hour commuters. When the train pulls in, it is a fight to the finish to grab a seat.

Murray sees an opening next to a young man with a shaved head, dressed like a gang member, who gives every appearance that he could kill you as soon as look at you. The rest of the commuters look over at the vacant spot and keep on going.

Murray walks up to the young man and says, "Say, do you mind if I sit here?" The young man glares at him and then turns his legs to the side, allowing Murray barely enough room to squeeze past him and take the spot near the window. After Murray sits down, the young man sighs, adjusts his jacket, and thrusts his head back in his best, "I am totally fed up with life" fashion.

As the train starts to pull away, Murray notices that two men who had boarded with him are now sitting in the seats directly in front of him. The one near the aisle appears to be in his early thirties, and is wearing an expensive-looking tailored, linen suit. His hair is precisely cut and styled, and he holds his body in the rigid and uncomfortable manner of someone about to hear some very bad news. The man near the window appears to be more at ease and somewhat younger, his suit considerably less expensive, than his traveling companion.

When the train has left the station and the noise has subsided somewhat, the man on the aisle begins speaking very loudly to the man near the window.

"Thanks for agreeing to meet me at the station. I never would have made it through this if you hadn't been around...What a *drag*. I can't *believe* you actually do this everyday," he says loudly.

"No problem," the one by the window says in a much softer tone.

Several seconds go by, and then the man in the linen suit begins to talk very loudly again. "I just can't believe you can actually *do* this everyday. I don't know how I would cope if I had to do this." He gestures his hands outward to indicate the train.

"Actually," the man by the window says, "I *prefer* it to driving. I'm from back East and where I grew up, everyone takes the subway."

"Yeah, well *here*," the one near the aisle says in a near-shout, "the only ones who take the subway everyday are *riffraff*...You know, people who don't even have money for a car, or people who have had their licenses pulled...and the unemployed, of course."

The man near the window shifts uneasily in his seat and surreptitiously looks around him. The gangster-looking young man sitting next to Murray sneers, sits up straight in the seat, and adjusts his jacket.

"How do you *do* it?" The one near the aisle asks loudly, his tone one of disbelief. "It's filthy, there's graffiti all over the place, and it *smells*."

The gangster-looking man lunges forward. His body stiffens, and his left hand clenches into a fist, and flexes again as he sits back in his seat. Murray notices he has the word, "TROY" and a symbol that looks like a dagger, tattooed on his hand.

"Well, you would never see *me* doing this if I didn't have to," the one near the aisle continues. "If my *Porsche* didn't cut out on me last night, *I* sure wouldn't be riding this thing," he says, shouting the word, "Porsche."

"When will it be fixed?" The one near the window asks.

"Oh, you don't have any idea what it's like to own a *Porsche*. It's not like having a *Chevy*. The mechanics for *foreign luxury cars* are *specialists*, so they never just go in and look at the one thing they think may be wrong. They always run a complete diagnostic, and it usually involves a few days while they check out several things. I'll tell you what though, I might just take the next day or two off until my *Porsche* comes back. I don't want to do *this* again," he says, several decibels louder than necessary.

"Oh, it's not so bad once you get used to it," the one by the window says.

"Well, it's not for *me*. I'll admit it. I can't handle anything *public*. I'm not used to doing anything with the *masses*," he says loudly.

Several people turn to look at the speaker. The woman sitting directly across from him rolls her eyes. The young man with the gangster-look mutters the word, "asshole" and shifts in his seat. The Porsche owner's traveling companion looks around uneasily and then stares out the window.

Several minutes go by, and then the one by the aisle sighs and begins talking very loudly again. "You just don't have any *idea* how hard this is. I mean, I'm used to driving my *Porsche* everyday. To be without it feels like...it's like a part of me is *missing*."

Murray takes his marker and writes in his notebook, "Part of you **IS** missing."

"P.S. **NO ONE CARES** about your Porsche, you half-wit!"

The young man sitting next to Murray watches as Murray writes. When Murray finishes, the young man snickers and motions to Murray to hand him the notebook and marker. When Murray hands them to him, the young man adds to the bottom of what Murray has written,

"**Stay off the subway**. If I see you here again, I'll slit your fucking throat, **Asshole!** "

He signs the note with something that looks like graffiti, tears the page off, and hands the notebook and marker back to Murray. The young man folds the note in half, then in fourths, eighths, and so on, until it is a one-inch square. Then he leans back and holds the paper tightly in his fist.

When the next stop is announced, the gangster-looking young man stands in the aisle just behind the Porsche owner. The train slows to a stop and the doors open. As the people standing near the door begin to exit, the young man taps the Porsche owner on the left shoulder and shoves the note at him. Reflexively, the Porsche owner reaches his hand out and takes the note. For one split second their eyes meet, and the Porsche owner's body stiffens.

The young man exits the train, and the doors close. He stands on the platform glaring in at the man for several seconds, then turns and pulls the collar of his jacket up around the back of his neck. The Porsche owner unfolds the paper and starts reading it, just as the train pulls away.

His body stiffens, and he turns sharply and strains to look out the window behind him, but the train has already begun to pass through the tunnel. He jerks his head around on either side behind him. Murray's face is buried in a book, the notebook and marker safely tucked away inside of his backpack.

"*Look* at this!" He exclaims to his traveling companion. "I can't believe it!" The man by the window reads the note and subtly looks around him.

"This is *exactly* what I am talking about!" The one near the aisle shouts. "Where is the conductor? How do I get hold of the conductor?" He shouts. The man near the window tells him that's not how things work.

"I need to reach *someone*. I'm going to report this to the *police*!"

Three nearby people snicker at the man's reaction. The woman sitting across from him shakes her head and says, "*Hmph*!"

"This is outrageous!" He continues. "I need to be able to *talk* to someone. I need to contact the police. He's not going to get away with this! This is exactly what is wrong with this country nowadays."

"You're going to have to just let it go," the man sitting next to him says. "He's gone now. There's nothing you can do."

"*Let it go*? He threatened to *kill* me! That's against the *law*, in case you don't know." There is a pause. "I'm getting off at the next stop. I *knew* I shouldn't try and take *public* transportation...I'm getting off here...I'm going to *report* this," he shouts, folding the note back up, and shoving it into the breast pocket of his suit jacket.

"Okay. I'll see you at the office later," the man by the window says. The man in the expensive suit does not respond.

The doors open and the Porsche owner gets off, looks left, then right, and then follows the crowd towards the stairs leading out of the subway.

Murray pulls his book tightly around his face and tries to stifle his laughs. Several minutes later, he is finally able to compose himself. He puts the book away, and stares out the window at the tunnel, as the train speeds by.

* * * *

Every day when Murray returns, Shadow greets him. He seems to have an uncanny sense for anticipating Murray's ever-changing habits of coming through the back door, then the front, then the back again.

Each day Murray is greeted with continual chatter from Shadow, and each day he listens carefully, and then fills Shadow in on his own adventures. And, each day Murray makes a beeline for the answering machine to see if there are any messages from Dolan. "Any day now," he tells Shadow, "I'm going to get the big call."

The black car appears again one day, right outside of Murray's apartment building. A man gets out and leans against the side of the car. He remains there for about forty minutes. When Murray looks out again, the man is nowhere to be seen, but the car is still there. Some time later, Murray is in his bedroom with Shadow watching the Bee Babe, when the doorbell rings. "*Ssshh,*" Murray whispers to Shadow as he turns the volume down on the television. The doorbell rings again. Murray remains frozen in his chair. Shadow sits next to him with his ears perked.

A few minutes later, Murray creeps into the living room and peeks out the blinds. The man is getting into the black car. Seconds later, he pulls away.

"I sure hope Dolan calls soon. Things are getting too close for comfort around here," Murray tells Shadow.

"*Rrraw*," Shadow replies.

The next day, while Kirby is at school, Murray is taking a shower when he hears the phone ring. "Oh," he tells Shadow, climbing out of the shower and wrapping a towel around him, "that might be the call we're waiting for from Dolan."

"Hello," Murray says.

"Hi. It's Mollie. You sound out of breath."

"Oh, I was just in the shower when I heard the phone ring."

"Sorry," Mollie says. "I was just calling to see if you were interested in seeing a private opening of an art exhibit with me next Saturday. I have two invitations for the opening and reception."

"That sounds like fun," Murray says.

"Some people from my group are having their work exhibited," Mollie continues. "The featured artist is this guy from Chicago. He's schizophrenic. The exhibit is called, "The Bell Jar Collection.""

"Hmm," Murray says.

"Yeah," Mollie continues, "it's a collection of artwork from the mentally ill...psychosis, all the way through to your garden-variety neurotic."

"I didn't realize they needed a special showing for that," Murray says. Mollie laughs. "I wouldn't miss it," he adds.

"Great," Mollie says excitedly. "Come over here first, and we'll go over to the gallery together...around five-ish?"

"Sure. I'm looking forward to it," Murray says cheerfully.

"Oh, I warn you, there'll be a lot of strange people there. A lot of artistic-types and what-not," Mollie says.

"A lot of people wearing black, eh?" Murray says, chuckling.

"Not to worry," Mollie says. "This is a very big event. I'm sure most everyone will remember to take their Prozac."

Murray chuckles. "Okay, then. I'll see you Saturday."

"Bye, bye," Mollie says.

"So long," Murray says.

Murray hangs up the phone and walks carefully around the puddles of water he has made. He returns to the shower, and has just turned the water on, when the telephone rings again. "Must be Mollie forgot to tell me something," he mutters. He turns the water off and heads back to the telephone.

"Hello," he says.

"Yes," a woman says, sounding very business-like. "I'm calling from the law offices of Carlton, Dusek, Wallerton, and Napersfield. I am trying to reach a Mr. Murray Bardos."

"He isn't here," Murray says without hesitation. "I'm afraid you are going to have to wait to reach him. He left week before last for New Zealand. He won't be returning for another twelve weeks."

"I see," the woman says, with irritation in her voice.

"I would be happy to take a message for him if you would like," Murray says pleasantly.

"Oh, do you expect to be hearing from him soon?" The woman says hopefully.

"No, but I could take the message and make sure that he gets it when he returns."

"Do you have an address or telephone number for him in…umm…you said it was New Zealand?"

"No. I'm sorry, I don't."

"Well, thank you for your time then," the woman says and hangs up.

Murray pads back towards the bathroom. "All right, Shadow," he says, "the next one is going into the recorder."

For the next several days, Murray runs to the phone each time it rings, and checks the answering machine every time he has been out or in the bathroom. "I hope Dolan will call today," he tells Shadow, his voice becoming a little more frantic with each passing day.

On Friday morning, Murray hangs out and talks with Kirby about the value—and lack thereof, as Kirby sees it—of what his professor calls, "deconstructing the patriarchal gender-based education system." After Kirby leaves for class, Murray tells Shadow that he is feeling especially hopeful about hearing from Dolan today, and so he will stick close to home.

Sometime in the early afternoon, Murray begins planning on where he and Shadow will be moving. He pulls out his map of the United States and spreads it out on the floor. "Okay, buddy," Murray says, "Pick a place. Where do you want to move to?"

Shadow walks over to the map and lies down across it.

"Oh, now, that's not helping us one bit," Murray says, rubbing Shadow's head. "Hey," he says after a little while, "I've got an idea. Come on. Let's go."

Shadow gets up excitedly and walks off the map. Murray picks up the map, and reaches into a box next to the typewriter, for some thumbtacks. He walks down the hall, with Shadow trotting along behind them.

When they get to Kirby's room, Murray stops and says, "Kirby won't mind." He opens the bedroom door and walks in. Murray goes over to the corkboard above Kirby's desk and tacks the map up across it. "All right, Shadow," he says, picking him up and cradling him in his left arm. "Here goes."

Murray closes his eyes and shoots a dart at the map.

"Let's see how we did, Shadow," he says, walking over to the map. "New Mexico!" He says. "What do you say to *that,* Shadow?"

Shadow answers with a "*Rrow*".

"Let's see exactly where it's going to be," Murray says, carrying Shadow up close to the map. "Hmm. Clovis. Clovis, New Mexico. Well, let's hope they have a Greyhound station there, Shadow. Because I have a feeling our play is going to make it, and very soon you and me can move. Would you like to live in New Mexico, Shadow?" Murray asks, taking the map off of the corkboard. "It's warm and sunny there. You can play out in the yard. Maybe we'll plant a garden...and a tree. We have to do *that*, right, buddy?"

Shadow looks intently at Murray, but does not answer.

By late afternoon, Murray is pacing. He walks to the telephone and picks it up several times and listens, to make sure there is a dial tone. After two hours of this, Murray looks up George Pelton's number in his phone book. "I can't take it any longer," he tells Shadow. "The suspense is killing me. Maybe George can call Dolan and see what's happening."

Murray dials George's number.

"George Pelton's office," a woman says.

"Yes, this is Murray Bardos. May I speak to him please?"

"Oh, I'm sorry, Mr. Bardos. Mr. Pelton is away on sabbatical. He won't be returning for another two months."

There is silence.

"Mr. Bardos? Can I help you with something?"

"Ah...no...well, could you leave him a message that says I have not heard from Dolan, and that I am calling to find out the status of my play?"

"Certainly. I'll give him the message when he returns."

"Thank you."

"Good-bye."

Murray lights up a cigarette and begins pacing the living room floor. In a few minutes, Shadow walks in talking. "Oh, it's all right, buddy. We're just going to have to wait a little longer to hear, is all."

* * * *

Murray arrives at Mollie's place just a few minutes before five. When she opens the door, he can't believe his eyes. "Wow!" He says. "You really look different dressed up with makeup on. I can hardly recognize you," he says, smiling.

"Yeah, well, it's my costume for the evening," Mollie says. "Do you think it's too much?" She asks.

"No. Not at all. I think you look great," Murray says. "The mini-skirt, the boots, all that black. It's a complete package," he says. "You really look like an artist."

"Well," Mollie replies, "in this business, it's crucial to look the part...at least during a showing."

"Say," Murray says hesitantly, "You suppose I'm dressed okay? I didn't have any black."

"Are you kidding? You're perfect. *Very* bohemian. They love that. You'll fit right in," she says confidently.

Murray relaxes a bit.

"You want a beer?" Mollie asks. "We've got time. They will be serving wine and hors d`oeuvres, but it's better to get loosened up *before* you arrive to these sort of things."

"Sure," Murray says.

Mollie goes to the refrigerator and brings back two bottles. "Here's to madness," she says, and the two of them laugh and clink their bottles together.

When they arrive, the gallery is already filled with people. There is the strong scent of patchouli, and some other woods scent that Murray cannot identify. A CD of world beat music is coming from the speakers that are strategically mounted, so as not to distract the viewer from the exhibits.

As expected, most everyone is wearing black. Several people look emaciated. Jewelry predominates on, as Murray put it, body parts that a few years ago, were reserved for those people appearing in National Geographic. People are milling about with plastic wine glasses, or standing in small groups, talking in low whispers as if they are in a library.

Murray and Mollie look around and try to get acclimated. "It's gonna' take me awhile to get my sea legs," Murray says.

"Don't worry," Mollie answers. "Everyone here is just as self-conscious and uncomfortable as you...they have just become experts at concealing it."

Murray turns left and walks to a smaller area, just off the main exhibit room. Mollie is just behind him. As he enters, he sees a table with several people gathered around it, and a man seated on the opposite side of the table signing autographs. The man is dark-skinned with a head full of short dreadlocks. He appears very large.

The man is talking and joking around with the people he is signing his name for. As Murray nears the table, the man looks up at him with an excited expression on his face. He says in a deep, bellowing voice, "Oh! You're here for me, aren't you? You're here to see *me*." The man stands up and approaches Murray. Murray notices the man is about six foot five, and weighs somewhere around two hundred seventy-five pounds.

"Hey, how you doin', man?" The man says, putting his hand out. He does a sort of handshake Murray does not quite know how to follow.

"Hi," Murray says, smiling. "Glad to meet you."

Mollie slides around behind Murray. "This is Wesley," she says in a low voice. "He's the featured artist from Chicago."

Murray nods and smiles.

"So come on over herea'," the man says, his voice booming. "I'll show ya' my work," he says, guiding Murray to the exhibit. "Here it is," he says proudly. "Which one do you want?"

Murray chuckles uncomfortably. "Well, I'll tell you my problem, Wesley," he says, leaning in closer to look at the sketches. "I don't have any money. But if I did..." Murray says, walking down the line of art pieces, "I sure would snatch one of these up."

Wesley laughs a hearty laugh. "Which one do you like best? Which one?"

Murray walks down the exhibit and looks at the sketches, twelve in all. "Well, I'll tell you, Wesley, I'd have an awful hard time choosing. You certainly have captured Chicago."

Wesley booms a laugh.

"But, if I had to choose, I guess it would be *this* one," Murray says, pointing to a large sketch done on poster-board. It is of Chicago Transit Authority buses whizzing down the Dan Ryan Expressway.

"You certainly captured the essence of speed and movement here," Mollie says. Wesley nods.

"All right," Wesley says with finality. "That's the one then." He reaches up and lifts the piece right up out of the exhibit. "I'm gonna' tell the gallery owner I need to finish this up. It's not done yet. I need to work on it some more."

He walks the sketch over to the table where he had been signing his autograph, and lays it down. Then he walks back to where Murray and Mollie are standing and looking over his other sketches.

"They really are quite good," Murray is saying as Wesley approaches from behind.

"Come on," Wesley booms. "Give Wesley a head-butt."

Murray looks at him confused.

"Come on. Head-butt! Head-butt!"

Before Murray can ask any questions, Wesley bends down to Murray's level and rams his forehead full-force into Murray's head. Murray reels backwards several inches and rubs his forehead, laughing.

"Come on! Again!" Wesley booms. Murray looks around the room. Several people in black are staring and laughing little laughs with their hands over their mouths. "Head-butt! Give Wesley head-butt!" He bends down and moves in like a bull ready to charge. Murray moves quickly towards him and the two men butt heads at full speed. Wesley lets out a ferocious laugh. "You all right, man," he says, "You all right!"

Next, Wesley turns to Mollie. "Give Wesley head-butt," he says. Mollie looks questioningly at Murray.

"Go ahead," Murray says, "but don't resist. It hurts less if you just go full throttle into it."

Wesley laughs. "Yeah," he says, "that's how it is."

Mollie laughs and says, "Okay." Wesley bends down and gears up. A second later, it is all over, and Mollie is rubbing her forehead and laughing.

"Let's go outside," Wesley says. Murray nods, and a few minutes later, the three of them are standing outside of the gallery watching the cars go by. They stand silently for several minutes, then Wesley turns to Murray and asks, "Can you write a script for meds?"

Murray looks shocked. He glances over at Mollie who gives him a secret smile. "No," Murray says.

They are silent again until Wesley says, "I want some Lager Meister. Let's go down the street here and get some Lager Meister!"

"I would," Murray says, "but we have to stick around here. Besides, should you be mixing alcohol with meds?"

Wesley lowers his head and shakes it. "Nah," he says.

"How long are you going to be in San Francisco?" Mollie asks him.

"Just this weekend. I only have enough meds for the weekend. Got to have my meds...don't want to flip out on the plane ever again...don't want to ever do that again."

Just then, someone from the gallery comes to the edge of the doorway. "Wesley, you're needed inside. There are some people here who want to meet you."

"Okay," Wesley says, "just let me finish up here."

The man nods, gives Mollie and Murray a once-over, and ducks back into the gallery.

Wesley finishes his cigarette and digs in his pocket. He pulls out a card from the gallery and a pen.

"Here," he says, writing something down on the card and handing it to Murray. "It's my address and phone number for the next time you come to Chicago."

"Thanks," Murray says, putting the card into his shirt pocket.

Wesley heads back into the gallery, ducking his head as he enters the doorway. Murray and Mollie watch as Wesley disappears from sight, and then turn to look at one another.

"Say," Murray begins, "how do you suppose he knew that..."

Mollie waves her hand and smiles, "Special radar," she says.

The two of them stand quietly for several minutes, lost in their own thoughts, and then turn to go back inside.

The main gallery is now crowded with people. Mollie and Murray make their way to the table and each gets a glass of wine. Murray studies the guests, and tries to figure out what each of them does for a living. Mollie points out several of the artists to him, giving him juicy tidbits about their psychiatric histories.

"You ready to see the exhibits?" Mollie asks after they finish their glasses of wine. Murray nods and the two of them head over to where the artwork is displayed. The first exhibit is a series of macabre paintings done completely in red and black. Each one depicts people with their heads cut off, as well as a variety of other forms of dismemberment. There is blood gushing everywhere from the dismembered parts. The faces on the decapitated heads have looks of horror.

"Fascinating use of color," a man says to his female companion.

She nods. "Agreed," she says. "Fascinating."

After the couple has moved on to the next exhibit, Mollie whispers to Murray, "No. What *would* have been fascinating is if he would have decided to use any color other than *red* for all that blood." Murray snickers.

The next exhibit is from one of the female artist in Mollie's group. It is a gigantic pair of papier-mâché` breasts. Hanging by chains, from the nipples of each breast, is a variety of miniature household items: an iron and ironing board, a tiny wash machine and dryer, a vacuum cleaner, and some tiny cans and bottles of various household cleaners. It is entitled, "Breast-Feeding Mankind."

"According to this," Murray says, "*woman*kind would just as soon do without a clean house or clean laundry."

Mollie snorts. "It's her new trip," she says, "to blame social injustices for her penchant to self-mutilate."

Murray rolls his eyes and they move on.

The two of them browse one exhibit after another, trying to figure out the correct diagnosis for each of the artists based on their pieces. Mollie points out that a series of eight particularly dark paintings, each featuring a self-portrait of a young man in various stages of committing suicide, is too obvious. "Depression," they both agree.

The last painting in the series shows the young man putting the noose around his neck while standing on a wooden chair.

"I guess if he ever decides to go through with it," Murray says dryly, "he'll have to get someone else to finish the part where the chair is knocked over."

Someone behind him does a "*tsk, tsk.*" Murray and Mollie look at one another and stifle their laughs.

The next exhibit is ten paintings, all of which are almost identical. Each features several narrow, brown rectangles standing vertically, with thin green triangles setting atop them.

"What do you call *this*?" Murray asks.

"Anorexia," Mollie says. "When she finishes therapy she's moving up to circles."

Someone behind them snickers and they move on.

At the next exhibit, Murray and Mollie study four paintings. All of them depict a large figure of a woman in the center of the canvas, with many different people connected to her by her hair, earlobes, hands, and so on. The other people in the painting are very tiny.

"What do you make of these?" Mollie asks.

Before Murray can respond, a tall, well-dressed man standing behind them answers. "Narcissistic Personality Disorder," he says with authority. "It's classic. Notice how the central figure is several times larger than everyone else in the painting...and how everyone else is somehow connected to the central character...Notice how everyone else in the painting is revolving around the key figure." He says, pointing.

Murray and Mollie nod.

"Oh," Mollie says, turning to the man. "Are you a psychologist?"

"No," he says dryly. "The artist is my ex-wife."

"Oh," Mollie says, biting her lip.

"I'm just kidding," the man says. "I wrote a book about the correlation between madness and art several years back. I've always had an interest in trying to help my clients by using art therapy...It's actually quite revealing."

Mollie nods.

As Murray and Mollie move to the next exhibit, the man follows behind them. "You see this," he says, gesturing towards the paintings in front of them. "Notice how the artist takes almost the entire canvas up for these self-portraits."

Murray and Mollie nod.

"It's always been my observation that the emotionally disturbed are a lot like the wealthy...they both take up an awful lot of personal space."

"Interesting," Mollie says.

The man nods and moves on.

Murray and Mollie walk over to a sculpture made of old, rusted wire-hangers, newspapers, plastic grocery bags, and wrappers, entitled, "Mother."

"Where did they get all that stuff?" Murray asks, motioning toward the sculpture.

"Oh, that's Andy's work. He's in my group. He calls it, 'Urban Art of Found Objects.' It's really just all the garbage that blows up on his driveway from Mission Street. He's been collecting it for a year."

"Well," Murray says, "maybe your friend Andy should have loaned some of his found objects to this person over here." He points to an exhibit entitled, "His-to-wreck-to-me." It is a sculpture of a hand holding a scalpel, reaching around a large naked woman who has a gigantic, gaping hole where her uterus would have been.

Murray points to the hole and says, "Maybe this artist could have used some of Andy's local garbage to fill in the gap...Then she could call it 'Womb Without a View.'

Mollie snickers and hits Murray on the shoulder. "You're really bad," she says, smiling.

Just then, Mollie spots her art instructor in the far corner of the room. "Oh, Murray, my instructor's over there, and I'm pretty sure that's an agent he's talking with. Do you mind if I go over there and introduce myself?"

"No, of course not. Go on ahead. Take as much time as you need...there's plenty here for me to entertain myself," Murray says, smiling.

Murray watches as Mollie makes her way across the crowded room. He looks around the main gallery, scratches his head, and then walks over to the side room where the food and wine are. He picks up a paper plate and begins scanning the food table. After he finishes choosing some cantaloupe pieces, he searches around the table some more. When he looks up again, he recognizes a familiar face at the very moment he himself, is recognized.

"*Mosh*! " The man says, laughing. "Fancy seeing *you* here."

The man steps around the table with his hand extended.

"Juno," he says. "From the playhouse, remember?"

"Oh...yes. Yes, of course," Murray says, shifting the plate to his left hand and shaking Juno's hand.

"Well, uh...what do you think?" Murray asks, gesturing in the direction of the main gallery.

Juno leans his head in close to Murray. "They should have called it, 'The Art of Lunacy'," he says.

Both men chuckle at the observation.

"*Ack.* I need a break. Let's go out for a smoke," Juno says.

Murray nods and follows him to the door. Once outside, they head across the street to a small park area. Murray munches on his food. Juno walks over to a circular concrete bench with a large planter in the center. He sits down cross-legged and lights a cigarette. After several minutes, Juno begins giving a piece-by-piece review of The Bell Jar Collection, replete with a prognosis for future success and future diagnoses for each artist.

Murray laughs and listens, and eats and laughs some more. Sometimes he laughs so hard that he begs Juno to stop.

"You know what their problem is, Mosh?" Juno asks after he is finished with his critique.

Murray shakes his head.

"These people," he says, gesturing in the direction of the gallery, "No, let me rephrase that...*most* people in the world...they lack Subway-vision."

"How's that?" Murray asks, lighting a cigarette.

Juno picks up a stick and begins drawing in the dirt that's inside the planter. "Take any event...like this art opening, for example. No two people will perceive it in precisely the same way. Each person perceives their own reality about what is happening, according to their own unique background, experiences, and expectations. You see, what is happening inside of there," he says, motioning his head in the direction of the gallery, "is something very different for *you* than it is for someone else...*me* for instance."

"Yes," Murray says, sitting down next to Juno, "but there has to be *some* consensus. I mean, we would all agree that it is an art showing."

Juno laughs heartily.

"Well, at least we would agree it's more like an art showing than a high-rise fire," Murray says, looking at Juno.

Juno laughs again. "Subway vision," Juno says, drawing more lines in the dirt, "is understanding and seeing that everyone creates their own unique version of reality...only they don't know it. They *think* it's objective reality. They think it's "real" because some of what they create is part of the *shared* reality. But it's only their *perception* of what is real. It's just what they have created in their own minds."

Juno puts the stick down and lights another cigarette. Murray notices that he has drawn something that looks like some sort of Japanese or Chinese symbol.

Juno inhales deeply, exhales, and then continues, "It is like what *you* might call 'the curse'. "

Murray flinches slightly. Juno pauses and goes on. "It is seeing that when the doors open and close, every person is riding the train for their own unique reasons. They may be sharing the same subway, but that's about it." He chuckles and takes another toke of his cigarette.

"Even the subway itself is an illusion," he continues. "It gives people the misperception that it's the destination, and not the journey itself, that counts," Juno says, before taking another drag from his cigarette.

"It's simple," Juno continues. "Subway vision is being able to see that this thing called 'reality' is no more than an illusion, because everyone has their own version of it. And who's to say whose version is the 'right' one?"

The two men sit silently for several minutes. Juno finishes his cigarette and crushes it on the pavement.

"So what's *your* version of reality?" Juno asks, looking at Murray.

"*My* version of reality?" Murray says, chuckling. He pauses and clears his throat. "That's not for public consumption, I'm afraid."

Juno's eyes twinkle. The two sit silently for a few minutes, then Murray gets up.

"Well, I guess I better get back over there. My friend is probably wondering what happened to me."

"See you around, Mosh," Juno says, smiling.

"See ya'," Murray says, and heads back towards the gallery.

When he approaches the front door, Mollie is waiting in the doorway. She is holding something the size of a poster board, wrapped in black plastic.

"*There* you are. I didn't know what happened to you. I thought that maybe you hated it so much, you went home," she says.

"Not at all," Murray says. "This has been a *very* enlightening experience."

"Are you ready to go?" Mollie asks.

"Sure. If you are," Murray says.

The two of them start walking towards the bus stop.

"Oh," Mollie says, stopping. "I almost forgot. This is for you." She hands Murray the poster board.

Murray looks confused.

"It's from Wesley. He said to tell you something...what was it? It was something odd...Oh yeah, he said he has another five-letter word for insane, and that he'll tell you it when you visit Chicago."

Murray's eyes open wide. He stands in the middle of the sidewalk shaking his head.

"What is it?" Mollie asks.

"Ah, nothing. Just some more of his special radar, I guess. Or maybe it's just another bizarre coincidence today...Let's see what we've got here." Murray pulls the black plastic cover off the poster board.

"Wow!" Murray says. "Will you look at *that!* It's the artwork I liked. He asked me which one I liked best, but I never dreamed..."

"That's really something, Murray," Mollie says, shaking her head and smiling. "That *really* is something."

VIII

For the next couple of weeks, Murray is relaxed. He stops checking the telephone for a dial tone, and tells Shadow he must just trust in his gut-instinct that the play will be picked up and that everything will work out.

Murray spends several days just hanging out reading, talking with Shadow, and watching Cable Public Access. He keeps one ear open for the phone, but does not even mention Dolan or the play. He tells Shadow that he has become so lovable that it is like having a completely different cat. Shadow responds by rubbing his front paws on Murray's pant leg.

At the next vet appointment, Dr. Noah is almost as excited as Murray about Shadow's status. He gives Shadow a clean bill of health, and tells Murray that Shadow's blood count is back to normal, and that he looks and acts just as healthy as can be. Yes, Dr. Noah had heard about animals whose personality and behavior completely changed after nearly dying, but he could offer no explanation for it—at least not one he was willing to discuss while he had the stethoscope around his neck.

When they get home, Murray gives Shadow a fist-full of new rubber bands and reminds him that it was just twelve weeks earlier that he almost died. Shadow jumps around and plays with the rubber bands as if nothing at all had ever happened.

On Monday, Kirby tells Murray that he and his buddies from school are going to Reno for an extended weekend vacation. He asks Murray if he wants him to place any bets for him. Murray considers, but then tells Kirby he better save his luck up for something else he's hoping for.

On Tuesday, George Pelton calls and leaves a message while Murray is at the market. When Murray returns, he calls George back. George is out of the office. Murray rewinds the tape and listens to George's message three more times, trying to determine what it all means by the tone in George's voice.

In the late afternoon, the phone rings. Murray jumps to get it before the end of the second ring.

"Hello?"

"Hello, Murray?"

"Yes."

"George Pelton here. I got the message you left a couple months back. I'm sorry I didn't get back to you sooner. I've been away on sabbatical."

"Yes," Murray says. "I know. Your assistant told me. It's not a problem."

"I didn't want you to think I had forgotten about you."

"No, no, I didn't," Murray says, pacing in anticipation.

"Murray...I'm afraid I have some bad news for you," George says gravely.

Murray stops pacing and remains frozen in place.

"I called Dolan when I got back and saw your message," George says. "It turns out, he never received your play."

"*What*?" Murray says with disbelief.

"I'm afraid it's true. And he's chosen his season's line-up already. The commitments have already been made." George pauses momentarily.

"What could have happened to the play?" Murray asks in a frantic voice.

"Well, I wanted to find that out myself before I called you. I called the messenger service that was supposed to take it over to the playhouse. They went through their records. It made it over there, all right. The ticket had Dolan's signature on it. So I called him back, but he swears he never saw your play. Now, Dolan can be a bit of an odd boy, to be sure, but I've never known him to be dishonest. I don't know what happened to it, but it never got into Dolan's hands."

Murray begins pacing the floor frantically and running his free hand over and over through his hair.

213

"Now, uh, look, Murray, I know this is real disappointing news, but there's always next year. Dolan will consider looking it over next year, I'm sure."

Murray mumbles something unintelligible. Tears are filling up in his eyes.

"What's that?" George asks. "I didn't catch what you said."

"That was my only copy," Murray says, his voice cracking.

There is a slight pause.

"You mean you didn't make a copy before you brought it over here?" George asks with disbelief.

"Uh...no...uh...there was something real important going on here at the time. Someone else dropped it off for me. I didn't think to ask her to make copies first..." Murray's voice trails off.

"Well, if I would have known...Rosa could have made a copy here...I just assumed..." George says.

"Do you have any of the copies left from the original reading the group did?" Murray interrupts, his voice sounding hopeful.

"No, sorry Murray. You said you were rewriting the second act. I didn't want to keep a copy of the play that you were going to rewrite. I didn't want to get it mixed up with your final version. As for the group's copies, Rosa shredded them for recycling. I'm awful sorry, Murray. If I would have known there were no other copies...it's just that with this tiny office and no real storage space..."

"That's all right," Murray says, clearing his throat. "It was my responsibility."

"Well now, you did type your name and address and phone number on the title page of the original you sent over here, didn't you?"

"Yes," Murray says.

"It's a long-shot, I understand. But it just may turn up. *Someone* has to have it. It has to be *somewhere*, right? Perhaps someone will give you a call or mail it back to you. There's always hope...I know how you must feel,

Murray. It was an awful lot of work...and a *great* play too...but perhaps you can rewrite it from memory..."

"Thanks for the words of encouragement," Murray says sadly. "I better go now."

"Tough luck, Murray. I *am* sorry. If there's anything I can do, just give me a call."

"Thanks," Murray says and hangs up the receiver.

Murray stumbles back into his bedroom, with Shadow following close behind him. He paces in circles and mutters. Shadow jumps up on the bed and watches him. Every so often, Murray sits down on his chair and rocks back and forth muttering, "Oh, God."

All through the night Murray paces and moans, and cries. He does not sleep. He does not eat. He does not respond when Kirby knocks on his bedroom door and asks if he is all right.

"Now what are we going to do, Shadow?" He cries. "That was our only hope."

Shadow stands on his back legs and rubs against Murray's leg with his front paws, but it is little comfort.

"Things can't get much worse, little buddy," Murray says, as he gets up to pace some more.

The next day is more of the same. Murray stays in a suspended state of confusion and despair. Shadow stays by his side, sometimes talking his cat talk, as if to give Murray assurance that everything will be fine.

"The only thing that's going to help us now is a *miracle*, Shadow. A damned miracle," Murray says, bending down to stroke Shadow's head, "and I've never exactly had a guardian angel. You don't know any guardian angels, do you buddy?"

Sometime that evening, Murray notices that Shadow has barely touched his food for the day. "Come on Shadow," Murray warns, "just because *I'm* upset doesn't mean *you* can go without eating. You have until the rest of tonight to finish this food here. If you don't eat, tomorrow morning I'll have to start force-feeding you again."

Shadow meows and turns his tail up.

The telephone rings twice that evening. When Murray picks up the receiver, no one speaks. The next time the phone rings, Murray lets it go into the recorder. Whoever it is hangs up without leaving a message. Murray shakes his head and mutters to himself.

That night Murray falls asleep from exhaustion, while still sitting in his chair.

On Thursday morning, Kirby is packing for his trip when Murray shuffles into the kitchen to make some coffee. Kirby tells Murray he'll be staying at the Reno Hilton, and that he'll be back sometime late Sunday night. Murray nods.

After Murray has his coffee, he realizes that Shadow has not been in to demand his breakfast. He opens a can of Shadow's favorite, Sea Captain's Special Delight, and goes into the bedroom to get him. Shadow walks to his food bowl, sniffs the contents and then walks away.

"All right, Shadow. That was your last chance. You're going to get a forced feeding."

Shadow trots down the hallway and disappears.

By the time Murray has dug out the syringes and mixed the special food, Kirby has left with his duffle bag for Reno. Murray calls Shadow's name several times, and then hunts the entire house to find him. After half an hour of searching, he finally finds the cat standing inside the bathtub, shielded by the shower curtain.

"Well, good try, buddy," Murray says, grunting to bend down and pick him up. "Very clever of you, I'll give you that. But you are still going to eat something. You don't want to get sick again do you?"

Shadow struggles ferociously as Murray carries him back to the kitchen.

The feeding is difficult and messy. Shadow is strong now and fights vigorously to get out of Murray's arms. When Murray tries to feed him, Shadow clamps his jaws tight. Murray must maneuver like an acrobat to hold onto the cat, hold the syringe, force his mouth open, and push the plunger down on the syringe, all at the same time. The feeding takes over half an hour. When it is over, Shadow runs off to Murray's bedroom. Murray cleans up the mess and tears off a piece of notebook paper to note the feeding time. He lights a cigarette and walks around the living room, sighing and running his hand through his hair. He stops to peek out of the blinds. The black car is directly in front of the window. Murray snaps the blinds closed and continues to pace.

After about an hour of pacing, Murray walks into his bedroom and begins riffling through drawers and boxes, pants pockets, and everywhere else he can think of, for old notes on the play. He is on his hands and knees looking around on the floor at bits of notebook paper, when he hears Shadow gagging.

"Hey, what's this?" Murray says, as Shadow throws up all of the food he has just been given.

Murray picks him up and holds him. After a few minutes, Shadow struggles and Murray sits him down on the bed. Murray starts cleaning up the mess.

"Now, whatever is the matter with you? You never threw up the food I force-fed you in all of the weeks I was doing it," Murray says, sounding confused.

Later in the evening, Murray feeds Shadow with the syringe again. Shadow does not fight to leave Murray's arms, but he keeps his jaws shut tight and resists the food. An hour later, he throws up all of the food again. Around ten, Murray tries again, with the same result.

Murray stays up the rest of the night with Shadow. At around midnight, Shadow goes to his water bowl and drinks all the water very quickly. Within ten or fifteen minutes he is gagging. His little body trembles. Murray watches in horror as Shadow vomits up all of the water. Murray picks him up and rocks him softly.

"You're dehydrated from all that vomiting little guy. You shouldn't have tried to drink the water so quickly," Murray says in a worried tone.

Murray gets an ice cube from the freezer and tries to get Shadow to lick it. Shadow refuses. Next, he puts a small amount of water in Shadow's bowl and tries to coax him to drink, but Shadow just lies down on the kitchen floor.

"Okay, buddy," Murray says, "I suppose you're pretty exhausted from all of that vomiting. Your throat is probably pretty sore. We'll try again in a while."

Murray picks him up and brings him into the bedroom and sits him down on the bed. Then he walks back to the kitchen and carries Shadow's water bowl and a syringe of food into the bedroom. Murray spends the next several hours, trying in fifteen-minute intervals, to get food and water down him.

Sometime around four in the morning, Shadow begins making moaning sounds. Murray lies down beside him and softly strokes his head.

"I love you, little buddy. I love you, Shadow," he says over and over, his eyes filling with tears.

They stay like this for three more hours. Around seven, Murray gets up, digs out an eyedropper, and puts a small amount of water in the side of Shadow's mouth. Several seconds later, Murray hears Shadow moan a deep, mournful moan that sounds like a human pleading, "*Noooo.*"

Murray picks Shadow up in his arms and watches in horror as Shadow's little chest suddenly heaves forward convulsively. Murray lies him down gently onto his pillow.

"Oh, God, Shadow," he says. Shadow's tongue hangs from the side of his mouth.

"What do I do? What do I do? Oh, God," Murray cries.

He begins massaging Shadow's chest over and over and over. He picks him up into his arms and Shadow's head falls back, limp. Murray blows into Shadow's mouth several times and then lays him back onto the pillow and massages his chest again. Shadow is silent, but after a while, Murray can tell there is a faint heartbeat. He lies down beside Shadow and strokes his head and face over and over.

"I love you, Shadow. I love you," Murray says, sobbing.

They lay still together like this, side by side, for nearly an hour. Then, Murray reaches out and rubs Shadow's head and mutters, "No...no...no." There is a gasping, gurgling sound, and Shadow's head falls softly back onto the pillow. "No!" Murray bellows out a bone-chilling moan. "No! No!" He shouts. He picks Shadow's body up and cradles it in his arms, tears pouring from his face. "Oh God, Shadow. What am I going to do without you? What am I going to do?" He cries out over and over.

Murray lays Shadow's lifeless body gently back onto the pillow and paces back and forth in the same small space, sobbing. He stops every few minutes and strokes Shadow's head and body. "You're my best buddy," he cries. "My Best Buddy ever."

Murray paces some more, and then picks up the phone and dials Mollie. No answer. He opens his bedroom windows, pulls a fan from his closet, sits it atop the bookcase, and turns it on. He looks over at Shadow again and begins weeping.

"I was just kidding about the guardian angel business," he says through his sobs. "We could have managed...I would have figured something out...Oh, Shadow!" he sobs, and drops to his knees beside the bed. He reaches over and strokes Shadow's head.

Just then, the dog next door lets out a loud, mournful wail. Murray looks up. There is another wail, and a series of strange barks. Within a minute, a dog at least a half a block down returns the strange wail. After a couple of more minutes, there is a wail from another dog, and then another, and another—all echoing the same sounds.

"The whole neighborhood knows now Shadow," Murray mutters, as he pets Shadow's head, crying.

Murray gets up and dials Mollie's house again; there is no answer. He paces for another half an hour, and tries once more.

"Hello," Mollie says, sounding out of breath.

Murray starts to speak. His voice crackles and then he begins sobbing.

"Murray?" Mollie says.

"Uh-huh," he manages.

"I'll be right over," she says, and hangs up the phone.

Murray paces, lights a cigarette, and sits down in his chair. He looks over at Shadow's body, and begins sobbing again. In a few moments he begins pacing. He is muttering over and over when the phone rings. He reaches over and turns the volume button up on the answering machine.

"Hello, Mosh? It's Juno. I've got to talk to you right away. I've got news. Call me as soon as you get in. Oh, and you should know, I changed your paradox of illusions into subway vision (the man laughs). Call me immediately, okay? Oh, here's the number..."

Murray turns the volume down and shakes his head. He begins walking around in circles, over and over, crying and talking to Shadow.

When Mollie arrives, Murray's face and eyes are red and swollen.

"Is it Shadow?" She asks.

Murray nods his head up and down.

"Oh, Murray...I'm so *sorry*," she says, putting her arms around him.

Murray leads her into the bedroom and tells her everything that happened over the past few hours. After a long while, Mollie walks into the living room, gets the telephone book out, and searches for pet cemeteries and crematories. She dials one of the numbers, talks for a while with the receptionist, and then goes back into the bedroom.

"Um," she says, hesitating. "Were you considering cremation?"

Murray looks up. "Oh," he says. "I hadn't thought about it, but...of course. No other way."

Mollie sits down on the edge of the bed next to Murray and gently touches his arm. "It's all arranged then. We just need to take him over there."

Murray nods slowly.

Mollie stands. "Did you have a special blanket or something?" She asks, her voice trailing off.

"Oh. Yes. Here. This was his favorite," Murray says, crying softly.

Mollie helps wrap Shadow in the blanket. She looks around the bedroom and walks over to a box with some books inside of it. She empties the contents and Murray gently places Shadow's body inside the carton.

Mollie walks into the bathroom, carries a box of tissues out, and then hands it to Murray. She digs in her pocket for the car keys. Murray walks into the living room, peeks out the window, and looks at the car.

"Where's Mary?" He asks, confused.

"She's with Todd for the weekend," Mollie says.

"You drove here *by yourself*?" Murray asks with disbelief.

Mollie nods as she locates the right key.

"But you don't have a..." Murray stops speaking as Mollie puts her hand up.

"I called Mary and told her there was an emergency. She said to take the spare key and use the car as much as I need."

Murray nods and walks back into the bedroom. A couple of minutes later, he is walking slowly down the hallway, carrying the carton and crying softly.

After they leave the crematory, Mollie takes the 280 to the Pacific Coast Highway.

"I thought we would take the coast south for a bit," she says. "It's a clear day for a change. The view should be nice."

Murray nods. Mollie pushes a CD of Mozart into the player and hits the repeat button. They drive along the coast without speaking. Murray just watches out the window. Occasionally, he takes a fresh tissue from the box and wipes his face.

When they get as far as Santa Cruz, Mollie suggests they get out and walk along the beach for a while. Murray nods. They stay until the sun is setting, just talking— mostly about Shadow.

When they get inside the car to go back to the city, Mollie tells Murray he will be staying at her place for the night, and that she will make him dinner.

On the way back, Murray says, "Mollie? Thanks for everything."

"Don't mention it," she says softly.

Sunday is not any easier for Murray. He leaves Mollie's in the morning and comes home to an empty and quiet house. He paces and smokes and cries for a while. Then he pulls up all of the bedding and puts it into the wash machine. Next, he gathers up all the syringes, bottles of medicine, cat food, and Shadow's bowls and litter box. He puts all of the items into a plastic bag and carries it out back to the trash bin.

Mollie calls twice to check in on him. He tells her it is hard, but that he is doing okay. He remembers the strange message from Juno, and wonders how Juno ever got his phone number. He tries to replay the message, but it has already been taped over by Karen leaving a message for Kirby.

Once he lies down and gives into the fatigue, Murray is finally able to fall asleep. He is sleeping so soundly, he doesn't even hear when Kirby gets back in, some time around two in the morning.

The next day, Murray receives a call from Mollie. Mary will get off work at three o'clock and she will drive all of them to pick up Shadow's ashes, she tells him.

When they arrive, Mollie is carrying a paper bag. "Here," she says, handing it to Murray. "I told you it was for something special."

Murray opens the bag and pulls out the contents. It is the antique, hand-carved box. Mollie has painted small angels all around the box. On the top she has etched the word, "Shadow."

"It's for his ashes," Mollie says.

Murray's eyes fill with tears and his jaw tightens. He nods his head up and down slowly. "I know," he says. "Thank you."

When Murray returns from picking up Shadow's ashes, Kirby is in the kitchen, cooking. Murray says hello, and then takes the hand-painted box into his bedroom. In a few moments, he returns to where Kirby is standing.

"Oh, Murray, someone came by here looking for you this afternoon," Kirby says, stirring his vegetables in the skillet.

"Oh?" Murray says.

"Yeah," Kirby says excitedly. "The guy said it was *really* important and that it was *urgent* he speak with you right away. He seemed upset you weren't here. He really seemed like it was some sort of emergency that you contact him right away. The guy left his name and phone number. It's written down on a piece of paper over there on the counter."

Kirby motions with his hand in the direction of the note.

Murray walks over to the counter and picks up the piece of paper.

The note says, "Must speak to you right away about urgent matter ~ J."

Murray reads the note again and looks at the phone number. "Curious," he mutters.

"Oh, hey, I almost forgot," Kirby says. "He said to tell you he is very sorry about your loss."

Murray's body gives a jerk.

"Do you know what that's about?" Kirby asks.

"Well," Murray says, clearing his throat, "actually, I have something to tell you...It's about Shadow..."

Kirby stops stirring his food and looks up at Murray's face.

"Ah, man...did he? I'm sorry, man...I'm really sorry."

Kirby and Murray spend the rest of the evening reminiscing about all of Shadow's antics. Murray is surprised that he is actually able to laugh a few times.

When it is time for bed, Murray walks into the bedroom and runs his hand across the top of the box with Shadow's ashes. Then he looks up towards the ceiling and says softly, "I know you'll always be with me now, Shadow. No more special buddy...but a special angel is even better, right? Right, Shadow?" And then he lies down on the bed and cries himself to sleep.

The next morning Murray is awakened by the sound of the telephone. He does not make it in time, and the call goes into the answering machine. Murray sleepily walks over and turns up the volume.

"This is Lyn Meyer with the Metropolitan Playhouse in San Francisco, calling for Mr. Murray Bardos. I realize this is highly unorthodox, Mr. Bardos, and I *do* apologize. It's just that we simply *must* have your signature on the contract...*today*, if possible, if we are to move forward with everything in time, and, well, we can't seem to be able to reach your agent. Please call me at..."

Murray turns the volume down and walks in a complete circle in the center of the floor. When the call has disconnected and the recorder has reset itself, Murray grabs a notebook off the table and replays the message again, this time taking notes.

When he has finished listening a fourth time, he sits down on the chair and mutters to himself. After a few minutes, he dials Mollie's number.

"Mollie," he says excitedly after she has answered. "Can you do me a favor?" Murray asks.

"Sure," she says.

"I can't go into the details now, but I need you to call a number and ask for someone, to see if a call I just received is legit."

"Okay," Mollie says. "What's the number?"

Murray gives her the number and says, "I need to see if this number is really someone from the San Francisco Metropolitan Playhouse."

"Hmm. This sounds hopeful," she says.

"I'll fill you in later," Murray says, "but first I need to know if there's even anything to talk about. If it's the Metro, ask for this guy...his name is...hold on...it's...Mr. Lyn Meyer."

"Okay. No problem," Mollie says. "What do you want me to do if it really is this guy?"

"I don't know," Murray says. "It's probably a joke...but, if it *is* legitimate, just...I don't know, say you're sorry, you were connected to the wrong office, and then hang up."

"You got it," Mollie says. "I'll do it right now, and then call you back and let you know what happened."

"Thanks, Mollie. Talk to you soon," Murray says.

He hangs up the phone, walks back and forth ringing his hands for a while, sits down on his chair, stands back up again, and goes back to pacing.

In a little while, the phone rings. Murray lets the call go into the recorder. When he hears that it is Mollie, he picks up.

"It's legit, all right," she says.

"What happened?" Murray asks excitedly.

"I called the number, and this woman answered the phone, 'Metropolitan Playhouse, Director's Office.' So I asked may I speak with Mr. Lyn Meyer, please, and she says, 'Who may I say is calling?' and so I made up some name, and then she asked if he was expecting my call, and I said yes. So she put me on hold and that's when I hung up."

"Wow," Murray says. "Wow."

"So, what does all of this mean?" Mollie asks. "This guy called you?"

"Yeah, but I don't know what it's about. I have no idea. I just wanted to find out if the guy was really who he said he was on the message, before I called him back," Murray says, running his hand through his hair. "Listen, I'll call you and let you know what's happening just as soon as I get to the bottom of this. Oh, and thanks again," he says.

"You better call me back," Mollie says. "Now I'm curious."

"Okay. I will," Murray assures her, and hangs up the phone.

Murray walks around the bedroom for several minutes muttering to himself, then gathers up some fresh clothes and heads into the bathroom to shower.

After he has showered and shaved, Murray makes some coffee, and then heads back into his room. He picks up the paper with the number on it, walks over to Shadow's box and rubs the top of it gently, muttering something, and then walks over to the phone and dials.

"Metropolitan Playhouse, Director's Office," a woman says.

"Uh, yes, I'm returning Mr. Lyn Meyer's call," Murray says.

"Who should I say is calling?" The woman asks in a pleasant tone.

"Murray Bardos."

"Oh, yes, Mr. Bardos. He's expecting your call. Would you hold, please, while I let him know?"

"Certainly," Murray says. He gently taps the edge of the table while he waits.

"Mr. Bardos? I'll put your call through now," the woman says.

"Mr. Bardos? Lyn Meyer. I apologize for disturbing you with this," the man says. "It's just that, like I said on my message, we have put through several calls to your agent and we can't seem to reach him."

"I see," Murray says, scrunching up his face in confusion.

"Well, we need your signature on the contract," the man says. "Normally, of course, we deal directly with the agent handling things. At any rate, we need you to sign before we can move forward. And we really need to get the advertisements and posters sent over for drafting, and the order together for the printer doing the playbills."

"Oh?" Murray says in a confused tone.

The man chuckles. "Well, I'm sure you are not aware of the details of the business end of things. Why would you be? That's why you have an agent." He chuckles again.

"But these things must be taken care of months before a play ever hits the stage. All of this behind the scenes business takes quite a long time, I'm afraid," the man says with authority.

"At any rate," he continues, "I'll patch you through to speak with my assistant, Carolyn. You can set up a time with her to come by and sign the contract. Your agent has already approved the final draft, that's why I was surprised when I suddenly had difficulty reaching him..." his voice trails off.

"Say," Murray says, "I have more than one number to reach him at, could you tell me which one you have been trying?"

"Sure," Mr. Meyer says. There is the sound of papers shuffling. "Here it is," he says, giving the number to Murray. "Can you ask him to call me right away when you reach him?"

"I sure will," Murray says.

"Very well, then," Mr. Meyer says. "Hold on and I will transfer you to Carolyn."

Murray shrugs his shoulders and shakes his head while he waits.

"Yes," the woman says, "Mr. Bardos? This is Carolyn Gentry."

"Yes," Murray says.

"All right, I need to set up a time for you to come in to sign...Is there anyway you can stop by later today?" She asks hopefully.

"Uh, let me see here," Murray says pausing. "What time were you thinking about?"

"Whatever time is convenient for you," the woman says. "It will only take a few minutes."

Murray sets up a time for later in the afternoon.

"Very good. That should do it," Carolyn says. "I look forward to seeing you later today. Oh, while I have you on the phone, I just want to verify we have the name spelled right, and that everything is in order. The way we set things up now will be how it appears later in the advertisements and on the posters and playbill."

"Okay," Murray says.

"The title is 'Subway Vision.' That's S-U-B-W-A-Y V-I-S-I-O-N. Is that correct?" The woman asks.

"Uh, yes," Murray says, shaking his head and looking more confused than ever.

"All right. And your name is Murray Y. Bardos, is that correct?" She asks, spelling it out.

"Yes," Murray responds.

"Having a 'y' for a middle initial is a bit unusual," the woman says pleasantly. "May I ask you what it stands for?" She asks.

"Yardley," Murray replies.

"Yardley," the woman says. "Oh, as in the soap?"

"Yes," Murray answers, chuckling.

"Okay, but you don't want your middle name spelled out, then? You just want, 'Murray Y. Bardos'?" She asks.

"Yes," Murray says. "Actually," he adds, "Can we just have my initials, 'M.Y. Bardos'?"

"Oh, certainly," the woman says. "Anyway you like it. Anyway at all."

"All right, then," Murray says confidently. "Make it m.y. bardos...all in small letters. Is that okay?"

"Certainly," Carolyn says. "m.y. bardos, all in lower-case letters. Well, that should about do it. We'll have the paperwork ready for you to sign when you come in this afternoon. Oh, did Mr. Meyer tell you to have your agent call us? I have left several messages, but he hasn't returned my calls."

"I know. I'll be sure to tell him," Murray says.

"We'll see you later today, then," she says. "Good-bye."

"Yes," Murray says, "Good-bye."

Murray hangs up the phone, darts into the kitchen, and grabs the note on the counter that Kirby left for him. He checks the number on the note against the number he just received from Lyn Meyer. Murray stands there for several minutes scratching his head.

"Juno," he says finally.

Murray walks back down the hallway towards his room, shaking his head all the while, and muttering the words, "Subway Vision." He walks into the bedroom, picks up Shadow's box, and cradles it gently. "I wish you were here, buddy," he says, rocking back and forth.

IX

Murray wakes up early on Saturday morning and checks to make sure Kirby's car is not out front. He makes a pot of coffee from Kirby's coffeemaker, and then showers and shaves. While he sips his coffee, he does a once-over of the apartment.

He had already been very careful to pack everything he wanted on Friday, before the shipping company came and picked up the cartons. Still, he had been in a hurry to get everything packed and get it out the door, before Kirby came back from class. Besides, Murray mumbles to himself, double-checking is good. You can never be too careful.

He walks into his bedroom to do one final check there. In the corner sits his backpack. It is filled with a few sundries, a book, some cigarettes, and a couple changes of underwear and clean socks. Inside the hidden compartment is Shadow's box, which has been carefully wrapped and tucked in between some clean shirts. The outer section holds his notepads and pens, and three envelopes, already addressed and stamped.

Murray sits down in his old, ripped, leather chair and looks around the bedroom. Only a very careful observer would notice that he was never coming back again. He had taken so very little from the rest of the house, that Kirby did not have a clue. The bed, chair, bookcases, most of the books, and television, were all staying, as was most everything in the kitchen, and the other beat-up furniture in the rest of the house. He would have dishes, silverware, cooking pots, and furniture at the furnished house he had just rented on a short-term lease.

All he had decided to pack and ship off were the few clothes he owned, a bound copy of his play, his tape recorder, several of his favorite books, a clock-radio and a telephone, his typewriter, some typing paper and notes, an ashtray and coffee mug, and his old metal coffee pot. Of course, the artwork of the buses whizzing by was shipped too. Murray had ordered a special box to be made for it, just so it could pass the shipping requirements.

He walks into the kitchen and pours a fresh cup of coffee. After a couple of gulps, he reaches into his pants pocket, and pulls out several new, hundred dollar bills. He opens up the never-used, porcelain cookie jar left behind from two roommates earlier, and drops in the money. Next, he reaches into his pocket for the apartment key. He takes if off his key-chain and drops the key in, along with the money.

He carries the mug of coffee over to his old chair in the living room and sits down. He stays there for several minutes, just looking around and occasionally muttering to himself. Suddenly, the ringing of the telephone interrupts his thoughts. Murray walks over and turns up the volume on the phone recorder.

"Mosh, Hi. Just calling to remind you...as if you needed reminding. (The man laughs.) The Big night...Opening night, *tonight*. I'll meet you backstage at the Metro. Four o'clock, sharp. Okay? Oh, just to let you know, I checked with Carolyn. It's confirmed. Full house tonight. For the entire run, as well. All sold out. See you then."

Murray smiles, erases the message, and walks into the kitchen. When he finishes the end of his coffee, he rinses the mug in the kitchen sink, and shuts off the coffeemaker. Then he walks into the bedroom, picks up his backpack, and does one final look around. "Come on, Shadow," he says to the air. "Let's blow this Popsicle stand."

He closes the bedroom door behind him, and heads out the back way. As Murray squeezes through the break in the fence for the final time, Jake runs over to the edge and watches. "So long, Jake," Murray whispers. Jake barks twice and wags his tail.

Murray takes the BART, and then the bus, transferring three times, to Pacifica. When he arrives, the tourists and the surfers have already taken over the beach. Murray climbs unsteadily down a steep hill, and walks alongside the ocean for quite awhile until he finds a private little alcove surrounded by large rocks.

He sits there for a long time watching the ocean, then reaches in his backpack and carefully takes out Shadow's box. "I always planned to take you to the beach someday, buddy," Murray says, chuckling. A few moments later, his eyes have filled with tears.

Murray sits watching the waves and talking to Shadow for well over an hour. Then he carefully wraps the box, and places it back into the backpack. Next, he pulls out his notepad, envelopes, and a pen. He writes the words, "Dear Mother" and then stops. He looks out at the ocean for several minutes, shakes his head, and then picks up the pen again and begins to write.

Dear Mother,

It will probably be awhile before you hear from me again. Don't try and contact me, I have left the Bay Area.

I am sorry for disrupting your version of reality. I should never have done that. Illusions are protection. I should have respected that. At the very least, everyone should have the right to exist in his or her own reality. I hope you accept my apology for upsetting you.

I will not tell you where I am going or what I will be doing. It's probably better if you just make up your own mind on that. I will write to you sometime, but I'm not sure when that will be.

Take care, and don't worry about me.

Murray

P.S. Shadow died.

Murray folds the paper, places it inside the envelope with his mother's name and address on it, and seals it. Then he picks up his pen and begins to write again.

Dear Kirby,

I am shoving off. I have left the utility money and an extra month's rent in the cookie jar, along with my key. You should have no problem finding a new roommate within a day or two...finding one who is not an odd-boy might take a bit longer (ha, ha!).

I am leaving you all of the furniture and kitchen things. Most of it is junk, but no sense in you having to go out and buy all that sort of stuff...I know you like to travel light.

I enjoyed our many conversations and have learned much from you. I will miss hearing your take on the "latest American myth", as you put it.

I am off, as you would say, to create a new reality. If anyone calls for me, tell them I died. For all intents and purposes, it is true.

Best wishes in your future endeavors,

Murray

P.S. I agree with your perspective that above all, we have to respect other people's choices.

Murray reads the letter, folds the paper, and places it inside the envelope with Kirby's name on it.

He picks up his pen and writes, "Dear Mollie," then he stops, lays the pen down, and lights up a cigarette. He sits thinking, and staring out at the ocean, for a long time. Several times he picks up his notepad and begins to write, but stops, and lays the paper down again.

Finally, after some half an hour, Murray picks up his pen and writes.

Dear Mollie,

A while ago I told you I might be leaving. That time has come.

I know you will have difficulty understanding why I had to do things this way, but you must know that I am doing what I have to do.

My life will never be the same for having known you. Those who have said you are held together with paperclips and rubber bands were WRONG. It is an erroneous perception. I hope that someday you too, will be able to see the complete picture.

I will miss your sense of humor and comforting smile, and I will never forget how you helped me through everything with Shadow.

I wish you the best with your paintings. I expect to see them in a gallery some day (though I would advise against having your opening with any artists whose focus is on body parts...ha, ha!).

I hope that someday you will be able to forgive me for leaving. The paradox of our illusions is that we all strive to fill the need to be connected, but in the end, none of us are.

Take care.
With love, Murray

P.S. I am sending you mental Gummy Bears.
Be happy, my friend.

Murray folds the last letter, places it inside the envelope with Mollie's name and address on it, and seals it. Then he puts all three envelopes and his notepad and pen inside his backpack, and takes off for one final walk along the ocean.

By the time Murray finally climbs up the hill and crosses the Coast Highway towards the bus stop, many of the tourists have left. Only a group of die-hard surfers, a few locals, and those determined to get the absolute most from their vacation dollars, remain.

Murray waits for the bus for nearly half an hour. Finally, he digs the schedule out of his backpack, and double-checks the arrival time. He gives it another ten minutes or so, then walks back to the Beach-Comber Convenient Store to check the time.

Murray enters the store and looks up at the clock above the cash register. Three fifty-two. "Oh, no," he mutters. "Damn it!"

He walks back outside, cursing and hitting his fist against his forehead. "You are such an *idiot*!" He yells.

Murray walks back to the bus stop and pulls out the schedule again. "The next bus does not arrive until 5:10. Shit," he says to no one. "What am I going to do? What am I going to do?" He mutters.

He waits for a clearing in the traffic, and then crosses the highway again to a parking lot with surfboards tied to the roofs of several vehicles. He stands at the exit to the parking area and sticks out his thumb.

Within fifteen or twenty minutes, a young man with sun-bleached hair who is slipping off his wetsuit beside a Jeep, yells over, "I'm goin' to Daly City. Where you headed?"

Murray puts his arm down and jogs over towards the Jeep. "The city," he says, out of breath. "But Daly City will be fine. I can take the BART in from there."

"Cool," the surfer says. "Actually, I go right past the BART station on my way home. I can drop you off there. I'll be a couple of minutes, though," he says pulling his jeans up and fastening the buttons. "Have to strap my board on."

Murray nods. "Okay by me," he says, smiling. "Thanks a lot. I guess I missed my bus and I'm suppose to be in the city at four o'clock."

The surfer looks up at the sun and laughs.

"*Whoa.* You're late, dude."

"I know," Murray says in a disappointed tone. "Can I give you a hand with anything?" Murray asks.

"Nah. You can just get in. I'll only be another minute or so," the surfer says, pulling the cord around, up, and over the board and looping it through the rack on the roof of the Jeep.

In a few minutes, Murray is flying down Pacific Coast Highway with the Butt-hole Surfers screaming something on the CD player about how we can never be sure just how we look through other people's eyes. Within twenty minutes or so, he is waiting at the BART station headed for San Francisco.

It takes another half an hour before Murray is climbing the stairs out of the subway. He considers walking the rest of the way, but when he spots a cab half a block away, he flags it down and hops inside.

"Metropolitan Playhouse," he says, out of breath.

The driver looks at him curiously. "You sure you want the Metro?" He asks Murray, eyeing his appearance up and down.

"Yes," Murray says emphatically. "I'm sure."

In another ten minutes, Murray is at the theatre. He tries opening the door at the back of the theatre. Locked. He heads around to the front of the building, and sees a crowd of well-dressed people entering the theatre, and several more milling about close to the door. He starts to climb the steps towards the main entrance when he hears, "Mosh! Over here!" He looks up and sees Juno motioning furiously with his hands. Murray walks over to where Juno is and follows him inside a back door.

The second bell sounds and people begin flooding in more quickly and taking their seats. Murray and Juno walk to the back of the theatre near a door marked, "No Entrance."

"Sorry I'm late," Murray says when they finally stop.

"You missed the entire first act!" Juno says. "You missed seeing the great reaction the people had to the first act!" He pauses. "I thought you were the punctual type."

"Yeah," Murray says, "I thought *you* were a jewel thief."

There is a pause.

"I *am*," Juno says, smiling. His eyes twinkle.

The two men are silent for several seconds.

Then, Juno says, "Listen, it's going *great*. The audience response so far is *very* positive. They laughed in all the right places."

"That's great to hear!" Murray says, smiling.

"Yeah," Juno says, "and I spotted three critics up in front." Juno motions with his hand. "They seem to be enjoying it as well."

Murray smiles broadly.

"But…" Juno pauses. "There *is* a problem, though."

Just then the house lights dim and the audience begin to "*sshhh*" one another.

Juno leans his head in close to Murray's and says in a low voice, "There's two men over there. Row M, about the middle,'" he says, pointing. Murray nods. "Very suspicious. They've been looking around a lot the entire time. They're with another guy in a black car. I went out for a smoke about halfway through the first act and he was sitting in the car talking on the phone."

Murray is silent.

"As soon as the second act ends," Juno whispers, "and the audience applauds and gets up, you take the exit behind the back stage, out. I have a car there waiting for you. He'll take you to the station."

Murray nods.

"I'll cover for you at the reception," Juno says. "You won't be disappointed you're not going, will you?"

"Like missing a dental appointment," Murray says, smiling.

"Here," Juno says, handing Murray an envelope. Murray looks inside. It is filled with cash. "It will tide you over until you get settled-in. There will be more, of course. Especially given the sell-out crowd here tonight."

Murray smiles. The theatre goes dark and the curtains open.

"Oh...and, Mosh," Juno whispers. "Be sure you call just as soon as you get to the end of the line. I want to know you made it there okay."

"I will," Murray says, smiling. "I will."

Murray and Juno face forward as the play begins.

~ ~ ~ ~

Subway Vision
Act II

The second act begins with the subway doors opening, and several people getting aboard. Eleven people take seats in the back of the train car, next to Diane's corpse. Several other people walk to the opposite end of the car and sit down. Some sit behind Barry and the Homeless Man, others sit on the other side of the aisle, behind the prosecutor.

In the center of the car, a man with a black robe, carrying a gavel, sits down behind a waist-high partition separating the seats from the exit. He faces in the direction of the defense (Homeless Man) and the prosecution (Mr. Corner). The seat directly across from the judge remains empty. Mosh moves over and sits in the seat directly behind Barry.

Judge: Are we ready to bring this court into session?

Prosecution: The Prosecution is ready, Your Honor.

Defense: Wait just a minute, Your Honor. We did not get to choose the jury. We don't even know who they are.

Judge: Well, of course you do. They are a jury of the Defendant's *peers.* There is nothing else you need to know.

Defense: But how do we know these are his *peers?* By the looks of them, they certainly do not seem like his *peers.* You would never hang out with these people, would you Barry?

(Barry shakes his head "no".)

Prosecution: Your Honor, I take issue with the implication here. We did the very best we could, given that, well, *look* at him. (Prosecutor gestures towards Barry) Does he look like a man who even has anyone who might actually *be* a peer?

Defense: Objection, Your Honor.

Judge: Sustained. I will remind the Prosecution to not discuss your personal observations in open court.

Prosecution: Well, in actuality, we did find twelve of his peers, Your Honor, but none of the people in the psychiatric ward were registered to vote.

(Several people snicker.)

Defense: At the very least, Your Honor, we object to the fact that one of the jury members is dead (points to Diane) and therefore, is unable to speak.

Judge: The way things are looking, Counsel, that is a factor that lies in your client's best interest. All right...where is the bailiff? Let's get this thing started.

Bailiff: All rise.

(The passengers stand. Defense/Homeless Man helps Barry, who is chained to the seat, to stand.)

Bailiff: This court will now come to order. The Honorable Judge Joseph P. Iniquitous, presiding. You may be seated.

(The passengers all sit down.)

Judge: Mr. Barry Yeldray, do you understand the charges of medical malpractice being waged against you?

Barry:	Yes.
Judge:	How do you plead?
Barry:	*Please, please.*
Judge:	Counsel, remind your client this is a courtroom.

(The Defense/Homeless Man whispers something to Barry.)

Judge:	Mr. Yeldray, how do you plead?
Barry:	Not guilty, Your Honor. Definitely, 100% not guilty.
Judge:	Duly noted. Are we ready for opening statements?
Prosecution:	Yes, Your Honor.
Defense:	We are, Your Honor.
Judge:	Very well, then. Let's begin.
Prosecution:	Ladies and gentlemen of the jury, we are here about a very serious matter. I would like to thank each and every one of you for stepping up to the plate and making a commitment to do your civic duty.
Juror #1:	(turning to Juror #2) I didn't realize we had a choice, did you?

(Juror #2 shrugs and shakes his head.)

Prosecution:	You are here today to determine if the Defendant here (gestures towards Barry) is guilty of medical malpractice...a very serious matter, indeed. We will *prove* to you, ladies and gentlemen of the jury, beyond a shadow of a doubt, that the Defendant, Mr. Barry Yeldray, is, in fact, guilty of

the crime he is accused of. The People of the United States government are relying on you, ladies and gentlemen, to do the right thing. And, after hearing the testimony of our witnesses, I have no doubt but that you will make this determination. (looking at the judge) That is all.

Judge: All right, is the Defense ready for their opening statement?

Defense: Yes, Your Honor.

(Defense/Homeless man walks over to where the jury is seated. He steps up to Juror #1 and holds up his fist.)

Defense: Rock, Paper, Scissors. Ready? One, two, three.

(Defense/Homeless Man and Juror #1 hold their hands out)

Defense: Ah-ha. I have scissors. Scissors cut paper. Sorry. You lose.

(Defense/Homeless man moves to the next juror.)

Defense: Ready? One, two, three. Ah-ha. I have rock. Rock smashes scissors. Sorry. You lose. Okay. Who is next?

(Several jurors raise their hands.)

Defense:	All right...You there, Juror #6. Are you ready? One, two, three. *Ohhh*, Sorry. I have paper. Paper covers rock. You lose.
Juror #6:	I thought rock was stronger than paper, so rock should win.
Defense:	It's an illusion. Besides, something does not have to be physically stronger to be superior.

(Judge nods)

Prosecution:	*Ob*jection! Your Honor, this is highly irregular.
Judge:	Over-ruled. Let's see where he is going with this. Proceed, Counsel.
Mosh:	(talking to Barry) These are definitely *not* your peers. You're much better at Rock, Paper, Scissors than this.
Defense:	Okay. Who would like to have their fortunes told?

(Several jurors and the Judge raise their hands excitedly.)

Defense:	Juror #8, then. Hold out your palm so I can read it. Hmm. Hmm...ah-ha...Oh!...Well, Juror #8, it appears you will be coming in to a lot of money.....Has your palm been itching lately? (Juror #8 nods) Well, then, that settles it. It will come soon. *Very soon.* All right. Anyone else?

(Several hands shoot up again.)

Defense:	Okay. How about Juror #12? (moves closer to the juror) Okay. Let me see your palm. Ah-ha...hmm...well, you will have a very long life...a healthy one at that. Are you healthy, Juror #12?
Juror #12:	Never been sick a day in my life.
Defense:	Well, there you have it. (several jurors clap and nod) How about Juror #9, there? (several jurors look towards Diane) She appears to be a little shy. Juror #8, would you mind holding her hand up so I can read her palm?

(Juror #8 complies)

Defense:	Oh...oh...oh, no...I'm afraid I have bad news, dear. For all intents and purposes, you appear to be dead as a doornail, Juror #9.
Prosecution:	Objection, Your Honor. The Defense has turned this proceeding into a dog-and-pony show.
Juror #5:	(whispering to Juror #6) Oh, I *love* dog shows!
Judge:	Sustained. Counsel, get to the point of your opening statement and stop wasting the court's time. Remember, Counsel, the Court must get off in four exits.
Defense:	Your Honor, ladies and gentlemen of the jury, we have no opening argument.

(Muttering comes from the jury.)

Defense:	And the reason is that we will prove there is no possible way the Defendant, Mr. Barry Yeldray,

could have committed the crime of medical malpractice. That is all, Your Honor.

(Defense bows to the Judge.)

Judge:	Very well. It's *your* funeral. Is the Prosecution ready to call their first witness?
Prosecution:	Yes, Your Honor. The Prosecution calls Ms. Michelle Holden to the stand.

(Witness is sworn in and takes the empty seat next to the Judge.)

Prosecution:	Would you state your name for the court?
Witness #1:	Michelle Holden...With an *"H."* (adds with importance)
Judge:	You don't say, Ms. Holden. I thought it was with a "W."
Prosecution:	Thank you, Ms. Holden. Now then, why don't you tell the jury just how you were acquainted with the Defendant.
Witness #1:	He was my doctor...my psychiatrist.
Prosecution:	And what was he treating you for?
Witness #1:	Anorexia Nervosa. But he also diagnosed me with Narcissistic Personality Disorder.
Mosh:	(in a low voice) It's a wonder she could tear herself away from the mirror long enough to be here.
Prosecution:	I see. Well, why don't you tell the jury about why you initially came forward as a government witness. What exactly, in your words, happened?

Witness #1:   Well, everything was going along fine. I mean, the first twenty sessions I spent telling him about all of my problems.

Mosh: Well, as much as she could *get to* in twenty sessions.

Witness #1:   He was good about just listening and not interrupting too much to ask questions. But then, one day, he said it was time for me to start making some changes and...well, I just could not believe it.

(Witness starts crying. Prosecutor shakes his head.)

Prosecution: I know it is difficult, but try to go on, Ms. Holden. The jury needs to hear this.

Witness #1:   (wiping away her tears and looking at the jury) He told me that I needed to stop thinking that I was...that I was...(cries some more, then gains composure) He said I needed to stop thinking that I was the center of the universe!

(Gasps and mutterings can be heard from the jury.)

Witness #1:   He said that I was *wrong* for getting upset and yelling at my girlfriend for canceling our plans on my birthday because her father died...she wasn't even that close to him. And it was *my birthday*!

(Witness cries some more. "*Tsk. Tsks*" can be heard from the jury. The Prosecutor shakes his head.

Mosh:	Ridiculous! You should have just marched right in to that funeral parlor with your cake and party hats. That would have shown her.
Judge:	(smacking his gavel down) Let's have quiet in this courtroom.
Witness #1:	(indignantly) Yeah, quiet. *I'm* talking. You should be listening to *me*. *I'm* the one who's important here.
Prosecution:	Go on, Ms. Holden.
Witness #1:	He said that I used food to draw attention to myself and to manipulate others. I couldn't believe it. He told me that I starved myself to make sure my father would pay attention to me because I needed to be the center of everyone's attention.
Juror #11:	(talking to Juror #12) Starving herself? Really? She looks a little chunky to me. (Juror #12 nods)
Prosecution:	And what was his solution to help you overcome your emotional disabilities?
Mosh:	She could start by taking the words "I" and "me" out of her vocabulary.
Witness #1:	He actually said, I couldn't believe it, that I needed to stop manipulating people and to stop feeling like everybody owed me something. He said I should start by seeing that I *wasn't that important* in the bigger scheme of things! (sniffles and wipes her eyes) I'll never forget those words!

(Witness starts to cry. Several jury members shake their heads.)

Witness #1:	He told me to eat something and to realize that I wasn't so important that everyone was always

248

looking at me. He said that if I gained fifty pounds no one would even care! He said that, in fact, I wasn't even that good-looking, let alone that important, so I should just get out of my fantasy world and realize it...and that if I couldn't do that much, that at the very least, I should refrain from ever having children!

(Witness breaks down in sobs. The jury gasps. Mosh snickers.)

Prosecution: And what has happened to you as a result of the Defendant's treatment?

Mosh: Now she's had to enroll in art school.

Prosecution: (giving Mosh a dirty look) Go on, Ms. Holden.

Witness#1: Well, I became so upset and depressed that I had to give up my job and move back in with my father so that he could take care of me.

Mosh: Do you think he'll do a better job the second time around?

Prosecution: (shaking his head in disgust) No further questions, Your Honor.

Judge: Does the Defense have any questions?

Defense: Ah, yes Your Honor. (gets up and approaches witness, unwrapping a candy-bar) Care for a candy-bar, Ms. Holden? (Witness shakes her head) No....I didn't think so. (turning to Barry) Barry, care for some candy?

(Barry nods his head and takes a piece of candy.)

Prosecution:	(standing up) Objection, Your Honor! Defense cannot just give his client candy in a willy-nilly fashion without sharing it with the rest of the court!
Defense:	Your Honor, I would like to invoke the attorney-client privilege.
Judge:	(nods) Very well.
Conductor:	(unintelligible announcement) ...reminding you that there is no eating on the train.
Defense:	Ms. Holden, isn't it true that the only reason the first twenty sessions went so well, in your opinion, was because *you* were doing all the talking about *yourself*? (shakes her head) *Ms. Holden?*
Witness #1:	No.
Defense:	(biting candy-bar) And isn't it true that the advice the Defendant gave you was the very same thing your family and ex-fiancé had been saying to you for *years*, Ms. Holden?
Mosh:	Fiancé? And just who was the pantywaist engaged to this woman?

(Several people turn and look in Mosh's direction.)

Witness #1:	He should have offered better advice.
Defense:	I see. And what would that have been, Ms. Holden? To help you to convince your family, friends, bosses, and neighbors that what *you* want and need should come *first,* above everyone else's needs?
Witness #1:	Yes. I mean no. I mean...
Defense:	(lighting a cigarette) Ms. Holden, I'm going to ask you to play a little game with me.

Prosecution:	Objection, Your Honor. I hope this isn't going to be more of his Rock, Paper, Scissors buffoonery.
Juror #10:	Actually, I kind of enjoyed playing that game.
Defense:	Ms. Holden, I want you to close your eyes and imagine that there is a fire in this court. (waves smoke in her face) Everyone but you is overcome with smoke. They are still alive, but just barely.
Mosh:	I like this game.
Defense:	(continues to wave cigarette smoke in her face) You have just enough time to escape and take just one of the jury members with you and save his or her life. Who do you take, Ms. Holden?
Mosh:	Take the dead one. No chance she'll steal the spotlight afterwards.

(Witness opens her eyes. She looks at the jury and then at the Defense attorney.)

Witness #1:	It's a trick. You're trying to trick me! (pauses) I can't help anyone else. If I take the time to help someone else, then I might not get out safely myself!

(There is muttering among the jury.)

Conductor:	(unintelligible sound) ...would like to remind you that for the convenience of our living passengers, smoking is prohibited on the subway.
Defense:	No further questions, Your Honor. (stomps out cigarette)

Judge: The witness is excused.

(The woman returns to her original seat.)

Judge: The Prosecution may call the next witness.
Prosecution: The People call Ms. Victoria Darnell, Your Honor.

(The witness is sworn and takes a seat.)

Prosecution: Would you state your name, please?
Witness #2:   Ms. Victoria Darnell. D-A-R-N-E-L-L.
Prosecution: Thank you, Ms. Darnell. Would you tell us how you are acquainted with the Defendant?
Witness #2:   He was my...my psychiatrist.
Prosecution: I see. Perhaps you could enlighten the jury as to why you were seeing him.
Witness #2:   Well, I was having a lot of problems. I mean, I came to him because my husband was cheating on me. (gasps come from the jury) And also, my boss was sexually harassing me, and I had to stay at that job because I was just fired from my previous job, and, well, there were just a lot of people out to hurt me like some of my coworkers, and my next door neighbor. Also, my family...
Mosh: Don't forget the Center for the Blind
Prosecution: I see. And will you tell the jury the Defendant's reaction to your cries for help?
Witness #2:   (sniffling) He told me, I remember it perfectly because it was really cold, he told me that everyone was always exactly where they wanted to be!

Prosecution: Those were his exact words, Ms. Darnell?
Witness #2:   Yes. Exactly. I was so shocked. I depended on him to help me figure out how I was going to protect myself from everyone who was trying to hurt me...
Mosh: Did you consider an Iron-Lung?

(Witness looks at Mosh and then sighs.)

Witness #2:   And *he* tells me, well, in essence, that I actually *wanted* to be hurt.

(Gasps and muttering can be heard from the jury.)

Prosecution: Did he give any logic, any reason for this assessment, Ms. Darnell?
Mosh: Besides the fact that you are a DOORMAT?
Witness #2:   He said I was a Professional Victim! (cries) I came to him for help, and he said I whined too much. And I didn't think that was true. I mean, it isn't my fault all of these bad things keep happening to me. But he said I had to start taking responsibility for my own life choices and actions. He said...(wipes her eyes and blows her nose) he said...

(Defense/Homeless Man gets out a violin and begins playing. A couple of jurors get up and drop money into his cup.)

Witness #2:	He said that I had a history of getting into situations where I played the role of victim. He said I must be getting something out of taking the victim role all of the time. I couldn't believe it! (she cries)
Prosecution:	So what method of treatment did he suggest, Ms. Darnell? What did he suggest you do to overcome your problems?
Witness #2:	He wanted me to make a concrete plan for getting out of the unhealthy relationship with my husband, and for getting out of the situation with my boss, and my problems with my family, and coworkers always taking advantage of me.

(Defense/Homeless Man leans over her and plays the violin loudly.)

Witness #2:	(shaking her head) People are always taking advantage of me. Even strangers. They must see me coming, I don't know. I've been mugged six times in the past two years. Maybe it's because I am so nice...
Mosh:	Your Honor, can we require the witness to look up "nice" in the dictionary? I think she means "stupid."
Judge:	(slamming his gavel) Quiet!
Witness #2:	Anyway, he wanted me to create what he called a "workable action plan." I could not believe it. I was paying him to help me, and here he is telling me *I* need to start taking responsibility for my own life choices and to make a plan to take action to change things. *That's no way to act when someone comes to you for help!*

Mosh:	No. You should make them a warm bath of Epsom salts and fix up the spare bedroom.
Prosecution:	And, Ms. Darnell, did this so-called therapy have any ill effects on you?
Mosh:	What about the therapist? Did she have any ill effects on *him*?
Defense:	(putting the violin down) Objection. Leading the witness, Your Honor.
Judge:	Sustained. Rephrase the question, Counsel.
Prosecution:	Did the Defendant's treatment or therapy have *any* results?
Witness #2:	Yes, there were results. Everything fell apart because of his advice and now my life is *ruined.* (starts crying) I just can't handle it when people are...forceful. I don't like to be around aggressive types of people. They make me...well, uncomfortable and that's what I feel like the Defendant was. I couldn't stand up to him, so I just did what he said and now...(she cries)...now, my husband has left me and I was fired again. All because of *him.* (she points to Barry and begins wailing)
Mosh:	Somebody ought to smack that chick.

(The witness wails louder.)

Judge:	(looking at Mosh) Silence in the court. One more outburst like that and I will turn you out at the next exit.
Prosecution:	The witness is obviously under duress. Obviously, her testimony thus far speaks volumes. No more questions, Your Honor.
Juror #2:	Did he just say the witness is under her dress?

Juror #3:	(shrugs) No, I *think* he said there's *volumes* under her dress.
Juror #2:	*Ohh.*
Judge:	Does the Defense Counsel have any questions?
Defense:	Yes, Your Honor. (stands and faces the witness) Could you tell the court, Ms. Darnell, about the time in your life when people were not trying to do bad things to you.

(There is silence.)

Defense:	Ms. Darnell? A time in which people were not out to harm you.

(Silence again.)

Defense:	*Ms. Darnell?*
Witness #2:	I guess there hasn't been any such time, now that I think about it. There's always been someone...even when I was a child, my sisters... (voice trails off, begins to cry)
Mosh:	Don't forget about Ken...and that *Bitch*, Barbie.
Defense:	So, Ms. Darnell, are you telling the court that you have been a victim your *entire life?*
Witness #2:	I...I guess so...yes.
Defense:	Do you know anyone else personally who has been a victim their *entire life?*
Witness #2:	No, not that I can think of. Not personally.
Defense:	If that's the only life you have ever known, being a victim, that is, then it must have been pretty frightening when someone suggested that you do

	something to *change* your life, wasn't it, Ms. Darnell?
Witness #2:	Yes. No. I don't know, I guess.
Defense:	Ms. Darnell, did the Defendant at any time ever suggest to you that with all of your whining about being victimized, that perhaps you should pack it all in and move to the Bay Area? Perhaps become a PBS lifetime member and buy yourself a subscription to the Utne Reader?

(Mosh snickers.)

Prosecution:	Objection, Your Honor! Badgering the witness.
Juror #6:	(talking to Juror #7) Oh, *badgers*. (shakes her head) We had a badger in our vacation home one summer. We thought we would *never* get rid of him. He would go through our garbage and make just an *awful* mess. Every night the noise would have me waking up my husband to search for prowlers.
Juror #7:	Are you sure it wasn't a possum?
Juror #6:	You know...maybe so...but either way, I sympathize with the witness.
Juror #7:	Me too. (both nod in agreement)
Judge:	We'll have to end testimony here because this witness's exit is coming up.
Defense:	Very well.
Judge:	(looking at witness as train stops at station and doors open) You may step down. The Prosecution may call the next witness.

(Woman exits the train.)

257

Prosecution:	We call Mr. Curtis Lendel to the stand. (Witness approaches, is sworn in, and is seated) Please state your name for the court.
Witness #3:	Curtis, that's with a "C", Lendel, L-E-N-D-E-L.
Prosecution:	Thank you. Now, Mr. Lendel, please tell the court just how you came to know the Defendant.
Witness #3:	Yes. He was my doctor. Well, actually, my shrink. You know, my psychiatrist.
Prosecution:	And what were you seeing him for, Mr. Lendel?
Witness #3:	I was having problems with my life in general. Managing my life, I guess you could say.
Mosh:	*Twit.*
Prosecution:	And how did that go? The treatment, or the relationship with the Defendant...was it satisfactory?
Witness #3:	Well, it was all right at first. I went to a lot of sessions and for the most part, he would ask me questions, and I spent most of the time answering them. You know, telling him about my problems with relationships, problems with my family, work problems, problems with people in general, and...my problems coping with life.
Mosh:	To remember "Continu*ous* ," think... "One-Unending-Stream."
Prosecution:	But there came a time when things were no longer going as you thought they should?
Witness #3:	Yes. (rolling his eyes) There definitely came such a time.
Prosecution:	Could you tell the jury about it?
Witness #3:	Well, I asked him what exactly was wrong with me and what I should do. He said I had "idiopathic nuttiness."

(Defense/Homeless Man chuckles.)

Witness #3:	I've since checked...There's no such thing.
Mosh:	There *must* be such a thing, because he's *definitely* got it.
Witness #3:	Anyway, he said I was only comfortable when my life was chaotic, so that I kept creating chaos over and over. Then he said what I needed to do...get this...was to stop wearing my mental illness around like a badge of honor.

(Muttering can be heard from the jury.)

Mosh:	(slapping Barry on the shoulder) Way to go, dude.
Prosecution:	And what happened to you as a result of the Defendant's treatment?
Witness #3:	My new therapist says, that thanks to the Defendant over there (points toward Barry) I may now be *permanently damaged*! I may be unable to ever really trust anyone who tries to help me ever again.
Mosh:	To remember "Histri*onics*," think..."Over-reacting-Nuts-In-Crisis."
Judge:	I'm not going to keep reminding you to be silent while this court is in session. (glares at Mosh) The Prosecution may proceed.
Prosecution:	I think the testimony of this witness has proven our case. No further questions, Your Honor.
Juror #11:	Now, whose side is this guy on again?

(Several jurors shrug.)

Judge:	Does the Defense have any questions for this witness?
Defense:	Just one, Your Honor. (turning to the witness) In your presence, Mr. Lendel, are you aware of anyone who has ever referred to you as a "Candy-Ass"?
Prosecution:	Objection, Your Honor.
Judge:	On what grounds?
Prosecution:	This line of questioning is irrelevant.
Defense:	Your Honor, the Prosecutor is irrelevant!
Judge:	Sustained. Are you finished, Counsel?
Defense:	(smiling) Just one more thing, Your Honor. (picks up panhandling cup and approaches witness, shaking it) Do you have any spare change?

(Witness makes a face & reaches in his pocket for spare change.)

Defense:	Bless you! I would like to give you this. (holds up a tattered badge) I know it's not quite as good as a mental illness badge, but someone dropped it in my cup last week. It's a Boy Scout badge for knot-tying.

(Witness takes the badge, then returns to his original seat.)

Judge:	Does the Prosecution have any more witnesses?
Prosecution:	Just one more, Your Honor. We would like to call Dr. Eli Vaughan to the stand.

(The witness approaches, is sworn in, and is seated.)

Prosecution:	Dr. Vaughan, would you state your full name for the court, please?
Witness #4:	Yes. Dr. Eli Vaughan. V-A-U-G-H-A-N.
Prosecution:	Thank you, Dr. Vaughan. Please tell the jury how you are acquainted with the Defendant.
Witness #4:	I worked with him. He was a colleague at Pitsore Medical School and Hospital.
Prosecution:	How long did you work together, Dr. Vaughan?
Witness #4:	Six years. We both started at just about the same time.
Prosecution:	When was the last time you saw the defendant before today?
Witness #4:	Not for a couple of years now. Not since he quit and left the hospital.
Prosecution:	Do you recognize this, (holding up object) Dr. Vaughan?
Witness #4:	Yes. It's the Defendant's stethoscope.
Prosecution:	And how did it get here?
Witness #4:	You asked me to bring it in.
Prosecution:	Your Honor, I would like to offer this stethoscope as Exhibit A. (holding it up again)
Judge:	Very well. Proceed.
Juror #10:	(leans forward to Juror #5) I can't see that from back here, what is that?
Juror #5	I can't think of the name, but it's that really important thing that doctor's need to tell them what's wrong with you. (both nod)
Prosecution:	Dr. Vaughan, tell the jury if you will, what your impression was of the Defendant's work.
Witness #4:	Well, I was aware there were complaints. The ones we heard here today. I felt it was my duty to report those complaints. My obligation. I immediately filed official reports with both the hospital and the medical board.

Mosh:	(mimicking witness's voice) And then I was so worked up I went inside my office and masturbated for half an hour from the excitement.
Prosecution:	So there were serious problems when you worked with him. Problems that could, in your professional opinion, be interpreted as medical malpractice?
Witness #4:	Yes.
Juror #1:	(to Juror #2) I'm not sure who it is we're trying, but somebody should *definitely* go to jail here.
Juror #2:	I think so *too*. I'm *definitely* voting guilty.
Prosecution:	That's all, Your Honor. The People rest.
Juror #10:	(to Juror #9) Oh good, I'm exhausted.
Judge:	Does the Defense wish to cross-examine this witness?
Defense:	Yes, Your Honor. (addressing the witness) You are a medical doctor, are you not?
Witness #4:	Yes. I am.
Defense:	Then let me ask you this. Why is it that when people get into car accidents, their shoes always fly off?
Prosecution:	Objection, Your Honor. Irrelevant.
Judge:	Sustained. Keep your questions to the topic, Counsel.
Juror #3:	(to Juror #4) It is *true,* you know. It happened to me.
Defense:	(smiling) Yes, Your Honor. (addressing the witness) Dr. Vaughan, isn't it true that you have a long history of reporting your colleagues for a variety of so-called offenses?
Witness #4:	Only when it has been necessary.
Defense:	Isn't it also true that you have a history of spreading nefarious rumors about colleagues who might, shall we say, get in the way of your career advancement?

Witness #4:	I don't recall.
Defense:	Let me see if I can jog your memory, Dr. Vaughan. Wasn't it the defendant who moved up the ladder in the department, leaving you behind? And wasn't it you who started spreading lies about him throughout the department *and* to his patients?
Witness #4:	I don't recall.
Juror #7:	(to Juror #8) I don't understand what use it would be to lie about the Defendant climbing ladders.
Juror #8:	What kind of ladder do you think it was?
Juror #7:	(shrugs) I don't know, some kind of ladder they keep in the department.
Defense:	In your line of work, Dr. Vaughan, professionally speaking, what do you call devious, manipulative and self-serving behavioral patterns?
Prosecution:	Objection, Your Honor. Irrelevant.
Judge:	Sustained.
Defense:	(smiling) That's all, Your Honor.
Judge:	The court will be adjourned for a brief recess before the Defense presents their case. The jury is admonished not to talk about the case during the break, and to follow all posted subway rules. (smacks gavel)

(People begin to get out of their seats and mill about.)

Defense:	(turns to Barry) Why so serious? Ride the snake, Barry. The best is yet to come.
Barry:	Where did you get your training?

Defense: (laughing) Same place as you, Barry. Same place as you. (patting Barry on the knee) Well, I'm going to go mingle for a bit.

(Laughter and talking can be heard throughout the train. The Defense/Homeless Man picks up the stethoscope and removes it from the exhibit bag. He walks over, places the stethoscope on the chest of each of the jury members and then begins giving them psychic readings based on the rhythm of their heartbeats.)

Mosh: Barry, do you remember that scene in The Graduate where Ben is looking through the glass as the wedding is taking place, and he's locked out, so he grabs a hold of those bars and shakes and shakes them, and screams, "Elaine! Elaine!" over and over?
Barry: Yeah?
Mosh: That was a great movie. Wasn't it?
Barry: (snickering) Yeah...it was.
Judge: (returning to his seat and banging his gavel on the metal partition that separates the exit steps from the seats) This court will come to order.

(Bangs the gavel again. Everyone settles into the seats.)

Judge: If the Defense is ready, you may call your first witness.
Conductor: Attention, for the safety of our passengers, gavel banging is prohibited while the train is in motion.

Defense:	Your Honor, we would like to call Dr. Prana to the stand. (Witness is sworn in and is seated) Would you state your name and title please?
Witness #5:	Dr. David Prana, Director and Chief of Staff, Department of Psychiatry, Pitsore Medical School and Hospital.
Defense:	And how do you know Mr. Yeldray?
Witness #5:	He was on staff in my department. For four years. He was already there a couple of years before I took over as Chief of Staff.
Defense:	And what was your impression of Mr.Yeldray's work?
Witness #5:	Very impressive. He was the best psychiatrist on staff. I referred many patients to him. Over the years, Dr., er...uh...Mr. Yeldray helped literally *thousands* of patients. I am aware of the three people who spoke here today. I have read their complaints lodged with the hospital, but I can only tell you that there are many, many people who are more than satisfied with Mr. Yeldray's work.
Defense:	And, if you would, Dr. Prana please tell the jury your assessment of Barry Yeldray's professional contributions.
Witness # 5:	Oh, well, considerable. He was quite the thinker. Published many articles in the field. Very creative. He regularly attended conferences and gave lectures. He was a faculty member and advisor and played an active role in our intern program. Very well respected, that I can tell you. We were very lucky to have him.
Defense:	I see. Was there ever a time when you considered Mr. Yeldray's conduct unprofessional or as possibly constituting malpractice?
Witness # 5:	No. Never.

Defense:	Thank you, Dr. Prana. No further questions. I would like to reserve the right to recall this witness at a later time, Your Honor.
Judge:	Very well. Does the Prosecution have any questions on cross?
Prosecution:	No, Your Honor.
Judge:	You may step down, Dr. Prana.

(The witness returns to his original seat.)

Judge:	Call your next witness, Counsel.
Defense:	We call Shamus O'Brien to the stand. (Witness is sworn in and is seated) Would you state your name please?
Witness #6:	Shamus O'Brien.
Defense:	How did you come to know Barry Yeldray?
Witness #6:	He dated my *mother.* That is, until TODAY.
Defense:	And during the time your mother was dating him, did he ever try and offer counseling or psychiatric advice to you of any kind?
Witness #6:	No.
Mosh:	Well, he damned well *should* have.
Judge:	Silence in the courtroom.
Defense:	That's all, Your Honor.
Judge:	Your witness, Counsel. Does the Prosecution have any questions?
Prosecution:	Yes, Your Honor. Shamus, if the Defendant *had* offered you psychiatric advice would you have taken it?
Witness #6:	No way, man. That guy's an Asshole.
Defense:	Motion to strike the last part of that response.

Judge: Strike the last statement. Members of the jury, you are instructed to ignore the comment about the Defendant being an "Asshole."

(Jurors begin murmuring.)

Juror #1:   (to Juror #2) Oh, we're supposed to forget that he's an asshole.
Juror #2:   (nodding and turning to Juror #3) Forget the fact that he's an asshole. Pass it on.

(Juror # 3 nods and passes the information on to the rest of the jurors.)

Prosecution: That's all, Your Honor.
Judge: The witness may step down.

(Witness returns to his original seat.)

Judge: Counsel, you may call your next witness.
Defense: The Defense calls Mrs. Amanda Paulsen. (The witness is sworn in and takes a seat.) State your name for the court please.
Witness #7:   Mrs. Amanda Paulsen.
Defense: Mrs. Paulsen, how are you acquainted with Mr. Barry Yeldray?
Witness #7:   He was my next-door neighbor for six years.
Defense: And during the time you were acquainted with him, did you have regular contact with him?

Witness #7:	Oh my, yes. All the time. We chatted all of the time, and went to one another's parties and barbecues. (looking at jury) You know, that sort of thing. (several jurors nod their heads)
Defense:	Mrs. Paulsen, during the many times you socialized with Mr. Yeldray, did you ever know him to introduce himself to people as "Doctor" Yeldray?
Witness #7:	Oh, no. Never.
Defense:	He never told people he was a doctor when he met them? Not at parties or barbecues or any social event?
Witness #7:	Oh, no. He never did anything like that.
Defense:	And when you were there, he was never compelled to brag about what he did for a living to other people?
Witness #7:	Never.
Defense:	And you didn't find that odd, Mrs. Paulsen, for a doctor to not tell people right away what his status was?
Witness #7:	Well, of course I found it odd. But it's not a crime to be modest.
Defense:	Mrs. Paulsen, did you ever see Mr. Yeldray wear this during his off time, when he wasn't on duty? (holds up the exhibit of the stethoscope)
Witness #7:	My word, no.
Defense:	*Never,* Mrs. Paulsen? Are you sure?
Witness #7:	Positive.
Defense:	A doctor who does not parade around with a stethoscope around his neck? That didn't make you the slightest bit suspicious, Mrs. Paulsen?
Witness #7:	I realize it is all highly unusual, but, well, it just didn't make sense to speculate.
Defense:	That's all, Your Honor.
Judge:	Does the Prosecution have any questions?

Prosecution:	No, Your Honor.
Judge:	The witness is excused.

(The witness returns to her original seat.)

Judge:	You may call your next witness.
Defense:	The Defense calls Mr. Mosh Pitt. (The witness is sworn and is seated.) State your name for the court please.
Witness #8:	Mosh Pitt.
Prosecution:	Objection, Your Honor. This man is dead. The Defense should not be able to call a dead man as a witness. It is unreliable testimony.
Defense:	On the contrary, Your Honor. It is the most reliable type of witness. Everyone knows that dead men don't lie.

(There is a pause.)

Judge:	You have a point there, Counsel. Proceed.
Defense:	Now, Mosh, why don't you tell the jury what your relationship with Barry Yeldray is.
Witness #8:	We are best friends. Or...we were, before I died.
Defense:	So you know him pretty well, then?
Witness #8:	Better than anyone.
Defense:	Suppose you tell the court then, did Mr.Yeldray ever tell anyone that he was a medical doctor while he was in your presence?
Witness #8:	(laughing) No way, man. He would *never* do that!
Defense:	And why not?

269

Witness #8:	Because...he thought most medical doctors were morons. (There is muttering among the jurors.) He thought most of them were reductionistic, you know? He said they could only see the world in black-and white. One variable, cause-and-effect, ipso facto, he always said. He said most of them lacked the ability to do abstract thinking. Didn't have a creative bone in their bodies. If something came up that wasn't in their repertoire of rote-memory, they didn't know the first thing to do. Nah, he would never tell anyone anything like *that.*
Defense:	Thank you, Mosh. In your opinion, did Mr. Yeldray ever act like he was a doctor...you know, maybe when he thought no one was looking?
Witness #8:	(laughing) You mean did he ever act arrogant to cover up the fact that he was just ordinary and mediocre? (laughs) No, man. Barry is the most insightful, the...wisest person I have ever known. He would never have a reason to *act* like he was a *doctor*! (laughs some more)
Defense:	One final question, Mr. Pitt. Could you tell us what Barry Yeldray's priority in life is? What, in your opinion, is the most important thing to him?
Witness #8:	Sure. That's easy. Happiness. The most important thing in the world to Barry is just to be happy...and *free* of course. He needs to have freedom. That's why all this stuff about him being a *doctor* is so funny.
Defense:	Thank you. That's all, Your Honor.
Judge:	Does the Prosecution have any questions for this witness?
Prosecution:	Yes, Your Honor. Uh, Mr. Pitt, just exactly what was it that you died from?
Witness #8:	Boredom.

Prosecution: (making a face) No further questions, Your Honor.

Judge: The witness may step down.

(The witness returns to his original seat.)

Judge: The Defense may call their next witness.

Defense: Your Honor, the Defense calls Mrs. Jennifer Yeldray.

(The witness is sworn in and sits down. Gasps are heard from the jury.)

Defense: State your name for the court, please.

Witness #9: Mrs. Jennifer Yeldray.

Defense: What is your relationship with Mr. Barry Yeldray?

Witness #9: He is my ex-husband.

Defense: I see. And how long were you married?

Witness #9: Five years. I married him about a year after he got his position at the hospital.

Defense: And you are divorced now, is that correct?

Witness #9: Yes. Of course. By default, you might say. He just up and disappeared. Moved out of state, I heard. After one year, I got a divorce on the grounds of "desertion."

Defense: Mrs. Yeldray, can you tell the jury, what was your lifestyle like with Mr. Yeldray? Did you live the upscale life of luxury and privilege that doctors and their families often enjoy?

Witness #9: *Hmph.* I should say not. Never. No one could have ever known he was a doctor by the way we lived. He wouldn't let us leave that awful neighborhood. I wasn't even allowed to replace the broken-down furniture. I don't know *what* he was doing with all that money he made, but *I* never saw any of it!

Defense:	I see...Mrs. Yeldray, now...you made a, shall we say, *surprising discovery* one day while your husband was away at a conference, didn't you?
Witness #9:	Yes.
Defense:	What *was* that discovery, Mrs. Yeldray? Could you please tell the jury?
Witness #9:	Certainly. I discovered that his medical credentials were fraudulent.

(Gasps come from the jury. A lot of muttering can be heard throughout the train.)

Defense:	Go on, Mrs. Yeldray.
Witness #9:	I saw them with my own eyes. It was plain as day. I held the originals in my hand. They had been altered. He never graduated from medical school!
Defense:	I see. And what did you do?
Witness #9:	I called his boss, the Director of the Department, Dr. Prana, there (points to Dr. Prana) *right* away and told him. I figured I should tell him and that he would know what to do.
Defense:	And did you ever discuss it with Mr. Yeldray?
Witness #9:	Not right away. I kept it to myself for a little while. I kept waiting to hear something from having reported it to Dr. Prana, but *nothing.* Eventually, it was so stressful just waiting for the other shoe to drop, that I finally told Barry. I told him what I

	had found, and that I had called the Director and told him about it.
Defense:	And what happened, Mrs. Yeldray? What did Mr. Yeldray do?
Witness #9:	Nothing. That was the odd thing. He didn't say a word. He just went into the bedroom and gathered up his paperwork and a few things, and then he left. I thought he was coming back later that night, so I waited up. But no. He just left. Just like that. Without a word. I never saw him again. That is, until now.
Defense:	That is all. Thank you, Mrs. Yeldray. Your Honor, we have no more questions for this witness.
Judge:	Does the Prosecution have any questions?
Prosecution:	(looking confused) No...No, Your Honor.
Judge:	Very well, then, the witness is excused.

(Witness returns to her original seat.)

Juror #8:	(raising hand) Uh, Your Honor, can we do something about Juror #9? She's starting to *smell.*
Defense:	We're almost finished here, Your Honor.
Judge:	Very well. Proceed, Counsel.
Defense:	Your Honor, the Defense would like to recall Dr. Prana to the stand.

(Mutterings can be heard throughout the jury. Witness is reminded of his oath and is seated.)

Defense:	Now, Dr. Prana, is it true that you received a call from Mrs. Yeldray informing you that Barry Yeldray's credentials were fraudulent and that, in fact, he never had a medical degree? I remind you, Dr. Prana, you are still under oath.
Witness #5:	Yes. It is true.
Defense:	And what did you do with that information, Dr. Prana? What was your reaction to the news?
Witness #5:	Well, (shifts uncomfortably in the seat) I took the necessary steps to check things out. I went on my own through the records on file.
Defense:	And what did you discover, Dr. Prana?
Witness #5:	I could not find any record of his credentials. No records at all. I was so shocked to hear his wife say that he had falsified his credentials. I was having a hard time believing it was so. Why...Dr...er, uh, Mr. Yeldray was the *best* psychiatrist we had on staff. The *very* best.
Defense:	I see. So did you ever do any follow-up on trying to verify his credentials?
Witness #5:	No. That was not necessary. Shortly afterwards, he gave his resignation, and then I never saw or heard from him again. I heard he had moved out of state. I knew it was not necessary to do any follow-up.
Defense:	Dr. Prana, is it true that medical doctors have an oath they must take prior to beginning their medical practice? The Hippocratic oath, I believe it is called?
Witness #5:	Yes. It is true.
Defense:	And, is it also true that if one does not graduate medical school, one cannot get a legitimate license to practice and does not take that oath?
Witness #5:	That is also very true.

Defense:	I see. Thank you, Dr. Prana. That is all, Your Honor. The Defense rests.
Judge:	Does the Prosecution have any questions for this witness?
Prosecution:	(distracted) No, Your Honor.
Judge:	Well then, the witness is excused.

(The witness returns to his original seat.)

Judge:	Is the Prosecution ready for closing arguments?
Prosecution:	Yes, Your Honor. (walking towards the jury) Our witnesses today have clearly demonstrated that the Defendant (gestures towards Barry) is guilty of the crime of medical malpractice. I hope that you, the members of the jury, will consider the extreme pain and suffering of these poor people, that you will weigh *all* of the evidence, and that you will vote your conscience when deciding this case. The People of the United States are depending on you to make the right decision. That is all, Your Honor. The People have concluded their Final Remarks.
Judge:	Is the Defense ready with their Final Arguments?
Defense:	Yes, Your Honor. (walking over to the jury) Well, ladies and gentlemen (chuckling) it seems that your job is already done for you. You do not need to spend all that time weighing the evidence and examining your conscience, as the Prosecution would have you believe. It has all been an illusion! The fact of the matter is, ladies and gentlemen, that the Defendant, Mr. Barry Yeldray (gestures his arm out) CANNOT be guilty of medical malpractice because (laughing)

Mr. Yeldray is not now, nor has he ever been a day in his life, a medical doctor!

(Several of the jurors chuckle.)

Defense: So, ladies and gentlemen, as Dr. Prana has confirmed, if Mr. Yeldray was never a medical doctor, then he could *never* have had a medical license, and he could *never* have taken the Hippocratic oath swearing to uphold the code of ethics in medical practice...and, as we all know, you cannot be guilty of *mal*practice, if you never practiced at all! You cannot be guilty of breaking an oath you never took, Ladies and Gentlemen!

(Defense/Homeless Man laughs heartily. Several jurors nod.)

Defense: It has all been an illusion! (laughing and shaking his head)
That's all, Your Honor. The Defense concludes.
Prosecution: Your Honor, I would like to call a sidebar.
Judge: Very well.

(Prosecution and Defense approach the Judge.)

Prosecution: Your Honor, ipse dixit. The assertion that the Defendant is not a real doctor has not been proven.
Judge: Speak English, Counsel.

Prosecution:	Your Honor, we had no idea that the Defendant was never a real doctor.
Judge:	The fact that the People came to court without doing their homework, or even checking the Defendant's background, is *not* the problem of this court. You may return now and be seated.

(The judge hits his gavel against the metal partition.)

Judge:	Members of the jury, you may now deliberate.

(The jurors stand up and huddle together for several minutes in the back of the train. Muttering can be heard. A few minutes later, one of the jurors approaches the judge.)

Juror #4:	Your Honor, we have reached a decision. We have a verdict.
	(hands the judge a piece of paper.)
Judge:	(reads the paper) Very well...Madam Foreperson, how do you find?
Juror #4:	We, the jury, find the Defendant, Mr. Barry Yeldray, **NOT GUILTY** of the crime of medical malpractice.

(Loud applause is heard throughout the train. Dr. Prana gives Barry the "thumbs up." The agent unlocks the handcuffs and leg restraints from Barry. The Homeless Man pats Barry on the back.)

Barry:	(looking at Homeless Man) Thanks. Thank you so much.
Homeless Man:	Ah, it was nothing. Someone has to stick up for the Misfits of the world.
Barry:	I never caught your name.
Homeless Man:	My friends just call me Mänes. It's a nickname from when I was a kid.
Barry:	(giving a start, then putting his hand out to shake hands) Well, take care, Mänes.
Mosh:	(approaching Barry) Put 'er there, man. (shakes Barry's hand)

(The doors of the train open.)

| Barry: | (turning to Mosh) Come on, man. Let's blow this Popsicle stand. |

(The two men exit the train. The curtain closes.)

End of Act II

~ ~ ~ ~

The curtains reopen. The audience applauds and whistles as the actors come onto the stage. With each new set of actors to walk on, the applause gets louder, and the whistles and shouts more intense.

"Well," Murray says, "that'll about do it."

"Don't forget to call me as soon as you get there," Juno says, shaking Murray's hand. The applause continues. The curtain closes. The audience stands up from their seats and continues to clap and shout. The curtain reopens. The actors join hands and take a bow. The audience continues to clap until the curtain closes again and the house lights go on.

"Oh, and don't forget, I'm leaving the end of this week. I'll be gone until the 30th. I'm going to the Cayman Islands on a little vacation of my own," Juno says, winking.

"Oh," Murray says, reaching into the pocket of his backpack and pulling out the three envelopes. "Would you mail these for me when you get to the Islands?"

"Sure thing, Murray," Juno says, putting the envelopes in the breast pocket of his jacket. "Now get out of here. Go the way I told you."

Ten minutes later, Murray is riding in the back of a black limousine, smoking a cigarette, and chuckling to himself.

X

Murray looks out the window of the Greyhound Bus as it speeds down Route 66. He holds the box with Shadow's ashes on his lap. Every so often he strokes the top of the box.

Just after they pass the sign pointing towards the exit for Lake Havasu City, Murray reaches inside the pocket of his pants for the packet. He carefully slips the rubber band, now tied together with knots, off the packet, and pulls a letter off the top of the stack of folded papers.

The letter is so old and worn from being opened and refolded, and from being carried around so long in Murray's pocket, that it is barely legible anymore.

Murray gently unfolds the paper. The letterhead is still clearly visible. His eyes scan it, "Pritzker Medical School." He starts reading what he can from the first paragraph, "...and I want you to know that no matter what has happened, I will always consider your work here to have been brilliant." Several more lines are unreadable, and then, "...the utmost respect for your significant contributions to the field and all of those you have helped..."

Murray struggles to make out the text in the middle, gives up, and moves to the bottom of the letter, which is still somewhat clear. He reads, "I leave you with the important words of the Dhammapada. 'We are what we think. All that we are arises with our thoughts. With our thoughts, we make the world. Speak or act with a pure mind, and happiness will follow as your Shadow. Unshakable'."

Murray reads the closing through tears in his eyes: "Best wishes in whatever world your thoughts create, Sincerely, Dr. D. Prana." Murray wipes his eyes with the back of his hand, gently replaces the letter in the packet, and places it back inside his pocket. Then he picks up the box, lays his head back, and closes his eyes. In a short while, he is asleep.

* * * *

Murray sets several cans of vegetables on the counter and reaches in the shopping cart for two packages of rice, a can of coffee, bath soap, toothpaste, and a package of toilet paper.

The man behind the counter rings up each item and announces the total.

Murray hands him the cash. "Say, you don't happen to know where there's a nursery in town, do you?" He asks.

The man behind the counter raises his right eyebrow and hands Murray his change. "Sam's. Up on Prince Street. Only one there is. He'll do good by you, though. Sam knows his business."

The man begins slowly packing the groceries. "Two sacks or one?" He asks.

"Huh? Oh, uh, two, please," Murray replies.

"You new in town?" The man asks suspiciously.

"Yeah, yeah. I am." Murray answers. "I am leasing Dr. Johnson's house while he is away from the university on sabbatical."

"Where abouts you from?" The man asks, raising his eyebrow again.

"Nevada," Murray says. "Carson City."

"Oh," the man says, relaxing somewhat. "The wife and I were there once. We stopped on our way over to Virginia City to see the Camel Races. Mark Twain lived there, they say. In Virginia City, that is."

"True," Murray says, smiling and nodding his head.

"So, what made you decide to move to Clovis, New Mexico?" The man asks, finishing up packing the groceries.

"Oh, I've always liked these parts," Murray says.

"Oh?" The man asks with interest.

"Yeah, my mother, God rest her soul, spent the last years of her life in Lubbock, Texas. I used to visit her a lot, and I just got to like these parts," Murray says.

"Lubbock," the man says, sounding pleased. "I'm originally from Amarilla' myself. Been here twenty-three years though. My wife got it in her head to move near her sister. That's why we came out here. You married?"

Murray lowers his eyes. "My wife died just this year. That's why I decided to come on out here. Thought a change of scenery would do me some good."

"Sorry to hear that," the man says. "Do you have any kids?"

"One," Murray says. "My daughter, Mollie. She's an artist," he says proudly. "She lives in San Francisco. I just went out and stayed with her for a bit before heading out this way."

"San Francisco!" The man shakes his head. "California," he says, still shaking his head. "You know what they say? If you tipped the United States on it's side, all the nuts would fall into California." He slaps the counter as he laughs.

Murray smiles. "Agreed," he says.

"So what do you do?" The man asks.

"Writer," Murray says. "I write plays. Say, there wouldn't be a playhouse in these parts, would there?"

"No, not an actual playhouse, but we do have plays from time to time. Over here at the college. Also at the university in Portales, next town over," he says, pointing his thumb in a southerly direction.

Murray nods and reaches for his groceries.

"Yeah," the man continues. "The wife and I went to see a play over at the college just about a month ago."

"Oh?" Murray says.

"Yep. Our Town, it was called," the man continues.

Murray nods and smiles.

"It was about this small town. Back in the old days," the man says, "when there was no craziness or drugs or crime."

The man shakes his head.

"The damnedest thing happened during that play," he continues, shaking his head again.

"What's that?" Murray asks with interest.

"Well, you know the main story-teller? I can't think of his name at the moment...but the one who comes out like a host and kinda' walks you through the play? He tells you what's happening as the play is going along."

Murray nods. "Yeah," he says.

"Well," the man says, "there comes this part in the play where this story-teller guy comes up close to the audience and starts telling us all about Grover's Corners...that's the name of the small town."

Murray smiles and nods.

"So, anyhow," the man says. "They have these actors planted in the audience, only the audience don't know it. And so the story-teller finishes his speech about how wonderful Grover's Corners is, and then he says to the audience, 'Does anyone here have any questions about Our Town, Grover's Corners?

"And then this is when the actors who are secretly planted in the audience stand up, one at a time, and ask questions. They stand up and say things like 'Do you have to lock your doors in Grover's Corners?' and 'Do you have many churches in Grover's Corners?' and 'Do you sell alcohol in Grover's Corners?'

"And so what happens? This young wise-assed teenager sitting next to me, he's not one of the actors, mind you, but nobody knows that, and so, this wise-assed kid, he stands up and says real serious, 'Do you have any *crack-babies* in Grover's Corners?' Can you believe that?"

Murray bites down on the inside of his cheek and shakes his head.

"Right in the middle of the play," the man says. "Well, I would 'a liked to smack him right across the head. The story-teller guy, he was a real professional, though. He just calmly says, 'No. We do not.' real serious, like it was part of the play." The man shakes his head.

"These kids today...I just don't know what gets into them."

"I know what you mean," Murray says, shaking his head also.

"Well," Murray says, "it's been nice talking to you."

He picks up his groceries and heads for the door.

"Oh, say," the man says. "What were you thinking of planting?"

Murray looks confused.

"The nursery?" The man says, finally.

"Oh, oh. A tree. Maybe one of those Pi–on trees. Dr. Johnson said to feel free to do whatever gardening and planting I liked," Murray responds.

"Oh, well, you can double check with Sam on this, but you're gonna' have to wait 'til next spring to plant it in order for it to take."

"Oh," Murray says. "Well, thanks."

"I'll tell Sam you'll be stoppin' by to see him," the man says.

"Thanks," Murray says, opening the door to leave. "So long."

"Oh, hey, I didn't catch your name," the man says.

"My friends just call me Mänes," Murray says. "It's a nickname from when I was a kid."

"Mine's Joe Ralston. Take care, Mänes. See you later."

Murray smiles and nods his head.

* * * *

Murray has just started to eat when he hears a horn blowing. He sets his plate down on the patio table and walks around to the front of the house.

"Did I interrupt you?" Sam yells from his truck.

"Nah," Murray says, "I was just sitting out back having some lunch."

"Now that spring has finally arrived, and the ground is no longer frozen," Sam says, walking around his truck, "I thought I'd bring that tree on by for you."

"Thanks. I really appreciate it," Murray says, helping Sam to lift it out of the back of his pick-up.

"Just follow the directions like I told you, and she should be fine," Sam says, slamming the tailgate shut.

Murray waves as Sam pulls away. He carries the tree as far as the mailbox, sets it down, and pulls out his mail. He shuffles through the pieces of mail marked "resident" and stops at a large envelope addressed to "M. Y. Bardos." It is postmarked from San Francisco.

"Juno," he says, smiling.

Murray carries the tree to the backyard. He lays his mail down on the patio table next to his typewriter, and walks into the shed to pull out a shovel and a screwdriver.

He looks around the yard for just the right spot, then walks over and thrusts the end of the shovel into the earth. He spends quite awhile digging a hole, then stands the small sapling tree inside of the hole and cuts the burlap bag, just the way Sam told him to.

Next, he walks over to the box setting on the patio table and carries it over to the tree. He carefully opens the box with the screwdriver and taps a small portion of Shadow's ashes into the Earth where the tree is standing.

"Listen, Shadow," Murray says, using his hand to scoop the soil over the ashes, "what I said in that letter was wrong. *We're* connected...in the only way that really counts. Right, buddy?"

Murray finishes packing the soil around the tree roots, gives the tree a good watering, and carries the shovel back into the shed. Then he heads back towards the table, sets Shadow's box down, and opens the envelope from Juno. Inside there is a letter, several newspaper and magazine clippings, a passport, a one-way airline ticket to Johannesburg, and a check. Murray reads the note.

Dear Mosh,

How are things going? They are going great on this end. I have enclosed the latest reviews of Subway Vision. As you can see, it is a hit. (Though one reviewer said your work feels like Tom Stoppard-meets-Bret Easton Ellis. I don't know how you feel about that.) We have a new contract with the Metro, with an option at the end of Fall. Also, a new commitment with the L.A. Repertoire Theater. Contract to follow.

Hope everything is going fine with you. Looking forward to reading the next draft of your new play soon.

Sorry the passport took so long. Have a good flight. Be sure to send me your new address as soon as you get all settled in.

STAY CONNECTED, Murray. Remember, we are all impostors. The paradox itself is what keeps it interesting. ~Juno

Murray gives a jolt when he reads the last part. He shakes his head and smiles. "I don't know *how* he does it, Shadow," he says.

Murray puts the letter down and looks out at the newly planted tree for several minutes. Then he picks up one of the newspaper clippings Juno has sent, and begins reading the underlined portion. "South African authorities say that problems arising from *conflict diamonds* (or "blood" diamonds) in recent years have created a void in the number of wholesalers participating in the bourses, or registered diamond exchanges." Murray studies the photo Juno has circled and the caption, "Diamonds prepared as gemstones." Then he lights a cigarette, leans back, and gives a wry smile.

Murray sits in silence for several more hours, gazing at the newly planted tree and listening to the sounds of insects. The sunset creates an impossible burst of bright orange and deep purple hues. 'Like the sky is filled with gemstones,' Murray thinks to himself. He silently muses about the sun in the southern hemisphere, wondering if sunsets look different there. Then he thinks about the new tree with Shadow's ashes at the roots, wondering what it will look like in twenty years.

Just as the light begins to fade, Murray sees what he thinks is a cat, slinking across the shadows. It creeps across the edges of the yard until suddenly it stops, seemingly drawn to the tree. The cat stays very still and then suddenly jumps straight up, into the newly planted tree. As Murray leans and strains to see, the cat sits motionless. And there the cat stays, until the shadows engulf it completely.